P9-CCW-057

The Corset Diaries

"Reality TV has never been more entertaining than here as the wickedly funny MacAlister has her heroine record her hilarious experiences with a quirky cast of characters and her passionate encounters with Max in a laughter-laced diary that is a saucy, sexy delight." —*Booklist*

"An enjoyable contemporary romance. . . . The story line is fun to follow. . . . Fans will enjoy this entertaining anachronistic look at displacement as the modern crowd struggles with life just over a century ago." —The Best Reviews

Men in Kilts

"With its wickedly witty writing, wonderfully snappy dialogue, and uniquely amusing characters, MacAlister's latest is perfect for any reader seeking a deliciously sexy yet also subtly sweet contemporary romance." —*Booklist*

"A fun, fast-paced, and witty adventure . . . *Men in Kilts* is so utterly delightful, I read this book nearly all in one sitting." —Roundtable Reviews

"Katie MacAlister sparkles, intrigues and is one of the freshest voices to hit romance. . . . So buckle up, for Katie gives you romance, love, and the whole damn thing—sheep included." —The Best Reviews

"*Men in Kilts* is filled with warm, intriguing characters and situations, and the atmosphere is fiery as Katie and her silent Ian irresistibly draw you into their story." —*Rendezvous*

"Wonderfully witty, funny, and romantic, *Men in Kilts* had me laughing out loud from the first page . . . a definite winner." —Romance Reviews Today

"This book hooked me from the first paragraph and kept me smiling—and sometimes laughing out loud—to the last page. . . . I thoroughly enjoyed *Men in Kilts* and recommend it highly." —*Affaire de Coeur*

Katie MacAlister

Light My Fire

An Aisling Grey, Guardian, Novel

A SIGNET ECLIPSE BOOK

SIGNET ECLIPSE
Published by New American Library, a division of
Penguin Group (USA) Inc., 375 Hudson Street,
New York, New York 10014, USA
Penguin Group (Canada), 90 Eglinton Avenue East, Suite 700, Toronto,
Ontario M4P 2Y3, Canada (a division of Pearson Penguin Canada Inc.)
Penguin Books Ltd., 80 Strand, London WC2R 0RL, England
Penguin Ireland, 25 St. Stephen's Green, Dublin 2,
Ireland (a division of Penguin Books Ltd.)
Penguin Group (Australia), 250 Camberwell Road, Camberwell, Victoria 3124,
Australia (a division of Pearson Australia Group Pty. Ltd.)
Penguin Books India Pvt. Ltd., 11 Community Centre, Panchsheel Park,
New Delhi - 110 017, India
Penguin Group (NZ), cnr Airborne and Rosedale Roads, Albany,
Auckland 1310, New Zealand (a division of Pearson New Zealand Ltd.)
Penguin Books (South Africa) (Pty.) Ltd., 24 Sturdee Avenue,
Rosebank, Johannesburg 2196, South Africa

Penguin Books Ltd., Registered Offices:
80 Strand, London WC2R 0RL, England

First published by Signet Eclipse, an imprint of New American Library,
a division of Penguin Group (USA) Inc.

First Printing, November 2006
10   9   8   7   6   5   4   3   2   1

Writing may be a solitary endeavor, but all of the readers who have written to let me know they've enjoyed Aisling's stories have left me with a warm, fuzzy feeling of happiness. I created the Dragon Septs Web site (www.dragonsepts.com) to keep Aisling's friends going between books—as well as to answer the many questions they had about her and the dragons—and it is to all the dragon fans that this book is dedicated, with much appreciation and gratitude for all the support.

1

"Just leave everything to me."

"Famous last words, Ash. Your record hasn't been too good so far, has it?"

The burly black shape in front of me that tossed the words over its furry shoulder didn't stop, but I did, frowning. Jim, my demon in Newfoundland dog form, might not be Little Mary Sunshine, but it didn't normally say things that it knew were deliberately cruel.

Around us in Green Park, people were flaked out in the rented park chairs or lying on the ground sunbathing, everyone happily enjoying the English September sunshine . . . everyone but my crabby demon.

"I have, if you haven't noticed, been rather busy these last three weeks getting moved from Oregon to London. But I said I'd find someone to dremel your toenails, and I meant it. There have to be dog groomers in England who grind away nails with a dremel rather than clip them."

"That last woman you took me to was nothing more

than a butcher," Jim snapped, marching forward with enough force to get me moving again. "I'm lucky I have all my toes. Minus the two you enchanted away, that is."

"I said I'm sorry fifteen times already—I'll say it for a sixteenth if it gets you out of this grouchy mood. I'm sorry she nicked your quick and made your toenails bleed. And that other toenail issue is *so* two months ago."

"Too little, too late," was the grumpy answer.

"Right." I stopped near a tree that was relatively private. "That's it. I've put up with your snarky comments the last couple of weeks because I know that transitions like the one we're making aren't easy for anyone. Lord knows I've heard nothing but horror stories from my family about Americans living abroad, but I expected better from you, Jim. You *like* Nora! You were looking forward to coming here. Why are you being so unpleasant about everything now?"

Jim turned to face me. I hadn't thought it possible for a Newfie's face to look sour, but Jim had pulled it off. "My heart is broken, in case you've forgotten! You shouldn't have, since you're the one who stomped all over it."

"Oh, that." I sighed and rubbed the back of my neck, stiff with tension.

"Yes, that."

"Well, I know it's no substitute for a corgi, but you've got a dog for companionship. You've got Paco now."

"Paco isn't a dog. Paco is a snack."

Secretly, I agreed with Jim. Nora's Chihuahua was nice enough but was a little light in the character department. Then again, Jim could have ruined me for all normal dogs. "I told you I'd take you to Paris to see Amelie and Cecile just as soon as I know . . ." The words trailed off to an awkward stop.

"As soon as you're sure that Drake is gone; yes, I know. But since he lives there, that's not likely to be for a long time, now, is it? And Cecile isn't getting any younger. I'd like to see her before she's dead, my lord."

I sighed again, leaving the slight shade of the tree to brave the crowds filling the park. During the four days I'd been in London, I'd learned to avoid the edge that borders Buckingham Palace. It was always packed with tourists, and the last thing I needed was for one of them to notice that the dog who marched so determinedly in front of me was speaking. "I hate it when you call me that, but we both know you know that, so I won't humor your bad mood by arguing about you trying to get in a few 'you're a demon lord now, Ash' digs. And since you've apparently forgotten, I'll remind you that Drake also has homes in Hungary and the Cayman Islands, and probably a couple other places that never came up during our short time together."

"Short because you walked out on him. *Again.*"

I ground my teeth. The park was too public a place to have it out with Jim. Nonetheless, I lowered my voice and whispered with as much threat as was possible, "I am not going to discuss my relationship with Drake."

"Ha! Relationship. Is that what you're calling it now? You two get together; you break it off. You get together again; you agree to be his mate; you take an oath of fealty to the sept; you get pissy; you leave him. Doesn't sound like much relationship is going on there."

Now, that stung. Jim knew full well the circumstances of my breakup with Drake. It had even agreed with me at the time that Drake had pulled a nasty on me and that I was fully justified in walking away from him.

"Demon, I command thee to zip thy lips until you get over your case of the grumps," I said instead of the gazillions of snappy comebacks that I knew would occur to me hours later. "I'm not going to defend myself or my actions. We're here, we're going to stay here, and I'll get you to Paris just as soon as I know the coast is clear. I'm sorry if that's broken your heart, not that demons have a heart to break, but it's the best I can do. Now, if you're done watering everything, let's get back to the apartment. Our stuff should be arriving today, and I want to get everything put away before Nora comes back from Liverpool."

Jim glared at me over its shoulder for a moment, but one of the fringe benefits of being a demon lord was that a demon in my control couldn't disobey a direct command, so we had a silent trip as we headed back to the three-room apartment that Nora had inherited from an elderly relative. Located above a chic combination bakery and bookstore, the apartment was a rare find in a city of overpriced, undersized housing.

"After I get the stuff unpacked, I'll call Amelie and let you talk to Cecile if you like," I said as we skirted a group of tourists gawking in an expensive shop's window. We took advantage of a break in traffic to hurry across the street. "Not that you deserve it. Honestly, Jim, you're just about the most aggravating demon I've ever had the pleasure to—bloody hell!"

I jerked Jim back as a black taxi ignored the laws regarding pedestrians in a crosswalk and screeched to a halt just millimeters away from my demon.

"That sounded very English. You are adapting well, yes?"

The oaths that I was about to crack over the idiot driver's head dried up on my lips as I peered through the window at the man behind the wheel. His voice was smooth, thick with a French accent . . . and very familiar.

"What . . . who . . . *Rene*?"

"Mais oui. C'est moi. Good morning, Jim. You look well. Did you have any trouble getting through customs?"

I stared at the pleasant-looking fifty-something man in the taxi, not sure I was really seeing him, my brain grinding to a halt at the sight. It couldn't be Rene. It just couldn't. Could it?

Jim glared at me in answer to the question asked of it.

"Ah," Rene said, tipping his head to the side as he blithely ignored the honking of horns from the cars stopped behind him. "She has ordered you to silence, eh?"

"Rene, what in the he—Abaddon are you doing here?" I asked, finally able to kick-start my brain into functioning.

He smiled and reached behind him to open the door. "I will take you to where you are going."

"Nuh-uh." I could ignore the backed-up traffic just as easily as he could. "Not until you tell me what you're doing here, in London, in a taxi. And it had better be good, because you showing up in Budapest a few weeks ago was really pushing the coincidence line."

"Get in, and I shall tell you all."

I gave him a long look to warn him he had better mean

it and opened the door to the taxi, herding Jim in before I followed.

"Now, spill," I said as the taxi started to move. "Oh, I'm going to 15 Warlock Close. That's located—"

"I know where it is. North of Bury Street, yes?"

"Yes. How do you know where it is? How do you know London that well? And what in god's name are you doing here? Why aren't you home in Paris?"

Rene's brown eyes twinkled at me in the mirror. I stiffened my immunity to his charm, sure something was going on for him to show up in yet another country driving yet another taxi. "You remember my cousin in Budapest, the one I was helping out during the week you were there?"

"Yes," I said suspiciously. "What about him? You're not going to tell me that he also drives a taxi here, in London?"

"No," Rene said, cutting across two lanes of traffic to turn left onto the short dead-end street where Nora's apartment was located. "His brother, my cousin Pavel, does, but that is not why I am here."

"Your cousin Pavel drives an English taxi?" I asked, refusing to budge when Rene pulled up with a flourish in front of our building.

"*Oui.* He is most good at it, as are all the men in my family." Rene didn't even bother trying to look modest; he just grinned at me in the mirror as he backed the taxi into a tiny loading area so it was no longer blocking the road.

"I'm not buying that, you know. Why are you following me? Are you some sort of really nice, helpful French stalker? You're not in love with me or obsessed with me or anything, are you?"

Jim snorted and rolled its eyes.

"You can speak if you have anything helpful to say," I told it.

"The sun will never rise on a day when I say something that's not worth its weight in platinum," my demon answered. "Hi, Rene. How they hangin'?"

"Free and easy, my friend," Rene answered, turning in his seat so he could reach to ruffle the top of Jim's furry black head. "It is good to see you both. You look well."

"No," I said, holding up a warning finger at Jim. "No long, maudlin tales of how your heart was broken because I didn't take you to Paris to see Cecile the minute we landed. Rene is telling us just why he's here. In a taxi. When he lives and works in another country altogether."

Rene laughed. "*Mon amie*, put your mind at the rest. I am not in love with you—I have a wife and seven small ones, recall you. And I am not a stalker, or obsessed with you, although I am very happy to see you both. I have missed you these last few weeks."

Now I felt like a great big heel. "I'm very happy to see you, too," I answered, leaning forward to hug him. "We were planning on seeing you when we got to Paris. How are you? How is your family? And what are you doing here?"

"I am fine. My family, they are fine as well, although my wife, she has the allergies of flowers and her nose does not march along happily because of it. And I am here because she stayed home so she could not come on our honeymoon."

"Your *honeymoon?*" Jim didn't look surprised, but I sure did.

Rene shrugged his familiar expressive Gallic shrug. "When we were married twenty years ago, we did not have the honeymoon. We put it off until we had the time and money, but by then the little ones were coming along. So it waited until now. We were to have a whole month touring England seeing the grand homes and gardens, but my wife, she does not want to see any more pollen, and the tickets are not exchangeable, so . . . here I am."

I wasn't buying it. It was too pat, too slick, too . . . *coincidental.* And he had used up all his coincidence tickets when he showed up to help me in Budapest. "OK. But why are you in a taxi?"

"My cousin Pavel." He reached behind him out through the window and pulled the door open. "He is taking his wife to stay in the Shakespeare town, using my reservation while I stay at his flat. He didn't ask me to take over his job, too, but *hein.* It is what I do best. Me, I am the taxi driver *extraordinaire.*"

"You're something, all right. And I'm going to find out just what it is." I rubbed the back of my neck, glancing at Jim. My demon did not normally stay silent for more than a second or two unless specifically ordered, but here it was letting an entire conversation pass by without any sort of comment. I couldn't help but wonder whether Jim knew who Rene really was.

"So suspicious," Rene answered, shaking his head as I got out of the car. Jim followed. "What makes you disbelieve me?"

"One," I said, ticking the items off on my fingers, "you

show up when I need help in Paris. Two, you do the same thing in Budapest. Three, you weren't affected at all by the Venus amulet I had there, which hit every other mortal man over the head like a lusty sledgehammer. Why is that, Rene?"

He just smiled at me.

"Uh-huh. I knew it. You're not just a taxi driver who happened to stumble into the Otherworld like I did, are you? You're . . . you're something else, right? Something not mortal?"

Rene smiled again.

"Ash."

"Sec, Jim. Come on, Rene. Out with it. It's no coincidence that you've shown up whenever I've needed you, is it?" My eyes narrowed as I thought about that. "Only I don't need you right now. Everything is hunky-dory in my life. I washed that dragon right out of my hair, I managed to smuggle Jim into the country by means of demonic limbo, and Nora is going to train me to be a proper Guardian, not one who falls into stuff without knowing what to do. So . . . why are you here?"

"Ash, there's someone at the door." Jim nudged my hand with its cold nose.

I turned to look at the man facing the outer door to the hall that led to the three apartments that graced the top floor of the building.

"I am not done with you," I warned Rene as I hurried over to the man, hoping it was the delivery of all my belongings cleared at last through customs.

"I will be around," he called after me. "You have my mobile number, yes?"

"Yes," I called back as he put the car into gear and

merged into the busy London traffic. "Sorry. Are you the man with my boxes?"

"Boxes? No." He turned to face us.

"Oh. Rats. Well, I'm afraid there's no one in the apartments now. One of the tenants is off on his summer vacation, and the other one is in Liverpool for the day."

The man held a business card in one hand and a pen in the other, evidently having been in the process of writing a note. A sharp, gray-eyed gaze swept over me. "A Guardian." He moved on to Jim, a slight frown pulling his dark brows together in a darker frown. "And a sixth-class demon."

"Yes, I'm a Guardian," I said, my hackles rising for some intangible reason. In the few months since I had found out there was a whole other paranormal side to the world I knew, including my own role as what amounted to a demon wrangler, I'd learned that appearances were more than a little deceiving. The man in front of me might look like a perfectly normal Englishman—high forehead, long face, prominent nose, gray eyes and brown hair—but power crackled off him, leaving the air static-filled around us. I'd also learned, however, that sugar would get me a lot farther than vinegar, so I slapped a pleasant smile on my face and prepared to make myself friendly. "Well, to be truthful, I'm a Guardian in training, but hopefully it won't be too long before I'm a full-fledged active member of the Guardians' Guild."

The man cast a glance at Jim again, his gaze sharpening. "You are Aisling Grey."

"Yes. Er . . . how did you know who I am?"

"All the Otherworld has heard of the infamous Aisling Grey, the woman who has the dubious honor of being a demon lord, Guardian, and wyvern's mate all at the same time," he answered, handing me his card. I gave it a quick look. On the front was his name—Mark Sullivan. Below it, in small, discreet print, was one word: INVESTIGATIONS.

"Yeah, dubious honor just about sums it up. You're a private eye? A detective?"

"No. I am the chief investigator for the L'au-delà committee. I have been asked to look into possible inconsistencies with Nora Charles, Guardian."

"Inconsistencies? What inconsistencies?"

Mark Sullivan gave me a long look that spoke volumes—of nothing.

"Nora is my mentor," I explained, my hands automatically drawing a ward of understanding on him. Maybe that would help. "She's training me to be a Guardian."

"Not anymore she isn't," Mark said, pulling a piece of paper out of his breast pocket. "This is an order prohibiting Nora Charles from acting as a mentor. Please see that she receives it as soon as she returns. From this moment on, she is forbidden to teach anyone anything—including her current apprentice. Good luck to you, Aisling Grey. I fear you are going to need it."

2

"I hate it when people do things like that," I grumbled as I slammed shut the door to Nora's apartment.

"What, act polite?"

"No, do that horrible foreshadowing thing that everyone around me seems to do." I tossed down Jim's leash and went to check Nora's answering machine to see whether there were any messages from the shipping company. "Just once I'd like someone to walk up to me and, instead of predicting disaster or bad luck or any of the myriad other unpleasant happenings that have been predicted for me, say, 'Aisling, you're going to win the lottery today. Or lose ten pounds overnight. Or fall madly in love with the next man you see.' Anything but foreshadowing."

Jim sighed. "It's all about you, isn't it? Never thinking about anyone else; only concerned about your own happiness."

I glared open-mouthed at the demon as a knock sounded on the door. I hurried toward it, glad I'd left the outer door unlocked for the delivery guys. "That is so totally off base, and you know it!"

"Fine, you want to be that way . . ." Jim scratched a spot behind its left ear, then considered its crotch as it said, "Aisling, you're going to win the lottery today, lose ten pounds overnight, and fall madly in love with the next man you see."

I opened the door on the last of its words.

The man standing in the doorway raised an eyebrow. "Hindsight, so they say, is twenty-twenty."

My jaw dropped. My heart speeded up. My lungs seemed suddenly airless. And my stomach wadded up into a small leaden ball.

A small fire burst into being on the nearby area rug. Jim ran over to stomp it out.

"Drake," I said on a gasp, air rushing once again into my lungs. "What are you—"

"You are hereby summoned to attend a synod of the green dragons tomorrow. Attendance is mandatory." Drake slapped a stiff black portfolio into my hands and turned to leave.

"Hey! A synod? Wait a minute—Jim, there's another one near the curtains."

Drake spun around again, his green eyes blazing with emotion—eyes that I knew so well, that had once seemed to hold everything I wanted. But that was before he betrayed me . . .

"Do you refute your oath of fealty to the sept? Do you refuse to honor your commitments, mate?"

"No," I answered, lifting my chin. I'd known all along that I was bound to the dragon sept that Drake ruled as wyvern. Even though we were no longer together, technically I was still his mate, and until I could find a way to undo that, I owed them my help when needed. I'd been braced and ready for this ever since I'd left Budapest. "No, I am not refuting my oath to the sept. I will attend the meeting as your mate. I simply wanted to know . . ." The words died on my lips.

He crossed his arms over his chest. "What did you want to know?"

Whether he missed me? Whether his heart hurt as much as mine? Whether he regretted betraying me like he did? Those were the first three things that came to mind, but there were others. All of which were questions that I would ask over my cold, lifeless corpse. So to speak. Luckily, before I had to try to think of an impersonal question, Jim stepped in to the rescue.

"You really are going to have to get a grip on controlling dragon fire, Ash. Hiya, Drake. Come crawling back, did you? Man, you are so whipped." Jim shambled over to give Drake a quick sniff. "I never met anyone so completely—fires of Abaddon! You don't have to barbeque me!"

"Don't set Nora's bathroom on fire," I warned as Jim raced off to put out the flames that burst into a corona around his head. I turned back to Drake, worried less about Jim's doggie form taking harm than about Nora's bath towels. "You get points for marksmanship but lose on effect. Roasting Jim alive won't do anything but leave the scent of burnt dog hair hanging around the apartment."

Drake looked thoughtful as he rubbed his chin. "Actually, I was off. I was aiming for you."

My eyes opened wide as his words filtered through the sudden love-anger-sadness cocktail that had recently become my usual emotional state. "You wanted to burn *me*?"

Drake moved so fast, it didn't even register in my brain. One minute he was standing several paces away; the next he was pushing me up against the open door, his body hard and aggressive, mine automatically answering by going all soft on him. "You cannot be under any delusion that you can simply walk away from me."

"I know I pricked your pride by leaving you," I said carefully, telling my body to stop mugging him and to behave itself so I could concentrate on reasoning with the most *un*reasonable dragon in human form that ever walked the planet. "But there is nothing more between us, Drake. It's over."

"It is not . . . over . . ." he growled, his lips so close to mine I could feel the heat of his mouth. The scent of him, spicy and masculine and uniquely Drake, went immediately to my head and made me giddy with want. But beneath that want there was heartache, a pain so profound, it all but crippled me for the week following our breakup. It had taken seven long days of nonstop sobbing to come to a point where I could get on with my life . . . without Drake at my side.

"Oh, man. He's going to pork you right here in front of me, isn't he? Jeez, and they say dogs have no shame."

"Demon, silence. And close your eyes," I ordered, unable to see whether Jim followed my command because Drake chose that moment to claim my mouth. He was a naturally arrogant, dominant man, and those qualities showed in his kisses. He wooed with a passion that left my knees weak and my toenails steaming. His entire body entered into the kiss he gave me, one hand sweeping up to cup my breast, the other sliding down my back to grab my butt, pulling my hips tighter against his.

Fire flamed to life in him, dragon fire, the familiar heat of it as welcome as manna as it roared through me, igniting my soul. My heart, my poor abused heart, wept with agony at the feel of us joining together in a manner that was so much more elemental than mere sex. It was as if our souls fit together, one completing the other, the two of us forming one brilliant, glorious being that would burn together for all eternity . . .

"No!" I cried, pulling my mouth from his. "You are not going to seduce me again! Dammit, you broke my heart, Drake. You can't piece it back together with glue made up of a few kisses and mind-numbingly fabulous sex! Over means over! I will honor my vow to the sept. I will present myself as your mate at the weyr and sept meetings. I will support your dragon decisions in any way I can. But I will not allow you to destroy me again!"

One of his long, sensitive fingers pushed aside my shirt to trace the rounded sept emblem that he'd branded into my flesh, marking me as a wyvern's mate. The emerald fire in his eyes slowly banked as he spoke. "You are mine, Aisling. You are mine today, tomorrow, and five hundred years from now. You will always be mine. I do not give up my treasures, *kincsem*. You would do well to remember that."

He stepped away, leaving me quivering against the door with so many emotions, I couldn't begin to separate them. I clutched my arms around myself as he left, wanting to sob out my pain, wanting to follow him and fling myself in his arms, wanting everything to be the way it was before he had stomped all over my heart.

That's how Nora found me a few minutes later, glued up against the door, slow, hot tears leaking from my eyes, dragon fire licking my feet.

"Hello, everyone. We're back a bit early. The kobold attack turned out to be a false alarm—Aisling? Oh, dear, you're on fire again." Nora set down the dog carrier she used to transport Paco. She squinted, adjusted the bright red glasses that perched so jauntily on her nose, and touched a finger to my shirt as I stamped out the last of Drake's fire. "Dragon scales." Her eyes lifted to mine, considering me in the cautious, thoughtful way she had. "A dragon visited you? A *green* dragon?"

I swallowed back a big lump of unshed tears and pushed myself away from the door, staggering over to collapse on her couch, my pounding heart slowly returning to normal.

Nora looked from me to the door, tipping her head to the side to examine it. "Judging by the Aisling-shaped outline that appears to be scorched into the door, I'd say it was *the* green dragon who visited you. How is Drake?"

"As stubborn as ever. Oh, Nora. I thought I was past this!" Both Jim and Nora watched me as I slumped into a giant wad of misery. Paco, released from his confinement, ran over to wrestle with my shoelaces, as was his wont. "I am so ready to move on. Here you are, poised to start my training—oh, that reminds me, there's something I need to tell you about that—and whammo. Two minutes with Drake and I'm a mess. How am I ever supposed to get over him?"

Nora sat down next to me, her dark eyes watchful as they peered at me out of her glasses. "Perhaps you are not meant to get over him," she said simply.

"Huh? Not get over him? Nora, do you have any idea how crazy that man . . . dragon . . . whatever he is—do you have *any* idea how crazy he makes me?"

"You know, normally I just can't get enough of you whining about Drake, or crying over Drake, or ranting about Drake, or any of the other gazillion 'about Drake' things you constantly do because you're obsessed with the man but refuse to admit it, but since you insist on starving this fabulous form I've taken simply because I'm a few pounds over the standard Newfie weight, I just don't have the strength for it today." Jim turned around and marched off to the room Nora had turned over to me.

She raised an eyebrow at the retreating demon. "What's gotten into Jim? I know you and it have a special relationship, but I've never heard it be outright rude before."

"It's mad that I won't take it to Paris because Drake is there . . . although he's not there; he's here. So I guess there's no reason not to go visit Amelie, except now I have this dragon thing to go to." I sighed and slumped even more, feeling far from the confident, self-assured person I so desperately wanted to be. "Nora, do I talk constantly about Drake? I don't sound obsessed, do I? I just sound . . . weary, right?"

Paco pounced on the paper that had fallen from my hand. Nora got it away from him before he did any damage to it, smoothing the sheet over her knee as she sat next to me. "Well . . . since you asked, I'm afraid I'm going to have to agree with Jim."

"What?" I shrieked, sitting upright in order to glare. I didn't, of course—for one thing, Nora was my friend, not just my mentor, and for another . . . well, there was a pesky little voice in the back of my head that was whispering its agreement with both Nora and Jim. The roots of denial, however, were strong and difficult to dig out. "You think I'm obsessed with him, too'?"

"I think you're in love with him, yes. And despite the differences you have, I believe you are meant to be together. Further, I believe that you know this but are too stubborn to admit it to yourself."

There's nothing like a bit of plain speaking to knock the wind from your sails.

"But . . . but . . ."

She shook her head, picking up the paper to glance at it. "I was going to address the issue with you in a few days, when we begin your training proper. A Guardian's strength comes from within, Aisling. To deceive yourself is to weaken your power."

"He betrayed me," I said, wanting to scream the words. "He broke my heart!"

"He betrayed your trust, yes. But you betrayed an oath to him. You both have to learn how to make compromises in order to happil—what on earth?"

The fury in her voice yanked me from the dark musings about my life. "Oh! I'm so sorry! That's what I was going to tell you, but then Drake came in and distracted me. A man named Mark Sullivan was waiting when Rene dropped us off at the door. He said he's with the committee, and he's slapping a restraining order or something on you that says you can't teach me because there's an investigation going on."

Nora nodded, her lips moving slightly as she read the letter.

"Rene?" she asked, looking up, a finger marking a spot on the letter. "You saw Rene?"

"Story for another day. Does the letter say what this is all about?"

She went back to reading, her face impassive. I hadn't known Nora long—it had been about a month since we'd met in Budapest—so I wasn't too good at reading her body language. There was no way to mistake the anger in her ebony eyes, however. They positively flashed black sparks as she crumpled the letter up and threw it on the ground for Paco to bat around.

I waited impatiently for her to say something. When she did, my eyebrows rose in surprise.

"The fools. The bloody ignorant fools. I've half a mind to curse the lot of them."

"I know how you feel. I was shocked when Mark said you were not going to be allowed to teach me. Why are they doing this?" I gave her arm a friendly pat as she looked blindly at her hands.

"It's Marvabelle, of course," she answered.

"Marvabelle? O'Hallahan?" I asked, even more surprised by the name she'd mentioned. "The Marvabelle who was in Budapest? The one with the wimpy oracle husband? The one who used to be your roomie when you were studying to be a Guardian? That Marvabelle?"

"One and the same." Nora jumped from the couch, striding across the living room with her chin high. She turned and paced back. "She's had it in for me ever since we were recognized for stopping the Guardian killings. She warned me then she would not stand around watching me have glory she felt she deserved."

"*She* deserved! She did nothing to catch the murderer!" I got to my feet and stomped around in sympathetic indignation, keeping a tight rein on my anger lest it manifest itself again in dragon fire. "We did all the work! We figured it all out. All she did was get in the way."

Nora stopped pacing in order to grab my sleeve as I stomped by her. "To be honest, you did all the work, and you figured it out. But I thank you for your outrage on my behalf."

"That doesn't matter," I said, waving away her thanks. "What does matter is that Marvabelle thinks she can mess with you. Us. I didn't know she had this sort of clout with the committee."

"Neither did I." Nora picked up a stuffed toy and managed to exchange it for the letter Paco was gnawing on. She smoothed it out and read it again. I peeked over her shoulder, my eyes narrowing at the officious language mentioning a complaint against Nora and the investigation that would hitherto follow.

"*In concordance with the precepts of the code of the Guardians' Guild, you are hereby ordered to cease and desist with any form of Guardian training until otherwise notified, pending the outcome of this investigation,*" I read aloud. "Oh, that is such bull!"

Nora nodded, folding the crumply letter and setting it

in a basket that held her correspondence. "I agree. But don't let it upset you. I have nothing to hide, and I have committed no violations of the Guardian's code. This is just a minor setback, and not worthy of our concern."

"Not worthy? It's utter crap, and I for one don't intend to sit around while . . ." I stopped at the determined look in her eyes. This was her profession, her life that we were discussing. Just because I wanted to punch the committee in the nose for believing Nora could do anything unethical didn't mean I could act on those desires. "OK. Just a minor setback. Gotcha."

"We will begin your training tomorrow, as planned," Nora said firmly as she deposited Paco's carrier in a closet. "Hopefully it will have the side benefit of helping you control Drake's fire."

"Er . . . I don't mean to question you, but didn't that letter say—"

"I do not intend to allow one spiteful woman to waste any more of our time than she has," Nora answered. She pulled a book out of the floor-to-ceiling bookcase that lined one wall and held it out for me. "Although it grieves me to do anything against the committee's dictates, in this I know they are wrong. We will proceed as planned." She paused in the doorway to the kitchen. "Unless you have had a change of heart?"

I laughed so hard tears wet my eyelashes. "Nora, I've broken just about every rule there is. I don't know why you'd think I'd balk at breaking another one."

She smiled, warmth glowing from behind her glasses. "I didn't think you'd mind. I'll make an appointment with Mark to discuss the issue. Now, as for your problems with Drake—why don't we have a nice cup of tea and talk it over?"

Whether I wanted to admit it or not, Jim's (and Nora's) words had hit me hard. I raised my chin and shook my head. "No, I'm through obsessing and monopolizing the conversation and whatever else I've been doing over that annoying man. I'm just going to have to work things out on my own. Er . . . would it help if I talked to the Guardian people, too?"

"It certainly couldn't hurt. Don't worry about that now—I'm sure we'll get everything straightened out once I can sit down and talk to them. And as for you . . . Aisling, I didn't mean you couldn't talk to me about your troubles," Nora said, opening the shutters that closed off a small bar from the kitchen area. "I will always be here to listen to you, if you need a friendly ear."

"Thanks. I appreciate that." I gathered up my things and the book she'd handed me and glanced at the clock. "I'll let you know if I need a shoulder to sob on. Right now I have an outfit to pick out for tomorrow's dragon conference, a book of demonic class types to memorize, and a demon to appease. If I leave now, I think there's time for me to zip over to Paris and make it back by midnight. I'll bone up on the texts you gave me once I get back."

She looked skeptical as I rushed into my room, grabbed my purse and passport, and ordered Jim to follow me. "Aisling, you'd really go all the way to Paris and back in twelve hours just to make your demon happy?"

"Paris?" Jim asked, shuffling its way out to the living room. At the word its ears pricked up, its eyes lit, and it suddenly looked a good ten years younger, not to mention five pounds lighter. "Did I hear that right? We're going to Paris? Right now?"

"Yes, I would," I answered Nora first. "Jim and you are both right—I have been obsessing and moody. I owe it a trip. By my voice, by my blood, by my hand, demon, I banish thee to Akasha."

Before Jim could do more than open its eyes wide with delight and surprise, it disappeared in a puff of black smoke.

"Man, that's a handy little spell," I said as I ran for the door, waving at Nora as I went. "See you later—I'll be back by midnight. Don't let the committee get you down. It can't be anything serious or we'd know, right?"

Honestly, there are times when I think I should be teaching a class called Famous Exit Lines You'll Later Regret.

3

Thanks to the swift efficiency of the Eurostar high-speed train running under the English Channel, three and a half hours after I had raced out of Nora's London apartment, I was standing on the street staring down a dark alley named rue des Furoncles sur les Fesses du Diable (aka Boils on the Buttocks of the Devil Street), a familiar view since that particular narrow alley was home to Le Grimoire Toxique, the cute little shop that catered to the wiccan and witch crowd in Paris. This area of town was heavily given over to occult-type shops, most of which were harmless places where non-Otherworldians came to buy incense and love spells. The shops given over to supplies used by those who knew what they were doing were hidden away on similar dark, out-of-the-way streets like the one where Amelie Merllain lived.

The tiny bells over the door to the Grimoire Toxique tinkled cheerily as I pushed open the door, a similarly cheery smile on my face. Two elderly ladies stood next to a bookshelf as a third woman, middle aged, with a slight amount of gray mixed into her short black hair, stood on a stepladder and fetched bottles from a top shelf.

"Bonjour, Amelie," I said in my best French (which admittedly was atrocious). I sneaked a peek at the slip of paper upon which I'd written a greeting gleaned from my seatmate during the trip to Paris. "Um. *Tu es que l'ombre de toi-même! Quoi de neuf?*"

Amelie's figure froze for a second. "I believe I am more than a shadow of myself, but not much is new here in Paris. Could it be that someone from out of town is asking?" She turned around with a warm smile. "Aisling, I knew it must be you. You have a way of speaking French that is truly . . . impressive."

I laughed and hugged her when she hurried down the stepladder, her hands full of jars that she set down on the counter. Speaking in quick French, she gestured toward me as she bustled around behind the long counter that served as her sales desk. The two ladies looked at me with pursed lips.

"Bonjour," I told them. They murmured what I assumed were polite replies. "Sheesh, Amelie, it's been forever since I last saw you!"

"You exaggerate. It has been under two months, I think. I will be with you in just one of the brief moments." Amelie doled out a pink powder, some dried herbs, and a handful of rose hips. "I told my ladies here that you are a friend from America, and are a powerful, much-respected Guardian."

The ladies looked anything but awestruck. "Then you are guilty of exaggerating as well." I hooked my foot under the rail on a tall wooden stool at the end of the counter, and plopped myself down on it. "Regardless of the time passed, I'm pleased to see you again."

"And I you," she said as she made up a neat paper package of all the herbs, giving them to the two ladies with a few hurried comments. "But where is Jim? Cecile will be deranged if she is not to see him."

"Oh, Jim!" I leaped off the stool, a little zinger of guilt lashing me. "I forgot all about it. I put it in the Akasha."

"The Akasha?" There was a little stereo gasp as Amelie spoke. The two ladies looked horrified and backed up a few steps.

"Yeah. The Akashic plain, actually. You know—the place everyone calls limbo? Where demons who don't eat their vegetables go?"

Amelie just looked at me. The two ladies stood clutching their packages, eyeing me warily as if they were afraid to go past me to the door.

"You are joking at me, yes?" Amelie asked.

"Um. About the veggies, yeah. I put Jim in the Akashic plain because of England's quarantine laws for animals. It's an easy way to get in and out of the country without having to worry about documents for Jim."

"But, Aisling . . ." Amelie looked taken aback for a moment or two. "The Akasha is steeped in dark powers. I know of many experienced members of the L'au-delà who will have nothing to do with it because it poses such a danger to them. Only the most protected of people access it. Who taught you to do so?"

"A . . . er . . . friend. He just taught me how to send and summon Jim from there; that's all."

"Still, you must be very powerful indeed if you are able to utilize it without it tainting you."

I stopped cold, wondering why I was always the last to hear things. The limbo I'd been parking Jim in was steeped in dark powers? Why hadn't Gabriel mentioned that when he gave me instructions on accessing it? How would I know if I'd been tainted? Why didn't Nora warn me about it when I told her that's where I was sending Jim? And *why* did I *always* end up in hot water doing something simple? "Uh . . . yeah, something like that. Why don't I just summon Jim and we'll move on?" I took a deep breath and swung open the door in my mind that was the portal to all my Otherworld powers. "Effrijim, I summon thee."

The air in front of me gathered together in a tight clutch, the motes of dust dancing on the afternoon sunlight cohering into a shape that quickly formed itself into that of a large, shaggy, black dog.

"Hounds of Abaddon, Aisling! Could you have left me dangling in limbo for any longer?" Jim glared at me for a moment; then its eyes opened wide when it realized where we were. "Amelie?"

The two ladies gave up all pretence and ran from the shop screeching something that I gathered wasn't a compliment on the form my demon had picked out above all others to wear in the mortal world.

"Where's Cecile?" Jim asked hurriedly, spinning around to examine the shop, its nose in the air as it tried to scent her. "Cecile? Baby? Daddy's home!"

"Cecile is having her rest upstairs—" was all Amelie got out before Jim went bounding from the room, heading for the back door and the flight of stairs that led to the apartment over the shop.

"The door is locked, isn't it?" I asked.

"Yes, but there is a window open," Amelie started to say, but the distant sound of tinkling glass interrupted her.

I sighed. "I'll pay for that, of course. I'd better go see if Jim managed to cut itself in its frenzy to get to Cecile."

"I believe I will take the early afternoon leave," Amelie said, going to the door to hang a CLOSED sign on it before locking up.

"Oh, but I hate to make you miss any customers." I hesitated by the beaded curtain that divided the front of the shop from the tiny back storage area.

"*Non,* it is an unexpected pleasure, your visit. One worth celebrating, yes? We will celebrate."

The celebrations took the form of a bottle of chilled white wine (Amelie remembered my favorite brand) and a plate of delicious cheese munchies. I sat back in the bloodred neo-baroque armchair and sighed happily. "I can't tell you how good it is to see you again. So much has happened in the last couple of months, I feel like a different person from the one who wandered in your door looking for information about a certain wyvern."

"Ah, yes. How is Drake? I heard that you were formally mated, and that you found a mentor, yes? This is very good news."

Jim looked up from where it was lying in a patch of sunlight with Cecile, Amelie's elderly, fat Welsh corgi. "News flash: Aisling broke it off."

"Again?" Amelie asked, giving me a surprised look.

"Yes, *again.*" That word was beginning to grate on my

nerves. "It's not like I didn't have a reason to leave him! He betrayed my trust."

"Hello, and welcome to *Aisling Heartbreak Hour*," Jim said, nuzzling Cecile's ear. "I hope you're comfortable, because this is likely to take a while."

"One more word, and you're going to find yourself back in the Akashic plain, tainted powers or no," I snapped, my patience worn thin by Jim's needling . . . and my own guilty feelings. Although Nora had been the first person to put it into so many words, I realized that I'd been hiding the truth from myself behind hurt feelings. "This is not going to take a while. Drake and I had issues. I left to think things over. I'm still his mate, I'm still bound to the sept, and tomorrow, as a matter of fact, I'm going to another dragon conference to stand by Drake while he does whatever he does at these gatherings."

"Gatherings?"

"Yes. Some sort of dragon shindig. Possibly involving wyverns, although I hope the more idiotic ones don't show."

Amelie sucked in her breath. "Idiotic? You speak so of the other wyverns? You dare much, Aisling. Do you know them well?"

"Not horribly well." I took another sip of wine, enjoying the fruity Riesling. "Fiat Blu I met here in Paris at the same time I met you. I met some of his men, as well. Did you know the blue dragons are psychics?"

She nodded. "*Oui,* I remember. And yes, they are known for their ability to find secrets."

"Yeah, well, Fiat is lovely eye candy, what with that whole blond god thing going for him, but underneath that handsome exterior beats the heart of a rat. He's trying to stir up trouble for Drake."

"Ah?"

"Fiat paired up with Chuan Ren. Have you ever seen her?"

Amelie poured more wine and shook her head. "No. I do not mix much with the upper echelons of the L'au-delà. I am happier in my own sphere of influence."

"Boy, do I envy you that. Well, the red dragon wyvern, Chuan Ren, is a . . . um . . . trying to find a nice word for her . . ."

"Bitch," Jim said, licking Cecile's ear.

I made a wry little smile. "Basically, yes. She's very powerful, very aggressive, and I don't think she likes Drake very much. I know she doesn't like me."

"Hmm."

"The fourth wyvern, Gabriel Tauhou, is a sweetie. He's a healer, like you."

Amelie smiled and nibbled on a cheese stick.

"Aisling has a crush on him." Jim's voice floated to us above the low drone of the air conditioner.

"Oh, I do not. I like Gabriel, nothing more. He helped me when Drake wouldn't, and he doesn't seem to want to stir up trouble, unlike the other two wyverns."

"That is very interesting," Amelie said, looking thoughtful. "And what of the fifth sept?"

"The what?" I frowned, setting down my wineglass. When I started mishearing things, it was time to switch to something a little less potent. "Fifth sept? There are only four dragon septs—red, blue, silver, and green."

"*Non,* there is a fifth sept. I heard that a black dragon

had been spotted in Germany. The local speculation is that he will claim the post of wyvern and bring the black dragons back."

"There's a fifth sept?" I looked at Jim. "Jim, how many dragon septs are there?"

"Now, or ever have been?" Jim answered. I ground my teeth a little. The dragons had a habit of answering a question with a question, and Jim had picked up that habit.

"Right now, how many dragon septs are there?"

"Four," Jim said, pausing a moment. "Five if you count the black dragons, but no one has seen any of them for a hundred and fifty years."

"Who's the wyvern?" I asked. Neither Jim nor Amelie had an answer. "Well, then, why did they disappear? What happened to them? Why hasn't anyone mentioned them before this?"

Amelie shrugged. Jim sucked ear. I glared at it.

"You never asked," my demon finally answered.

"I believed you would receive answers to your questions from your mate," Amelie said. "I am not au courant with all that goes on in the dragon world. I can only tell you what the gossip of the moment says."

"Well, you can bet your bootstraps I'll be asking Drake about that. If there's another wyvern out there I have to make nice to, I'd like to know about it first."

Amelie smiled again and switched the subject. "I know this will be of interest to you, since you had something to do with it the last time you were here—the office of Venediger has not yet been filled, although there have been challenges for it."

"Oh, really? You know—silly me—I never was quite

sure exactly what the Venediger does. It's a position running the French Otherworld?"

"France, yes, and the rest of what is now the common
market. Mostly all of Europe. It is a very big position,
you know? Very important. To be Venediger means to
have much control, much power. The challengers for it
have been strong, but not strong enough." She slid me an
odd little look that I couldn't read.

"Really? What happened to them?"

"They killed each other," she said simply and held out
a plate of cold, marinated mushrooms. She made a little
moue at the horrified expression on my face. "Yes, it is
shocking, but unfortunately, the people who first come
forward at a time like this are not ones we want in control.
Now that the feverheads and rogues have done away with
themselves, the serious challengers will come out and battle for control."

"I guess you've got to be a hothead if you end up fighting to the death for a job," I said slowly, wondering what
sort of person would end up in control of western Europe's Otherworld society.

Amelie agreed. "But Aisling . . . there has been some
talk."

"Oh? About what? Oooh, stuffed tomatoes! Thank
you, they look delicious."

I popped a tiny tomato into my mouth while she sat
down opposite me, her hands folded together.

"Do you recall what I said the last time I saw you?"

"The last time? Hmm." I thought back a couple of
months. "Bon voyage?"

"Before that. It was right after you solved the murders of the Venediger and Madame Deauxville."

I put down the scrumptious morsel of tomato and cheese, my blood running cold. "You said that since I had defeated the person who was going to take over as Venediger, that meant I was a candidate for the job, but it's not going to happen, Amelie. I have enough on my plate as is."

"It is the opinion of many here that you would be perfect for the position," she said stubbornly as she poured herself another glass of wine.

"Much as I appreciate such a thought, I wouldn't be perfect for it. I don't even know what a Venediger does, for cripe's sake!"

"You are a smart woman. You would learn quickly."

I set my glass down and took a deep breath. "Thank you, but no. Seriously, no. It's all I can do to keep up with Nora and the dragons—anything else would be absolutely out of the question."

She shrugged, and without saying anything more on that topic, turned the conversation to personal subjects. I told her what I'd been doing the last couple of months, about our time in Budapest, and gave her a brief update on the situation with Drake.

"He . . . betrayed you?" she asked, clearly surprised.

"In a manner of speaking. He kind of tricked me into becoming his mate while leading me to believe he would support my Guardian training."

"That is very wrong of him . . . but very like a dragon," she said after a moment's thought.

"Yes. I will admit that he was in a hard place, and perhaps I wasn't noticing warning signs as well as I might, but hindsight and all that."

"Hmm. It is difficult."

By the time we were through dissecting my love life, discussing all the gossip of the Paris Otherworld, and allowing Jim to have quality Cecile time, I had only an hour and a half left before I had to get to the station to catch the high-speed train back to London.

"Would you like to go to G&T?" Amelie asked as I helped her clear the dinner table after we'd eaten a lovely meal of poached smoked haddock and potatoes, and wild mushroom ravioli that had me gibbering with pleasure as it melted in my mouth. "If it has bad memories for you, I will understand, but it is still the premiere place in Paris."

"I'd love to. I don't hold the bar at fault for all the stuff that happened there," I told her as we gathered up our things. Jim was torn between leaving Cecile and missing out on potential snacks from unwary patrons at the Goety and Theurgy bar, where so much had happened a few months ago. In the end, it decided that although love was eternal, a sleepy Cecile was not as entertaining as G&T.

"I want a drink, though. And some snacks. That mushroom thing isn't going to hold me over until morning," Jim said as we headed for the metro.

"If you'd eaten the food Amelie provided, you wouldn't be hungry now," I said in an undertone, pinching its ear to remind it to keep its voice down in public.

"That was dog food!" Jim's voice was rife with disbelief. "Do you have any idea what they put in that stuff? It's, like, all ground-up lips and butts! I'm not putting that in this magnificent form!"

"Fine, I'll buy you a hamburger once we get to G&T, but if I find you begging from anyone, it's straight back to the Akashic plain with you!"

I was mildly surprised to see that G&T looked no different than it had before but was reminded with a jolt, at the sight of the previous Venediger's picture on a wall near the bar, that the events I'd remembered were only a few months in the past. Despite the former owner's brutal murder, and the manager's spiral into madness, everything looked exactly the same. I half expected to see Drake and his two redheaded bodyguards lounging in the corner.

"I know it's silly, but you'd think it would look different after everything we went through." My gaze roamed the club, looking for some sign that the events we'd participated in had some sort of lasting effect. "Everything's the same, though—same low, pulsing music you have to yell over to be heard, smoky air that leaves you craving a ventilation system, and people slinking around looking as normal as can be despite the fact that they're anything but."

"The band is different this week," Amelie said, waving a hand toward a small stage at the opposite end of the club. We walked down the few steps into the room, prepared to squeeze our way through the dense wall of people who stood among the bar, tables, and dance area. I expected we'd have to use a few elbows to get through, but as I stepped forward, an aisle through the mass opened up as if by . . . well, magic.

"This is odd," I whispered to Amelie as I took advantage of the strange phenomenon. Before me, people stepped aside to make way for us. Behind, the path closed up seamlessly after Amelie and Jim. "This happened to me once before here—what gives with everyone? Why are they acting like they don't want me to inadvertently brush against them? I'm not a leper!"

"No, but you are a person of much importance in the L'au-delà," Amelie answered in a soft tone. "You are a demon lord, a wyvern's mate, and a Guardian. There has never been a person who was all three—that is why many people believe you would be a good Venediger as well. They are simply showing you the respect due your position."

"Hey, if Aisling is a celeb, does that make me one, too? Will someone ask for my picture, do you think?" Jim asked, looking around for potential paparazzi. "Should I set up my demon-jim.com Web site now?"

"*Oui,* you are known as well. All have heard of you: You are the demon who serves your master well."

"Hrmph," Jim said. "Lassie I'm not! Fame can wait if all I'm going to be known as is a trusty sidekick. What's this biz about Ash as the V?"

"Just silly talk, nothing more. I'm not going to complain about making it through a crowd easily," I whispered to Amelie, "but it still gives me the creeps. I'm not anyone important at all, and for them to treat me this way is . . . oh, look, a table."

We grabbed a couple of chairs and a small table in an out-of-the-way corner and accepted menus from the waitress.

"Drinks?" she asked in broken English.

"I will have a cognac," Amelie told her, handing back the menu.

"Er . . . dragon's blood," I said with an apologetic smile.

"And for ze demon?" she asked, giving Jim a bland look.

Jim drooled on her foot.

"It will have a club soda in a bowl and a hamburger with all the trimmings."

"No onions. I have Cecile to think of," Jim corrected me.

"So? How does it feel to be back?" Amelie asked once the waitress left, tipping her head to the side as she looked at me.

I looked around again. Although the music pulsed, conversation ebbed and flowed around us, and people generally went about their evenings, I had a feeling that everyone in the room knew exactly where I was sitting. It was an uncanny, unnerving feeling, and it made me extremely uncomfortable. "It feels . . . kind of odd. The first time I stepped foot in here, I had no idea of what this world was made of. I guess what's bothering me most is that the club hasn't changed—I have."

"But changed for the better, no? Now you see all the possibilities."

I smiled. Amelie was the first one who'd told me to look beyond the obvious into something she called the "possibilities"—which I'd gathered meant that anything that could be, might be. It was all very quantum physics, and I did my best to try not to think too hard about it, just accept that there were things existing that I had never thought possible.

"Oh, look. There, do you see? The man at the end of the bar, next to the troll."

I squinted through the smoke and tried to pinpoint the

figures Amelie was indicating. "There's a troll here? The kind with green hair and stumpy legs and a big pot belly?"

She gave me a look like I had suddenly sprouted antlers. "What are you speaking? No, of course a troll does not have green hair and a pot belly. The woman in the Birkenstocks and patterned capri pants. That is the troll—her name is Trude. She comes from Bavaria. But that is not who I want you to see—it is the man next to her. That is Peter Burke."

"And Peter Burke is . . . '?"

"He is said to be a most powerful mage. And one of the . . . what is the word? Contenders? For the position of Venediger, *hein*?"

"Ah." I looked at the man she indicated. He turned at that moment and looked directly at me. I smiled. He frowned and looked away again. "He doesn't look like a powerful mage. He looks like . . . well, kind of Alan Alda-ish. Placid, almost."

"You are not seeing the possibilities within him," Amelie said dryly.

I admitted that was so and, clearing my mind, swung open the door to my powers and released them in order to really look at the mage.

As it always did, everything seen through my super-Guardian vision looked so much brighter, so much sharper, as if the everyday world was slightly grayed out and blurred. I moved my eyes along the people in G&T, noting that a woman who sat apparently alone with two men actually had a spirit shape hovering protectively behind her. The woman Amelie named as the troll had a faint sparkle of something all over her skin—it reminded me of mushroom spores. My gaze shifted to the man next to her, and I jerked as his head turned once again to me. For the space between seconds a black tendril of power seemed to snake off him, but it was gone so quickly that I wondered if I had imagined it.

"Huh. Interesting. I've never seen that before, but I don't see anything that screams mage. Then again, I've never met one. Maybe there's something about them I don't know to look for."

"He is not a popular man," she said quietly.

"Really? If there's such a powerful mage all ready to step into the Venediger's shoes, why on earth would anyone want me to fight for the job?"

"We do not know who he is. No one knows for certain." Amelie leaned close so I could hear. "But it is rumored his power comes from a dark source."

Something bothered me about Peter Burke, but I couldn't put my finger on what it was. Perhaps Amelie's forebodings were getting to me. "Hmm. I can see why people wouldn't want someone with one foot in Abaddon in control of the Otherworld, but if you want to get technical, I am a demon lord, so that should let me off the hook, too."

She shook her head. "Everyone here knows about you and Jim. You are not a prince of Abaddon, nor do you have ties to them." Her gaze shifted across the bar to where Peter Burke sat. "The same cannot be said about others."

"Hey! I sensed an insult in that statement!" Jim said, looking up from the bread sticks I'd given it. We both ignored the demon.

"Well, it's a moot point. I can't take the job." I continued my perusal of the room, greatly enjoying seeing beneath the surface of the denizens of the Paris Otherworld. "Wow. This is fascinating."

"I wish you would think about it . . . oh, dear."

"Oooh, there's a faerie over there. She has translucent wings that are almost invisible even to my supervision. Cool."

"Ash, you're going to be sued if you keep it up."

I ignored Jim. It always exaggerated. My gaze shifted past the faerie and her companion (also fey), wandering around the room, enjoying seeing people in their true forms. A little ripple of excitement caused everyone to shift, a wave of cool air curling through the crowds as a hush descended over everyone.

"That's odd. I wonder who's causing that . . . oh, no!"

"Aisling, you must stop now. This is getting out of hand," Amelie said.

"It's Fiat," I groaned, recognizing the man at the doorway of the club. "Damn. I was hoping to avoid him."

"Ash, you may want to drop the menu before it burns you."

"Hmm?" I looked from where Fiat was gliding his way down the steps, two of his guards in tow, to the menu I still held in my hand. It was on fire.

"Criminy dutch!"

The mental door slammed shut as I dropped the menu on the floor and stomped on it a few times to put the flames out. I looked up to apologize and explain to Amelie that although as Drake's mate I could pull on his dragon fire, I had yet to really learn how to control it, but the look on her face as she gazed around the room stopped me.

Every menu in the place was alight. People stood silently with them burning where they had dropped—on the tables, the floor, and the bar itself. To a man, they all turned to look at me.

"I see you have made your presence known in your own distinct manner." A smooth voice with an Italian accent floated from the far side of the room. "Welcome back to Paris, *cara*."

4

"Aisling Grey," the dragon who stopped in front of me said, a smile touching his lips. I ground my teeth together. A name, as I have learned, has power, and the emphasis Fiat put on my name made it seem as if he had some sort of hold over me.

In his dreams.

"Sfiatatoio del Fuoco Blu," I said, deliberately using Fiat's full name. He ignored that and clutched my hand, pressing his lips to the back of it, nodding to Amelie when I introduced her.

He pulled out a chair without waiting for an invitation. "*Cara,* it has been so long. What, two weeks since we have last been together?" Fiat's cool fingers trailed across the back of my neck. I shivered and scooted to the side, aware that I was being less than polite. The blue dragons' element was air, and Fiat always seemed to be a good ten degrees cooler than his environment. "An eternity."

"Yes, two weeks, although you could hardly say we

were together. You were trying to disrupt the peace conference, and I was there supporting Drake."

"Such a fierce defense of him. What fire you have." He reached out and tucked an unruly strand of hair behind my ear. I fought down the desire to smack his hand and told myself he was purposely trying to rile me. I wouldn't give him the satisfaction of giving in to the temptation. "And yet, I have heard that all is not well with you and your mate. You have been living in the States while he remains in Europe, no?"

"No," I said firmly, smiling at the waitress when she brought our drinks. She brought Fiat a dusty dark green bottle and small aperitif glass as well, clearly a standing order. I lifted my glass and touched it to Amelie's, then acknowledged my manners and did the same with Fiat. "*Santé.*"

"*Santé,*" Amelie murmured, her eyes wary as she watched Fiat.

"I had also heard that you were moving to London to be nearer your mentor." Fiat sipped at his drink, some sort of golden wine. "Is Drake accompanying you? Or are the rumors true, and you are at odds with your mate?"

I said nothing but ground out a smile. It was pretty insincere, but it was a smile nonetheless. Although I wanted nothing more than to tell Fiat what I really thought of him, I held my tongue. This wasn't just about me now—I had the green dragons to think of. Drake wouldn't thank me if I insulted Fiat so greatly that the blue dragons refused to cooperate at any further peace discussions.

Fiat's eyes narrowed. He leaned toward me, sniffing. "Why is it you smell different?"

"I really don't think a discussion about my choice of deodorant or bath powder is at all enlightening, but if you really want the names of both, I'll be happy to give them to you."

"No," he said, suddenly lunging at me until his nose was buried in the crook of my neck.

"Hey!" I said, trying to push him away. Minding my p's and q's was one thing—full frontal sniffage was another! "Knock it off! Um. *Please* knock it off."

"You want me to rip him a new one?" Jim asked. Amelie looked confused.

"Of course not. Don't be silly," I said, trying for a light, dismissive laugh. The last thing I wanted was for anyone to get bent out of shape, even though this really was over the line. "Fiat is just overly impressed by my perfume. I'll have to write the makers a testimonial letter."

Jim snorted in disbelief.

"It is not perfume or chemicals you have applied to yourself that I smell," Fiat answered, finally giving in to my (polite) shoves. He sat in his chair for a moment, his fingers stroking his chin as he watched me. "It is something about you that has changed. Some . . . chemical change in your body." Crystalline heat flared to life in his eyes. "Are you breeding?"

"What?" I squawked, in so loud a voice that several people looked over at us. Amelie smothered a much more quiet gasp.

Jim wasn't anywhere near as subtle. "Now. Let me rip him to shreds now. Pretty please with sugar on top?"

Everyone ignored the demon.

"Are you breeding Drake's child? Are you pregnant?"

It took me a few minutes to get myself under control. "You know, I think I'm just going to pass on answering that question. My personal life, my relationship with Drake—anything that doesn't have a bearing on the peace between the dragons—is not going to be a topic I will discuss with you."

Under the table, out of sight of Fiat, Jim leaned over and drooled on his expensive, shiny shoes.

"Hmm." Fiat's finger tapped on his chin as he continued to inspect me as if I might sprout a BABY ON BOARD sign. "You are human. Drake is a wyvern . . . no. You are correct. Any dragonkin you have will not have a bearing on the future. They will not become wyverns."

"Well, I'm glad you're seeing it my way, but I've got to say I don't see Drake as an old man handing over control of the sept to anyone but a child of his—not that we're having any, but as long as we're being hypothetical, I think you're wrong. He certainly would want one of our children to be wyvern after him."

Fiat rose from his chair with swift elegance. "You have much to learn of our ways, *cara*. Your ignorance is almost as dazzling as the whiteness of your breasts."

I looked down at my chest for a minute, making sure my boobs weren't suddenly popping out of my sundress. They weren't. I bit back yet another retort.

"Such rigid control you have over yourself," Fiat said, shaking his head. "Not only is your mind perfectly blocked from mine, you will not even play that delightful teasing game we have so enjoyed in the past. I wonder how long it will last?"

I let that go, too. Words—in this instance—couldn't hurt me. Fiat was right in that I had slipped my mental barriers into place the instant I saw him. He had a particular talent for mind reading, and I wanted to be sure that he knew my mind was definitely off limits.

"What about now?" Jim asked, glaring at Fiat. "Please? That boob comment was over the top."

"No. Nice to see you again," I said noncommittally to Fiat as he stepped back from the table. I struggled to summon up one last bit of polite banter. "Are you staying in Paris for a while?"

His fingers caressed the stem of the wineglass, his eyelids dropping until he gazed at me with a look so sultry, it set off the hairs on the back of my neck. "Drake has broken your spirit. I preferred you fiery and uncontrolled. I must see what I can do to restore you to your former state, breeding or not."

"*Now*?" Jim asked, a plea in its voice.

I shot it a glance that told it to be quiet. "Fiat, you know well that if you laid one little finger on me, Drake would bring you down. So, much as I enjoy this bandying of wits, I'll simply say good-bye. Au revoir."

"Pah," he said, a flicker of annoyance visible in his eyes for a moment before he stalked off to where his bodyguards were waiting.

I gave the three of them a polite, tight smile of recognition and turned back to Amelie with a sigh of relief. "Whew. That was hairier than I thought it would be. Breeding! Have you ever?"

"Fire hounds of Abaddon, Aisling! What's with you? You let him get away without once siccing me on him!" You wouldn't think a Newfie's face could express many emotions, but the way Jim worked, it could have been on the stage. Outrage, frustration, and speculative malignancy each took a turn on its face.

"It's called acting like an adult, and since when are you so hot and bothered to defend me to a dragon?"

Jim sniffed and turned away.

Amelie gave it an interested look. "What class of demon are you, Jim?"

The demon was silent.

"I'm sorry, Amelie; it has no manners tonight," I told her. "Jim, I realize you don't have to answer questions that anyone asks you other than me, but in the polite world, when someone asks you something, you answer. Please do so."

"So, are you preggers?" Jim asked instead, looking up when the waitress brought it a hamburger on a pretty yellow plate. "That would explain a lot."

I set down the glass of spicy, fire-inducing (often quite literally) beverage that only dragons and their mates could drink without dire consequences and laid my hands flat on the table, looking Jim firmly in the eye. "Not that this is anyone's business, but no, I'm not pregnant."

"Are you sure?" Jim spat out a bit of pickle. "You haven't gone psycho hormone woman and demanded gallons of chocolate ice cream in what . . . six weeks? That sounds pregnant to me."

"Oh, for god's sake . . . one more word about this, and you're off to Akasha until I get home."

"I wonder what Drake is going to say when he finds

out?" Jim asked between licks of the now-empty plate. "I bet he goes nuts—heyyyyy . . ."

I spoke the words that sent the demon into limbo so quickly, it had no time to do anything but look startled.

"Sorry, Amelie. Jim's been a bit, well, off the last few weeks. It kept telling me its heart was broken, and we both know that demons don't have hearts, but even so, I think it really was unhappy about not seeing Cecile. Looks like we're going to have to set up regular visits to keep it happy."

Amelie blinked at me a couple of times. I figured she was making all sorts of mental comments about Americans and their snarky demons.

"I do not believe I have ever met anyone like you," she finally said.

"Is that good? It sounds like it could be a compliment, but knowing Jim, maybe you meant that in a less than sterling way."

She just looked at me with mild brown eyes.

I sighed. "Gotcha. You mean that I'm weird. It's OK. I've pretty much come to grips with that. Moving on . . . what did Fiat mean about one of my kids—not that I'm going to have one anytime soon, and I'm not sure that Drake and I are going to be able to work things out, but assuming that miracles can happen and we do, what was all that about one of our kids not being wyvern after Drake?"

"That is something for you to talk to him about," she said, her lips making the thin line that I knew meant she wasn't going to be forthcoming with any further information.

"But you know the answer?"

She nodded.

"Criminy. Why does no one ever want to tell me anything?" I groused quietly to myself as I took another sip of the dragon's-blood beverage. Heat roared through me, causing a few stray flickers to erupt from my fingertips. Absently, I slapped them out. "It's like some sort of guessing game and everyone knows the rules but me. I hate that sort of thing. It makes me want to take my ball and go home."

"You still do not have a true understanding of what it is you've agreed to do," Amelie said, shaking her head. "Aisling, this is not a game you play. You hold many people's lives in the flat of your hand, and I fear that one day, you will destroy them without knowing it."

Her words hit me like a bucket of ice water. "I'm sorry, Amelie—I didn't mean to appear flip. You may not believe it, but I'm very cognizant of my responsibilities to the dragons. Hence my rather strained restraint with Fiat earlier. And I know Jim would say I'm whining, but sometimes I feel like everything is stacked up against me, and there's no way I'm ever going to find my way out."

"You will," she said, signaling for the check. She plopped a couple of coins on the table. "You must simply embrace all of the possibilities."

"Right. Like the possibility that I'm not going to go insane, and someday, I will understand everything." I snatched up my purse and followed Amelie through the crowded floor of the club to the door. Once again, a magical aisle opened up for us, and I was aware again of being the focus of many people's attention. It was a very creepy feeling.

"That is one possibility, yes. How much time do you have?" she asked as we made our way out of the club into the soft evening air, bright lights, and nonstop low drone of chatter that make up Paris on a summer night.

"Eeek. About twenty minutes. Is it far to the train station?"

"*Non*. We will walk there."

Security issues being what they are, we had to part at the outer lobby of the train station. Amelie embraced me, her smile warm and empowering.

"You will do what is right, so long as you always leave yourself open to the possibilities. Be true to yourself, and everything will fall into place," was her parting advice. I wished her well in return and told her I'd give her a call in a few days to set up a time when Jim could come to visit Cecile again.

I'd arrived earlier than required at the train station, had ample time to get through customs, and soon found myself wandering around the departure area, waiting for our slightly delayed train to arrive. Even though it was late at night, the station was crowded with English tourists returning home after a day spent shopping and sightseeing. The station was a cacophony of the usual train station noises—people talking and laughing, children running around screeching as they played tag or just generally got in the way of people trying to move through the mass of bodies, music coming from the fringes, where several street musicians had set up competing stations, and occasional blasts of static-filled, unintelligible announcements from the train company, in what I assumed was French, English, and German.

Since I wanted to get a good seat facing forward, I edged my way along the platform until I found a tourist-free spot near the far end—away from most of the crowds, but not positioned so I'd end up at the dining car.

"Aisling! What is the most charming Guardian of my acquaintance doing in Paris? I thought you had gone to London to train with Nora."

I spun around at the deep, slightly accented voice, more than a little startled to behold a familiar face flashing a dimpled smile at me.

"Gabriel! What on earth are you doing here? Your last e-mail said you had to go home to take care of something."

"I did, but I've been summoned by your mate. Is that the train?"

A cheer from the waiting passengers and a whoosh of noise and air heralded the arrival of the now-late train. I stepped to the edge of the platform to see around the crowd, turning back to tell the silver wyvern that the train was in fact coming.

The words never left my mouth. Before I could turn completely, I was struck by a tremendous blow on the small of my back, sending me hurtling onto the train tracks, directly in the path of the arriving train.

5

Pain burst into glorious life on my side, pain that exploded into agony as my arm was damn near yanked out of its socket. Before my brain had time to process the fact that I'd been knocked onto the track, I was off it again, jerked beyond it to the other side of the platform.

A couple of people nearest me screamed, but the noise was eaten up with the arrival of the train as it came to a stop a few scant feet behind me.

A shriek of horror mingled with pain burbled up as I found myself pressed against a hard, unmoving body. My brain finally caught up to reality, causing me to shake with the nearness of my certain demise.

"Oh, my god," I said, clinging with desperate gratitude to the man who had saved me. Thank god for Gabriel. I had no idea what he was doing at the train station at that moment, but I would, until my last days on the earth, be grateful he was there when I needed him. "Oh, my god, oh, my god. Oh, my god."

"Not god, *cara*. The next best thing, though."

"I was almost killed," I told Gabriel's chest, great, huge, heaving sobs of terror and relief trying to rip free of my constricted throat. My arm and rib cage hurt like the very devil, but all I could think of was how nice it was to be alive and feeling pain considering how near I had been to death. "Oh, my god. I almost died."

"You are a wyvern's mate. Death does not come easily to one such as you, although I will admit you could well have been decapitated by the train, and that would indeed have been the end to the brave little Guardian."

Horribly vivid, gruesome images came to mind that had me clutching Gabriel even harder. Two train officials ran up to ask questions, but Gabriel spoke rapidly in French I couldn't begin to follow, and before I knew it, he was trying to pry me from his chest. "We are attracting unwelcome attention. Come, *cara*, I will escort you home."

"I know I'm immortal, but that train could have smashed me to pulp. Or cut me up into a gazillion pieces. Or . . . or . . . oh, my god!"

Gabriel gently unclasped my arms from where they were wrapped around his waist, easing me back from his chest.

My brain did a mental jaw drop that just about had me on my knees in surprise. The man who had saved me from certain death wasn't Gabriel—it was Fiat.

"What . . . what . . . *Fiat*?"

"Ah, your wits return to you. Excellent. This way, *cara*."

My wits hadn't returned. That's the only reason I can think of that Fiat got me almost out of the train station before I realized what he was doing.

"Wait," I said, pulling my arm from his grasp, looking around me wildly. We were at the entrance of the departure area, next to a bank of metal detectors and security people checking everyone who came into the station. "This isn't right. I'm going home."

"*Si*. My home. Renaldo?" Fiat inclined his head toward the big blond behemoth who had been in front of us. I recognized him as one of Fiat's bodyguards, a man who, like his wyvern, was utterly ruthless when it came to getting his own way.

"I am not going home with you," I said in a low, determined voice, taking a few steps to the side so Fiat couldn't grab me. "Look, I appreciate the fact that you just saved my life—I'm more grateful than I can ever say—but I am not going home with you. I'm going to my own home, where I can sit and cry for a good day or so to work through the horror of being shoved in front of an oncoming train. So, thank you a thousand times for the rescue, but no thanks to the domestic arrangements."

I turned to walk away, but Fiat grabbed my arm, pulling me up close to his body. I was reminded again just how well built the man was—I swear there wasn't an ounce of fat on him anywhere. He was as rock solid as Drake. "*Cara*, you owe me your life. You will come with me now so that we might discuss how you can pay this debt."

His fingers bit hard into my upper arm. I turned my head slowly and narrowed my eyes at him, meeting his sapphire gaze without a single waver. "If you do not let go of me in the next three seconds, I am going to scream."

"You will not make a scene," he answered, yanking me hard toward the exit.

"One, two, three," I said quickly, then opened my mouth in an eardrum-piercing scream. "He's got a bomb!" I pointed at Fiat. "Terrorist!"

Fiat swore under his breath as he dropped my arm and spun around, his hands up as the security people rushed toward him, guns at the ready. A second before they reached us, Fiat's mind brushed mine.

I am not through with you, cara.

Goose bumps marched up my arm despite the warmth of the evening. I rubbed them as the swarm of security people descended upon us both, three-quarters of them pouncing on Fiat, the rest surrounding me, belting me with questions in French.

Five hours later I dragged myself from a ubiquitous black London taxicab, bruised, battered, exhausted, and on the verge of what felt like a breakdown. I weaved slightly.

"You are sure you are all right, *mon amie*?"

I nodded and waved a limp hand at Rene. "Fine. Pay you tomorrow."

"Peh. The payment, she is not important. You are. Get some rest, and then call me tomorrow and tell me exactly what happened."

"K. Night. Thanks for picking me up," I answered wearily, staggering slightly as I headed for the door to the stairs that would lead me up to sanctuary.

"Anytime, my friend, anytime." Rene sped off in a cloud of diesel fumes as I crawled my way up to Nora's apartment, too tired to dig the key out of my purse. I thud-

ded on the door a couple of times, leaning heavily on it as
my brain whirled around in a circle of residual shock and
horror, pain, and exhaustion.

"Aisling? Is that . . . oh, my lord. Are you all right?"
The door suddenly swung open, causing me to stagger
into the living room. I righted myself and stood swaying
for a moment, blinking in the bright lights Nora had
turned on.

"Yeah, I'm OK. Just sore and tired. Going to take a
bath."

"But—what happened to you? Is your French friend
all right?"

"Fine," I said, stumbling to the bathroom. "Tell you all
about it in the morning. Jim, I summon thee."

My demon appeared in a puff of black demon smoke, its
mouth open to harangue me for leaving it so long in limbo,
but for once Jim had the foresight to not light into me.

"You look like Abaddon," was all it said.

"Feel worse," I answered, then closed the bathroom
door in its face and gave myself over to a long, hot soak.
I knew I'd have a lot of explaining to do to both Nora and
Jim, not to mention mulling over what had happened in
the train station, why Gabriel hadn't grabbed me, and
why Fiat *had* when my death was sure to mean the death
of Drake, his arch nemesis. But all that could wait until
the morning. Things always looked more manageable in
the morning.

I am so often wrong about things like that.

"Morning, Nora . . . oh. You're going out?" I stifled a
yawn as I squinted across a small kitchen made bright by

the morning sun. Jim was flaked out in a pool of sunlight, cocking an eyebrow at me, but saying nothing as it read the morning paper.

"Yes, I got a call this morning that there's been an imp outbreak near my portal," she answered, taking a last sip of coffee before rinsing out the cup and setting it to dry. "Jim went out for a walk with Paco and me earlier, so it shouldn't need to go out right away."

"Oh. Thank you. Um . . . imps. In Green Park? I should come help with them."

"You have dragon business to attend to," Nora interrupted, putting Paco in his traveling carrier. She snapped it shut, then laughed when she saw me. "Such a guilty expression! Aisling, I knew when I took you on as an apprentice that there would be times when you would be unable to assist me as a normal apprentice might. This is one of those times, and since the imps aren't dangerous in any way, I have no problem whatsoever in taking care of them myself. I'm just going to remove them, then I'll catch a train to Chichester to deal with the kobolds I mentioned yesterday. It was a false alarm then, but I want to keep an eye on it. With luck, I should be back by dinner."

I glanced at the clock. I had the dragon thing to go to in a couple of hours. Nora might be generous enough to excuse me from helping her with the imps, but I was too conflicted to do that. Obviously she'd gotten along just fine without me up to that point, but now that I was signed on as an apprentice, it was my duty to help her wherever and whenever she needed me. "I've got a few hours yet. Do you think the imps will take long?"

"They shouldn't, no. But, Aisling, you don't need to

come with me. I understand how important this dragon meeting is to you."

"Be right out," I said over my shoulder, hurrying to my bedroom. "Jim, stop reading the paper and get ready to be my trusty sidekick."

"Yes, kemosabe," it answered, turning the page.

Fortunately, Nora's portal was only fifteen minutes away on foot, located in a slim belt of trees that lined an edge of Green Park.

"And your portal is where?" I asked, searching the ground at the spot Nora had pointed to for something that looked like an open conduit to Hell.

"Here," she said, standing next to a squat, prickly pine tree. I walked around the tree, scouring the ground for the portal.

"Where? I don't see it. Is it hidden or something?"

"No, it's right here," she said, touching the tree.

"The *tree* is the portal?"

Her eyes glittered behind her glasses. I was learning to read her expressions, and that particular glitter meant she was smiling to herself. "Yes. You expected a gaping maw to Abaddon, filled with brimstone and the screams of the eternally tormented?"

"Well . . . yeah. Something like that. Or at least like the portal that popped up in that restaurant in Budapest. Jim—" I turned to ask my demon a question, but it wasn't there. I scanned the surrounding area. No demonic Newfie was anywhere in sight. "Where'd it go?"

Nora set down her Paco carrier and extracted a slim black case from her inner pocket. "It was here a minute ago. Does it normally go off on its own?"

"No, hardly ever . . . oh, there you are. Where have you been?"

Jim smirked. "Miss me?"

"Immeasurably. What were you doing?"

"I smelled some imps nearby. Being the exemplary sort of demon that I am, I thought you'd like me to locate them for you. So I did. There were only a few so I took care of them for you."

Nora's eyebrows rose. "Jim is trained to destroy imps?"

"Trained isn't exactly the word," I said, squatting next to the demon. "Open your mouth."

"What?" Jim asked, trying to back away, but I caught its collar and twisted it tight. "I haven't done anything."

"You ate those imps, didn't you? Dammit, Jim, you know how high in fat they are! The vet said your cholesterol was that of an eighty-year-old man. I told you imps were off your diet!"

Jim snarled something unintelligible, made so because it clenched its teeth together as I pried its flews apart so I could see along the edge of its teeth.

"Aha! What's this?" I picked out a minuscule little item from the depths of its lips and waved it around in front of its face.

"I don't have the slightest idea what you're yammering about," Jim grumbled, looking away.

Nora adjusted her glasses and examined the bit of partially chewed blob on my fingers. "That looks to be part of an imp's hand."

"It is. It is also proof positive that someone has been

breaking its diet. No doggie fake bacon strips for you tonight, buster!"

Nora bent even closer over my hand, holding it steady. "Jim . . . the imp you ate. Was it wearing jewelry of any sort?"

"Jewelry?" I asked, peering at the remains of the imp hand. It was an odd shade of light blue, with the usual (for imps) three fingers. There was no sign of imp rings or bracelets on it. "Why jewelry?"

"Did you have a chance to read the field guide to imps that I gave you the other day?" Nora asked.

I shook my head. "I meant to yesterday on the train, but things got kind of out of control. What's with the jewelry?"

Nora looked at Jim.

"If I had eaten an imp, and I'm not saying I did, because Aisling could have palmed that onto my lips to make me look guilty, but if I had, and it might have had a nasty little bit of gold on it, what of it?"

I shook the imp hand in front of Jim's nose. "Bad demon! Bad!"

It rolled its eyes.

Nora took a deep breath and grabbed Paco's carrier. "Show us where you found the imp nest," she ordered Jim.

It looked at me.

"Do it," I said, demons being able to take orders only from their demon lord.

"If you had read the field guide," Nora said as she followed Jim into the clutch of trees, holding aside branches as she ducked into some dense shrubberies that lined the fence, "you would know that imps of that particular color belong to the suzerain. In addition to the unique color, they are marked by the gold jewelry they wear."

"Great. So Jim ate an important imp?"

She squatted on her heels next to a small rhododendron, picking something out of the dirt. I knelt down to look at it. The object in her hand was a dirty bit of gold. It looked like a doll's ring. "Not just an important imp. *The* important imp. This is a crown."

We both looked from it to where Jim sat perfecting its look of innocence.

"I'm very much afraid that your demon has eaten the reigning imp monarch. I shudder to think of what sort of retribution they will seek against you."

I glared at Jim for a few seconds. It had the decency to look embarrassed. "Lovely. Retribution from imps. Just the sort of thing I need in my life, a bunch of imps pooping in my shoes and stealing my hairbrush, and whatever other sorts of things they do to people who piss them off."

Jim looked even more uncomfortable.

"Aisling," Nora said, brushing off her knees as she got to her feet. "You do not understand. This is not some minor matter of revenge. Your demon has eaten the imp monarch."

"Yeah. I'm really sorry about that, and you can bet I'll order Jim to a strictly imp-free diet from here on out."

"Aw, man!" Jim groaned.

Nora put her hand on my arm. "Imps may appear harmless, and most of the time they are. But I cannot stress to you enough the dire nature of this act against them. The entire imp nation will rise up against you in revenge."

The hairs on my arms stood on end. "Good god. How many imps are there?"

"Worldwide?" She shook her head. "Thousands. Hundreds of thousands. And I'm afraid you've just become their public enemy number one."

"You're talking about actions more serious than hiding my toothpaste and short-sheeting my bed, aren't you?"

"I'm talking about imps destroying you, Jim, and everyone near you in a manner that would make medieval torture look like a pleasant way to pass an afternoon," she answered, her voice grave.

I turned slowly to fix Jim on the end of a glare so pointed, the demon should have been skewered up against the tree behind it.

Jim burped. "Sorry. It seemed like a good idea at the time."

I lectured Jim all the way home. Nora left to deal with the threat of possibly more kobolds, and Jim complained of a bellyache (no doubt the imp king was not digesting easily), so a half hour later I headed out by myself to visit a nearby bookstore Nora had recommended, figuring I'd use the hour before I had to meet Drake to bone up on Guardianish things. I was so caught up in my own concerns, I didn't catch my name the first time someone said it.

A little zing of pain shot up my back the second time, instantly attracting my attention to the man who stood next to a bench in the small green square through which I was strolling.

"Aisling Grey   if you have a moment of time, I would like to talk with you."

I recognized the man immediately. The curly dark brown hair and dark eyes, square chin, and slightly above-average height were nothing out of the ordinary, but the aura of power surrounding him was palpable even several yards away. I stopped and allowed him to approach.

"We have not been introduced, I think, although naturally I have heard of the famous Aisling Grey." He smiled faintly, his voice a bit husky, tinged with a faint Irish accent. "I am Peter Burke."

He didn't hold out his hand, something I'd learned quickly was standard with people in the Otherworld. Drake had told me that too many people could pick up on things when they touched you, so only good friends or close acquaintances shook hands.

"Nice to meet you. Is there something I can help you with?"

"Indeed. Can you spare me a few minutes?" he asked, giving me a polite, tight little smile.

"Sure. Are you in London for business?" Obediently, I took a seat on the bench he indicated.

"In a manner of speaking. I have been attending to my concerns elsewhere for the last few months and only recently returned to Paris. There I discovered that Albert Camus had been murdered, and you were instrumental in discovering his murderer's identity."

"I had a bit of help, but that's more or less true," I agreed. Peter's eyes bothered me—something about them wasn't quite right, but I couldn't put my finger on exactly what it was.

"Regardless, you made an impression on the members

of the Paris Otherworld." His face was oddly expressionless, making me uneasy.

"Ah, now I see what you want," I said, the truth dawning. The reassuring smile I flashed at him fizzled when he didn't respond to it in the least. "You're worried that I want a shot at the Venediger's job, right? Well, you're worrying needlessly. I have enough going on in my life and have no desire to be Venediger. My friend Amelie said something yesterday about people thinking I should take the job, but that's not going to happen."

"I see," Peter said, the faintest hint of amusement showing in his eyes. I relaxed at the sight of it, relieved that he was showing some sort of emotion. "Naturally, I am greatly reassured to know that you have no designs on the position so well suited to me, and loath though I am to disturb you at a time when you are so busy, I had thought that since you are held in such high esteem by the Paris Otherworld, you might assist me."

"Assist you?" I cleared my throat and shifted on the bench, Amelie's concerns still fresh in my memory. "I don't know how I could do that. I think you're grossly overestimating just how much influence I have."

"Nonetheless, it would give me the greatest pleasure to know I had your support in my campaign to become the next Venediger."

I had to tread warily here—dragon politics had taught me that much. "I'm going to be honest here, since you seem to be a reasonable man. I am flattered that you think I can help you get the job, but I don't know you. I barely know anyone in Paris, and nothing of the history of the Venedigers, let alone exactly what the job entails, so it's out of the question for me to throw my support behind you. Or anyone else for that matter," I added quickly, just in case he was pricked by my refusal. "It's nothing to do with you personally. I'm just not qualified to recommend anyone for the job."

He pursed his lips for a moment. "Are you aware of the laws governing the Otherworld regarding the position of Venediger?"

"No, I'm not. And that's just one more reason why it would be stupid of me to recommend someone—"

"The laws of the Otherworld state that the position is granted to the person who has beaten all other challengers. If there are no challengers, then the position is put up to a vote by the membership of the L'au-delà. In short, the popular vote wins."

"Very democratic," I said as noncommittally as I could. If Peter thought I was going to march around Paris soliciting votes for him, he was quite, quite mad. "I don't, however, see what this has to do with me. As I said, I have no intentions of trying to get the position."

"You don't need to. If there are no other challengers— and to date, I am the sole contender, the two other individuals who were interested having killed each other in an ill-fought challenge—then anyone who is voted into the position will be declared the new Venediger." He paused to let that sink in. "Even someone who is apparently unwilling to take the position."

"They can't make me be Venediger against my will," I said quickly.

"You think not?" His eyebrows rose. "There is precedent for it, in fact. In 1518, a friar was made Venediger when the man who sought the position was proven to have participated in a number of human sacrifices. The members of the Otherworld refused to accept him and picked instead a man they felt would not abuse the position."

"That has nothing to do with me. I'm not going to be Venediger, period."

"My travels to explore the mystic side of myself have sent me into the Far East for so many years, I'm afraid I am unacquainted with most of the people in the L'au-delà now. They do not know me, but they know—and apparently trust—you. I very much fear that unless you make it clear you support me, you may find yourself in the very position you so fervently wish to avoid. As you can see, it would benefit us both were you to make a public stand."

The weight of the world settled onto my shoulders, making me slump with weariness. Just how much was any one person supposed to bear? Wyvern's mate and demon lord and Guardian . . . and now Venediger? My mind balked at the thought. I couldn't do it. I just couldn't take on one more responsibility. I hadn't yet proven I could handle the ones I had!

"I'm sorry," I said, getting to my feet and shaking my head. "This is not something I can become involved in."

"You already are, Aisling Grey."

"No, I'm not; you just think I am. And I'm not going to be. Good-bye, good luck, and happy election or whatever it is you have to go through."

He said nothing as I walked away, but I could feel his curiously unemotional black eyes on me until I was out of sight. I pushed away the twinge of concern our conversation had brought me. Peter Burke and his desire to become Venediger had nothing to do with me, nothing at all.

Or so I prayed.

6

"So you're saying there's nothing short of a blood sacrifice that will satisfy the imps and get them to leave me alone?"

"If you convince them that your demon acted without orders from you, and if you offer them sufficient compensation for the loss of their monarch, and if you allow them to witness the sacrifice, if they agree to all that, then, yes, it may allow you to survive this atrocity with relative success."

I slumped back against the chair in Nora's small kitchen, the phone clutched to my ear. "OK. I'll send them a message explaining everything and offering them . . . what did you call it?"

"The historic term is *danegeld*. But it's basically a punitive payment for the loss of life of their leader."

"Right. I send them an abject apology, explain what happened, and more or less let them run amok with my Visa card. I can do that."

"I hope so. Because the alternative is unthinkable."

Nora clicked her tongue, muttered something about late trains, and wished me luck with the dragon meeting. "I shouldn't be gone above a few hours. You can tell me about the meeting when I get back."

"Will do. Good luck! Have fun hunting for kobolds."

"You look moderately less pissed," Jim said after I hung up the phone, tipping its head on the side to consider me. "Are you going to forgive me and move on, or keep giving me those nasty little looks for the rest of both our days?"

"I haven't decided yet." I poured myself a second cup of coffee, leaning up against the kitchen counter to sip the blessed life-giving fluid. How on earth was I going to explain to the European population of imps about Jim's snacking habits?

"Which means the latter." Jim sighed. "Change of subject time—you wanna tell me what was up last night, or do I have to break out the crystal ball and divine it? And why did you come back from your trip to the bookstore looking so grumpy?"

"Don't be silly. Demons can't divine."

"Where *do* you get your ideas?" Jim shook its head and drank a little water from the dogs' water bowl.

I squinted at it. "You mean they can divine? I thought you had to have a soul to do that. Demons don't have souls."

"Newsflash: Not all demons are created equal."

My squint turned into a pointed look. "What on earth does that mean?"

Jim's furry shoulders shrugged.

I decided I'd had enough of arguing with it, and instead gave myself up to the bliss of coffee as it scorched its way down. "I want to marry Mr. Starbucks and bear him many children."

"You don't think that's going to conflict with all the kids you and Drake will have?"

"Stop staring at my stomach," I said, closing my eyes to allow the beverage to work its magic on my still-tired brain. "I'm not grumpy or pregnant."

"Uh-huh. Who was the one who was telling me her boobs were hurting?"

I mulled that over for a moment. Jim was right that my breasts had been a bit more sensitive than normal, but I chalked that up to a period delayed by the stress of moving to the other side of the world. "Boobs hurt when you have your period, you who have no uterus."

"Right, but you haven't had that in over a month, have you? According to *Cosmo,* one of the seven classic signs you're preggers is sore boobs."

"We are not having this conversation," I told the demon before I headed toward the bathroom. "We've got ten minutes before we have to leave. Go lick whatever it is you have to lick in order to be presentable in public."

Jim's reply was thankfully lost in news from a radio I flipped on before stepping into the bathroom to comb my hair. A few minutes later Jim and I stood on the sidewalk, waiting for our ride to the dragons' meeting.

"So what's this all about, anyway?" Jim asked as a black car pulled alongside us. I climbed into the car after it. "And why did you come home last night all ragged and bloody and smelling to high Abaddon?"

"We're going to some sort of sept meeting. I don't

know exactly what it's about, but Drake felt it was important I be there. Hi, Rene. Thanks for picking us up."

"Bonjour, Aisling and Jim. I, too, am interested to hear the tale of your activities last night."

I heaved a little inner sigh but was secretly warmed by both Jim's and Rene's apparent concern. Even if it was only a demon and a mysterious taxi driver, it was still nice to be worried about. "Someone tried to kill me last night by shoving me in front of an oncoming train," I said quickly, pausing for their reactions.

"Who would do such a horrible thing?" Rene asked when he was through swearing. "And why would someone try? Do they know not you are a wyvern's mate, and now immortal?"

I thought for a moment but couldn't remember ever telling Rene that I was immortal. And yet he seemed to know that was one of the benefits of being a wyvern's mate . . . just more proof that he wasn't what he seemed to be. I filed it away under my mental evidence folder and succinctly recounted the events of the past evening.

"*Mon dieu.* You think it was the silver wyvern who pushed you?" Rene asked, his eyes watching me in the mirror.

I pointed at the road in front of him as he narrowly missed mowing down several pedestrians. "No, of course not. Well, possibly. Oh, I don't know what to think! Gabriel is a friend. He wouldn't try to kill me. It had to be someone else or an accident . . . and I really don't think it was an accident."

"Hmm," Rene said thoughtfully as he negotiated his

way across London. "That is most interesting that someone would want to kill you."

"Yeah, it's a barrel-full-of-monkeys sort of fun, but I
could do without murder attempts right now."

"Ah. Because of the *bébé*?"

My jaw dropped slightly at the last word, spoken with
a delightful French accent. My head whipped around to
glare at Jim. "What have you been telling him?"

To my surprise, Jim's eyes were filled with righteous
indignation. "Nothing! I didn't tell him anything!"

"You just had to spout off about your wild theory
about me being pregnant—which, I assure you, isn't so,"
I said, turning to face Rene. "If Jim didn't tell you its silly
idea, why did you say that? I don't look pregnant, do I?"

"*Non*," Rene said hurriedly as I tugged the fitted
bodice of the dark green viscose dress, one of a couple I'd
bought for dragon affairs. "I thought I heard someone say
you were *enceinte*."

"Who would say something like that about me?" I demanded to know, intending on giving the rumormonger a
piece of my mind.

Rene gave me an unreadable look. I pointed a finger at
him. "When I'm done with all this dragon business, you
and I are going to sit down and have a long, long talk."

"That will be very agreeable," he said.

I ignored that. "What I meant to say earlier was that I
have enough stress in my life right now without trying to
figure out who's trying to knock me off."

"Ah," Rene said, but I noticed his gaze flickering in the
mirror to my abdomen.

"I'm not pregnant!" I practically yelled. "Honest to Pete! Don't you two think I'd know if I was?"

Jim rolled its eyes. "Ash, sweetie, honey, babykins—you're not the most astute person in the world."

"No, but I'm sentient enough to know if I'm pregnant or not."

"My wife did not know for three months with our first one," Rene mused. "But her monthly time, it was not very stable, you know? Yours is perhaps more reliable?"

I slumped back against the seat and rubbed my head. "I can't believe we're having a conversation about this."

"I've only been with her for a few months, but she seems to be pretty regular," Jim said. "Every three and a half weeks she'll come home with a big bag of potato chips and lots of chocolate, and I know the next few days will be major grouchyville."

"I'm going to wake up now. This is a horrible dream. Right. I'm waking up."

"It is bad for her, the time? My wife used to be much worse, but having the little ones seemed to cure her of most of the trouble," Rene said.

I wanted to bean him on the back of the head.

"You answer that, and there will be no lunch for you," I told Jim, who had opened its mouth to answer. It hrumphed instead and looked out the window. "Rene, will you be available this afternoon? I don't know when the meeting will get out, but I assume it'll include a meal, so I'm guessing three or four hours."

"You call, and I will be here waiting for you in no more than ten minutes," Rene said, flashing me a charming smile.

"Great. I'm sure Drake will offer us a ride home, but . . ."

"I will not abandon you to him, have none of the fears."

I opened my mouth to thank him, but at that moment, a white panel van slammed into the taxi, sending us with a horrible barrage of crumpled metal, breaking glass, and screaming tires crashing directly into a cement zebra-crossing barrier.

7

The screeching noise of the accident echoed in my head as I lay gasping with pain on the floor of the taxi. My first instinct was to go straight into full panic mode, but I haven't been working on meditative exercises for nothing. Despite my brain shrieking at me to claw my way out from the twisted remains of the taxi, I kept a grip on my emotions and slowly tried to sort out my impressions.

My ribs hurt where I had fallen in front of the train, but no worse than they had earlier, which meant nothing there was broken. I was trapped under something big, heavy, and hot . . . which breathed, so it wasn't the car seat, as I had thought.

"Jim?" I asked, wiggling my feet to make sure my legs weren't broken. "Are you OK? Is anything hurt?"

"Aaaaagg," a familiar grumpy voice groaned. "Did anyone get the number of that wrecking ball?"

I breathed a tiny sigh of relief. If Jim could crack wise, then it was all right. "Get off me if you can; you weigh a ton. Rene? Are you all right?"

"I think he's unconscious," Jim said, the tremendous weight lifting off me. A shower of glass sprinkled down as the demon struggled to get out of what remained of the taxi. "There's blood all over and he's slumped into the steering wheel."

I swore under my breath, flinching when I used my right hand to lever myself up off the floor. Around us, voices called out questions, horns honked, and far in the distance, an ambulance's siren sounded. "Crapbeans. I wrenched my hand. Can someone help me?"

Hands reached in through the broken window to pull Jim out. I got to my knees and looked over the back of the front seat at Rene. Two men were trying to open the driver's door, but it was smashed against the barrier. The door on the other side escaped the impact from the van that hit us, however, so the Good Samaritans quickly got it open and gently pulled Rene out of the car.

"Don't move him," I yelled as another man and a woman helped me through the broken window. I held my right hand close to my body but shrugged off the man's request that I sit and allow him to check me over.

"Rene? Oh, god, there's so much blood!" I crawled over to where he lay on the pavement, surrounded by our rescuers and interested bystanders. "Is anyone here a doctor?"

"I have first aid training," a serious young man said as he handed his messenger bag to a young woman. He knelt down on the other side of Rene and did a quick examination. "He's breathing."

"Is anything broken? Does he look like he's seriously hurt?" I asked, using the hem of my dress to wipe some of the blood off Rene's face. A gash near his hairline explained the blood all over his face . . . but curiously, the wound wasn't bleeding anymore.

"It's difficult for me to tell," the young man said, gingerly feeling Rene's arms and legs. "But I don't think anything's broken. Internal injuries are beyond me, however."

Rene's left leg twitched. I was in the process of using an unbloodied bit of dress to put some pressure on his head wound, but instead I sat watching with stunned wonder as the wound closed itself and melted into nothing.

Two brown eyes opened to meet my astonished gaze.

I leaned close and whispered, "Who *are* you?"

"A friend," he whispered back, a little twinkle flashing in his eyes. The siren of an ambulance grew louder and closer as I sat back, wondering for what seemed like the umpteenth time just who he was and why he was in my life.

I allowed the paramedics to pull me aside and check me over for injuries without one murmur of dissent. Rene, however, argued with them that he was just fine, and that the blood must have come from a slight cut in his scalp.

"Everyone knows how the wounds of the head, they bleed like the pig running around without its brain," he told the nearest paramedic.

The woman looked a little surprised but couldn't argue with the evidence Rene presented—he looked hale and hearty as he told everyone that he didn't need further examination.

"I'm sorry about your cousin's taxi," I said a short while later, after signing a release form and getting a lecture about being checked out at the nearest hospital. I waved at the paramedics as they left. "I don't know if it's shock from the accident or what, but I'm not quite exactly sure what happened. All I remember was seeing a flash of white, then boom!"

Rene stood with his hands on his hips as he surveyed the wreckage of his taxi. A couple of nearby policemen were directing traffic around it, while in the distance I could see a tow truck making its way through the backup. "The car is not important. My cousin will be angry, but that is what the insurance is for, no? Do not derange yourself over it. You are certain you are not hurt?"

"Immortal, remember?" I said softly, calling out my thanks to the serious young man as he and his lady friend finished talking to another policeman. He and the girl walked over to matching motor scooters. "It takes more than a little hit-and-run to do me in."

"*Oui,* but you can still be injured, as can Jim."

Jim glared.

"Yes, you can talk," I told the demon, "but keep it low. I don't need any more attention from the straight guys."

"Meh. You worry too much about what other people will think." Jim ruined its disinterested tone by rubbing its furry head on my leg. I knelt down and gave it a big hug, tears pricking my eyes in aftershock.

"Man, a little bang up, and she goes all girly," Jim said, giving my neck a quick swipe with its tongue. "I've seen bunnies fiercer than you, oh mighty demon lord."

"I'm sorry; I'm a girl. I'm strong, professional, and

capable of dealing with life on my own, but that doesn't mean I can't indulge in a bit of happy tears now and again. Do you think we can get another cab in this mess? I'm late already, and Drake is going to kill me if I miss this meeting."

"It is important that you be there," Rene said, spinning around to examine the massive traffic jam. "*Non*. It is not possible here, but there"—he pointed to a pedestrian mall that ran at right angles to us—"that is how you shall get out. I will arrange for it."

I have no idea what he said to get the serious young motor-scooter guy and his friend to give Jim and me a lift, but before I could think of any one of a thousand rational reasons why I should not find myself perched on the back of a scooter, Jim crushed between me and the driver as we illegally zipped through a pedestrian-only area, we were through it and on the road again.

"Thanks again," I told the young man a few minutes later, pushing a couple of pound coins into his hand. Jim shook itself, shot me a few looks to let me know it didn't appreciate the mode of transportation we'd been forced to take, marched over to a nearby shrub in a big cement urn, and peed on it.

I waved off the couple with more thanks, smiled at a doorman helping an elderly woman out of a taxi, and sailed through the revolving door to the lobby of London's famed Putnam Hotel just as if I wasn't bloody, battered, wrinkled, and missing one sandal.

"You are late," a man's voice growled at me as I limped up to the reception desk.

"Hello, István. Nice to see you again. How's life been treating you?"

The red-haired dragon who was one of Drake's two ever-present bodyguards looked me over from the top of my head down to my one bare foot.

"Better than you. You are hurt?"

"No, this isn't my blood."

István nodded and turned to Jim. He said something in a language I didn't understand. Jim bared its teeth in answer. Without another word, István turned and walked toward the elevators.

I smiled brightly at the people nearest us, all of whom were gawking with unabashed curiosity.

"I'm a professional," I muttered under my breath as we followed István to the bank of elevators. "I am a Guardian, and a wyvern's mate, and a demon lord. What other people think of me walking into a nice hotel covered in dirt, blood, and powdered glass is immaterial."

"Maybe, but I bet you're turning a few eyes with the tear up the back of your dress. Hot pink undies, eh?" Jim said from behind me.

I hastily grabbed at the back of my dress, whirling around so my butt was toward the elevators. Which, of course, meant that I was staring out across the packed lobby.

Everyone was staring back.

"Why can't I ever go anywhere without being embarrassed, attacked, or confronted?" I asked as I backed into the elevator.

István shrugged as he punched a button. The couple

next to him took one look at Jim and me and hastily bailed out of the elevator.

"You are different from all others," István said, folding his arms over his chest as he gave me a dark look. "You should be happy you are wyvern's mate."

"I would be happier if I were a wyvern's mate who didn't have a torn dress and a bunch of imps out for my blood," I answered, closing my eyes and trying to get ahold of myself. I had to face Drake, and that took immense energy, even when we were in agreement about life.

"What?" István asked.

"Nothing."

We were almost to the meeting area when István let it slip that Drake had brought along clothing for me (why, I wasn't ready to consider yet). Rather than make a fuss over him pulling his usual arrogant crap, I allowed István to take me to Drake's suite, quickly picked a new dress from the collection that hung in one of the closets, and even sent a little mental thank-you that I wouldn't have to go before the entire sept grubby, disheveled, and torn.

The dragons had evidently booked a small theater for their sept meeting. I had expected a few key players to show up, but I was stunned by the mass of people milling around, most streaming up and down the aisles looking for seats. At the bottom of the theater was a stage set up with two tables, each with three microphones, flanking a center podium.

"Good god. How many people are here?" I asked István as we stood in the doorway at the top of the theater. Long rows of steps led down to the stage. Most of the lower seats had been filled and more and more people pushed past us, some of whom stopped to look at us briefly before they found seats.

"There are more than two hundred here today," István said, giving me a none-too-gentle shove toward the steps down. "You sit at bottom."

"Hmm. Just how many green dragons are there altogether?" I asked, squeezing through clumps of people clogging the aisle.

"Two hundred and thirty-one."

"Wow. So few. I thought there would be thousands of you. So almost everyone came to this meeting? Is it that big of a deal?"

"Yes," István said, snarling something at a group of people that had their backs to us. They hurriedly parted and allowed us through.

"I wonder if Drake needs an MC," Jim said, marching beside me as I made my way down the stairs. "I used to do roasts for one of my previous masters, and everyone had a great time. I was particularly known for my brilliance in mimicry. Oh, look, there's Pál."

I waved at the second (and much friendlier) of Drake's two bodyguards, pausing to look at Jim. "One of your previous masters? You had a demon lord other than Amaymon?"

"Huh? Where'd you get that idea?"

Jim marched on, ignoring my obvious curiosity.

"From—pardon me, sir, I didn't see your elbow—from you, you annoying little demon. You just said you used to do roasts for one of your previous masters. Who was your other demon lord?"

Jim didn't answer, just kept hopping down the steps. I

grabbed its collar right before we were at the bottom. "Jim, I order you to answer me—who else was your demon lord?"

"No one," it answered, its eyes avoiding mine. "You going to stand there choking me until I hack up a hairball like a cat, or are we going to go get one of the good seats up front, next to the podium?"

"No, you're going to . . ." The words dried up on my lips as Drake emerged from behind the curtained wings. He stepped out onto the stage and with a typically Drake possessive manner, began to scan the crowd. By the time his attention had focused on my side of the room—and me specifically—all thoughts of threatening Jim had melted away.

"Say what you will about the man, he has a hell of a presence," I whispered to Jim.

"Yeah. And an ass you could bounce bricks off of," Jim whispered back. When I widened my eyes at him, he coughed and added, "Well, that's what you said before you dumped him for the umpteenth time!"

"Remind me to order you to wipe your memory each night." I watched as Drake walked across the stage to the small flight of stairs that led to the theater floor. The way he walked should be outlawed—all sinuous, sleek power, more like he was a panther than a dragon. Yes, it helped that I knew well just how fabulous his human form was, but even fully clothed he was gorgeous. Today he wore black—or what I thought was black until he got close enough for me to see the material of his shirt and pants. The shirt he wore opened at the collar, a beautiful silky creation that had my hands twitching with the need to touch it.

"Mate," he said, stopping in front of me, nodding briefly to István. "You wore the clothing I bought for you."

"She was in accident," István said, surprising me. It wasn't like him to make an excuse for me. "She was very dirty and bloody."

Drake's green-eyed gaze narrowed on me as he examined me. "I see no injuries. You were not hurt?"

"The idiot driver didn't hurt us, no," I said, carefully skirting the issue of the incident in Paris. I needed time to mull over exactly what had happened before I decided what steps to take. Unable to stop myself, I touched the material of his shirt sleeve. "That's a lovely shirt. I thought it was black, but it's a shadowed pattern of very dark green, isn't it? Oh. It's . . . is that moving?"

I watched in disbelief as the vaguely discernable pattern in the shirt seemed to shift and rearrange itself within the cloth.

"Yes. It is dragonweave. It is worn by only the most powerful members of the sept. I have a dress made from it for you. You're late, but if you were in an accident, I will allow the insult to pass without punishment."

"Thanks; it wasn't exactly my choice of ways to start the day, either," I said, hackling up a bit at his high-handed attitude. Why had I ever thought Drake could change? It was obvious he was set in an unyielding mindset of arrogance, dominance, and all-purpose dragon-knows-best. To expect him to compromise in a relationship was . . . well, it just wasn't awfully realistic.

"Hi, Drake. I'm here, too, in case you didn't notice. I wasn't hurt in the accident, either, although Rene was for a bit, but then he healed himself. Can I have a collar made of dragonweave?"

"No," Drake said, waving a hand toward the stage.

I sighed an inner sigh at having to take my place on the stage, where more than two hundred dragons would have me in their sights, but reminded myself that I had agreed to be his mate, and that meant I had to take my place at his side for formal functions such as this.

"What exactly is going on here today?" I asked quietly as I took a seat at the end of one of the tables. István, Pál, and a couple of other dragons filled the other spaces. Drake stood between me and the podium, his arms crossed as he watched the audience. A potent silence fell. The last couple of people who had been standing in the aisles greeting one another and chatting hurriedly took their seats.

"I call to order this meeting of the sept of the green dragons on this fourteenth day of August in the year one thousand eight hundred and twenty-two."

"1822?" I asked, leaning to the right slightly, to where Pál sat next to me.

"The dragon year begins with the formation of the first weyr. Eighteen hundred years ago the black and red dragons formed a weyr."

I wanted to ask Pál about this mysterious black dragon sept, but Drake began speaking again, so I sat looking attentive, professional, and thoroughly supportive of whatever it was he had to say.

"We will conduct this meeting in English for the

convenience of certain people present," he said, turning to look at me. I smiled a bit hesitantly, not sure whether I was supposed to thank everyone for that courtesy or not. "The first order of business is the formal recognition of the wyvern's mate, Aisling Grey."

Drake's hand clamped down on my shoulder. I rose, smoothing down the pretty green dress, grateful I didn't have to do this all bloody and torn. "Do I say anything?" I whispered to him.

He shook his head, pulling me so that I stood smashed up against him. My brain went into Drake-deprived overdrive, filling me with all sorts of new pain, longing, and a sad, hopeless feeling that I'd never be able to work things out with him, or entirely let him go.

The dragons rose as one giant group, looked at me for the count of three; then all of them, men, women, and children, knelt down and bowed their heads. It was totally unexpected and, for some reason, touched me greatly. I knew that to many of them, I was an unknown, a stranger to their sept, but that they'd accept me so easily made me feel incredibly warm and fuzzy. I sniffled back a couple of happy tears.

"You know, frequent bouts of crying are another sign of early pregnancy," Jim's voice whispered from where it sat on the other side of Pál.

I glared Jim into silence, but judging by the shocked look on Pál's face, followed by his quick inspection of my midsection, he had heard what the demon had said, dammit.

"Dmitri Askov, you do not recognize my mate?"

Drake's voice rumbling next to me brought me out of a

lovely daydream in which I was sending Jim back to its former demon lord. One man, one lone man, stood in the theater of people all kneeling to honor Drake and, by extension, me. The man had the same ageless quality of all the other dragons, appearing to be in his mid- to late thirties, but was probably several hundred years older than that. I hadn't yet met a dragon under eighty.

"I do not," the dragon named Dmitri said in a noticeable English accent. Like Drake, he stood with his arms crossed, his dark hair swept back from his forehead in a similar fashion. He was probably a few inches shorter than Drake but was built a bit heavier. I squinted slightly, noticing a faint resemblance in the man's jawline. All in all, he was a pretty handsome man but not nearly as drop-dead gorgeous as Drake. Could this be a relative? I was shocked for a moment at that thought. I'd never considered Drake having any relatives, despite the fact that he must have had parents at the very least. What happened to his family? "I do not recognize this human as your mate. You have violated the rules for the last time, Drake Fekete. This time you must pay. As will this human you think to inflict upon us!"

8

I sucked in my breath at the anger in Dmitri's voice, peeking at Drake from the corner of my eye. I needn't have wondered whether he was going to explode. Drake's anger was always controlled, unlike my lamentably explosive temper. His was slow burning and long to become fully inflamed.

"There are no rules regarding the species of a wyvern's mate," Drake answered evenly. "If that is your only objection—"

Dmitri laughed and stalked down the stairs to the stage. "It is but the beginning, *cousin*."

Well, *that* explained a lot. The way he spat out the word explained even more.

"Like the rest of the sept, I grow weary of your mismanagement, your bad decisions, your inability to keep the peace as you swore to do. You are more human than dragon now! Your ineptness, abuses of the sept in general, and clear acts intended to inflame relations between septs exhibit your unsuitability for the position of wyvern. All that we could excuse, but it is your parentage that demands your removal." Dmitri sauntered onto the stage and stopped in front of Drake, waving a hand at the audience.

Parentage? What was all that about? I kept my mouth shut, knowing that Drake would not welcome my defense of his character and actions, no matter how well meant it was. I had an inkling of what was coming next, though. Drake did, as well, because he didn't move a muscle as the familiar words were spoken.

"By the laws that govern the sept, I, Dmitri Alexander Mikhail Askov, sergeant in the green dragon militia, do hereby issue a formal challenge of transcendence to Drake Fekete, the one who falsely claims the position as wyvern of the green dragons."

"Oh, you do not want to be doing that," I said in a low voice, quiet enough that just the people nearest me could hear it, but not so loud that the microphones picked it up. Dmitri's head snapped around to look at me, his dark eyes narrowing in scorn as I spoke. "Look, I've been in your shoes, and I can tell you from experience that Drake takes challenges very seriously. Obviously you have some issues with him, but take it from someone who knows— you don't want to do the challenge thing. The payback on that is a real bitch."

"I do not recognize you as a member of this sept," Dmitri said, then spat on me. I was so stunned by his action, I just stood there with a glob of spittle splattered on my collarbone.

Drake's reaction was instantaneous. He was a blur, one moment standing between me and the podium, the next ten feet away, the theater ringing with the sound of the backhanded slap he delivered to Dmitri.

Slowly, Dmitri turned his head to look at Drake, his eyes bright with fire. "So be it," he snarled, turning on his heel to march off the stage.

"That's just about at the top of the gross-o-meter, and you know, I've seen a lot of gross things in my time," Jim said, nudging aside a pitcher of ice water and bringing me the folded linen napkin that was underneath it.

I took it, wiping the spit off my chest. For some reason, my hands were shaking, as if I had been the sole focus of Dmitri's obvious animosity.

Drake returned to the podium, raising an eyebrow at me. I gawked at his control for a moment, then took a cue from his apparently calm demeanor and hurriedly resumed my place on the chair between him and Pál.

"The second order of business I have to announce concerns the red dragons. This morning I received a statement from Chuan Ren that as of this date, the red dragons have withdrawn their acceptance of the current peace treaty and have declared war against members of this sept."

"Holy cow," I said on a nearly silent breath, leaning over to Pál to ask, "What happened? I know things were dicey when I left Budapest, but I didn't know it was bordering on war."

"Things suffered much when you left," he said, his eyes filled with sadness. A band tightened around my heart.

"I'm so sorry. I never thought things would go downhill without me. I was sure Drake had things in control, or I wouldn't have walked out. I had no idea Chuan Ren was serious about declaring war," I whispered, miserable and bowed by guilt.

"The wyvern of the red dragons is serious about everything. Particularly so where it concerns Drake," Pál whispered back. I wanted badly to ask why, but Drake had been shooting quick little annoyed looks at me while he read the formal declaration of war. It was, like others of its ilk, couched in all sorts of grandiose language, but what it boiled down to was the red dragons were pissed and wanted the green dragons to be their servants.

I snorted and said under my breath, "Ha. In her dreams."

"As most of you have been through this before," Drake said, lifting an eyebrow slightly at me, "you will know how to safeguard your family and property. The militia will be in contact with each family to ensure the full resources of this sept are available to those who need them. Due to the stranglehold the red dragons have in the Far East, travel to Asia should be undertaken only in the direst of situations, and with ample protection."

I leaned over to Pál. "When was the last time you guys were at war?"

His brow furrowed in thought. "One hundred years."

"Is that all?"

Drake shot me another, more prolonged, annoyed look.

"Yes," Pál answered after a few moments, leaning so his mouth was close to my ear. "Drake defeated Chuan Ren in trial by combat in order to gain peace."

Hmm. That explained why the red wyvern seemed to

have it in for Drake. I bet losing to him didn't sit well with someone with her warrior pride.

The rest of the meeting was pretty much a summation of the last year's major events, septwise. There were three births to announce, one death by accident when a dragon was caught in a car bombing in Egypt, and a list of academic and professional achievements that had me squirming in my seat with inferiority.

I was a Guardian, dammit. And a demon lord. Fancy degrees or economic honors and respect of the sept were not important to me. I was trying to convince myself of just that when there was a brief spattering of applause and everyone stood up, the front row filing onto the stage. One by one the members of the sept stopped in front of me, shook my hand, told me their names, and moved on to be greeted by their wyvern. It took almost three hours, and by the time it was done my hand ached, my brain swam with names and conversational inanities, and my stomach rumbled almost as loud as Jim's grousing.

"Are you going to feed us?" I asked Drake when the last sept member left. "Or do I have to apply an emergency hamburger to Jim so we can make it home without it expiring of starvation?"

"Feeeeeeeed me," Jim moaned, flopping on its side in apparent exhaustion.

Drake's eyes glittered dangerously. I knew he must be as tired as I was, more so since he had talked to everyone twice as long as I had. I just administered conversational cocktails while they waited for the main course. "I would be happy to feed you. I was not aware you were welcoming my presence in anything but a purely formal situation."

"Yes, well, I need to talk to you about that, amongst other things, but right now, we need food. Is there somewhere nearby we can go?"

There was. A short half hour later, I squeezed a slice of lemon into a tall glass of iced tea and sighed with dry-throated relief. Drake lounged across the table from me, consulting a menu. He'd managed to get us a private room, going so far as to bribe the restaurant manager to allow Jim in.

"Are István and Pál not joining us?"

He turned the menu over and scanned the back of it. "They are eating in the other room. They wished to give us privacy."

"Oh, good. That means you guys are either going to talk relationship or get naked. Either of which should distract me while my steak is being cooked."

"You're having a chicken sandwich, not a steak. And just remember what the phrase 'Effrijim, I command thee' can do."

I swear Jim grinned at Drake. "She's crazy about me."

"I can see that," he answered dryly, turning his attention to the menu when a waiter slipped into the room. I gave an order for Jim and myself, toying with my iced-tea glass while Drake grilled him about the freshness of the salmon. There were so many things I wanted to say to Drake, so many questions I had, so many wicked, wanton acts my tongue wanted to engage in with him . . . but my brain, that ever-trusty organ, reminded me where those sorts of urges had led me in the past and warned me to make my way cautiously. Drake had broken my heart twice. I knew it couldn't survive a third time.

"Jim, when I order you not to listen to me, what exactly do you do? Hear the words but just don't pay attention? Don't remember anything?"

The demon sighed. "I knew you were going to do that. I can't hear anything when you do that. It's an order, and I can't violate an order. So the words just aren't there for me to hear."

"Oh. Good." I set down my glass. "Effrijim, until further notice, you are not to hear anything Drake and I say."

Jim groaned and laid its big furry black head on its paws, giving me a nasty look. I ignored it. "We have some things to talk about. I dearly want to know what's up with that Dmitri guy, but first things first."

Drake leaned back in his chair, an obstinate look on his handsome-as-sin face. "Yes, first things first—what did you mean when you told Pál that you'd been pushed in front of a train?"

I hate it when Drake pulls the rug out from under me, conversationally speaking. "Oh, that. He asked why I was favoring one side when I had said I wasn't hurt in the car crash. There's not much to it—someone tried to kill me. Or rather, you, since no one would benefit from my death."

"You think not?" Drake's eyebrows rose a little, but he didn't explain. He just gestured at me to continue.

"No, there's no reason for anyone to want me gone unless it's to try to get to you. To be honest . . . oh, man, I don't know what to think. Gabriel was there, right next to me, so he could have been the person to push me. But he's my friend!"

"Gabriel?" Drake frowned to himself as he thought that over. "Describe to me exactly what happened."

It took a good ten minutes to go over everything. Drake asked several questions about who was standing next to me on the platform and how Gabriel had suddenly appeared.

"I have always thought of him as an ally, it is true," Drake said at last. "But he is the wyvern of another sept."

"You really think he pushed me?" I set down the piece of bread I'd been toying with. "But why? He's always been so nice to me. I *like* him."

"I am merely exploring the possibilities, not stating it as a fact," Drake answered, his voice the teensiest bit censuring. "I have had no indication that Gabriel means to do anyone harm."

"Well, then, who did it? I didn't fall, Drake. I know the difference between a fall and a push. Someone slammed into my back, knocking me down in front of the train. If it wasn't Gabriel, then it had to be Fiat. But if that's the case, why did he save me right after I fell? And why didn't Gabriel say anything to me afterwards? He must have seen Fiat push me. You'd think he would have something to say about that."

"It has been many decades since I have understood the way Fiat's mind works," Drake said slowly. "The blame does not necessarily fall on him, however. The red dragons take the status of war very seriously, and I have no doubt whatsoever that they will make several attempts to harm you in an attempt to make me yield. I suspect they are the ones behind the hit-and-run accident, as well."

"Great, that's all I need—the red dragons on my back."

"You need not fear on that score, *kincsem*." His eyes glittered at me with restrained heat. "I will allow no one to harm you. What else did you have to discuss with me?"

I shifted my mental gears from murder attempts to more intimate matters. "Something a bit more personal. I want to talk about what happened in Budapest and what it means to us now."

"Ah." He sat back, giving me a long look. "I take it you're about to lambaste me again for your lack of foresight."

I took a deep breath. No other man—no, no other person—in the entire world left me simultaneously frustrated, enraged, and so much in love it made me giddy with joy just to look at him. "No, I'm not going to lambaste you again for anything. I realize now that I went into this arrangement blind, and although it would have been nice to have someone tell me what exactly was going to be expected of me as a wyvern's mate, I am willing to take my share of the blame for not asking enough questions."

A light flared for a moment in Drake's eyes, dying almost immediately. "If only you had been this reasonable in Budapest."

I carefully set down the table knife I'd been gripping. "You're not going to bait me into an argument, Drake. I want to talk to you about what's going on, but if you have no desire to participate seriously in a discussion about the possible future of our relationship, then this is a waste of time."

He was silent for a moment, his fingers drawing lazy circles on the tablecloth. I shivered a little, knowing the sort of fire those fingers could stir within me. "You wish to negotiate?"

"Yes." I nodded. *Negotiate* was as good a term as any, and one to which Drake responded well. "Things got out of hand in Budapest. I'm the first one to admit that and to admit that I was as much to blame for it as you were."

I waited to see whether he'd object to that, but he didn't say anything, just inclined his head for me to continue.

"But I've had some time to think, and sort things out, and really work through what it is I want from life."

"You wish to be a Guardian," Drake said, his face impassive. I was instantly suspicious.

"I *am* a Guardian. There's nothing anyone can do about that now. I may not be formally trained, and I may not ever be recognized officially as one, but I've made my peace with the fact that I was put on this earth to wrangle demons and watch over portals to Hell."

"Is that so?" Drake asked in a deceptively soft voice. He was silent again for a moment, but there was a banked fire in his eyes.

I opened myself up to it for a moment, embracing that dragon fire that seemed so natural to me, watching with amazement as my fingernails burst into flame. One by one I doused the dragon fire by dipping my fingers in my water glass.

"I take it you believe there is another reason for my

existence?" I smiled to myself as I sipped my iced tea. I knew exactly what he was going to say.

"Do you know how wyverns are born?" he asked, causing me to choke on a piece of chipped ice. That'll teach me to be smug wherever Drake was concerned.

"You said that dragons are born in human form, not . . . er . . . hatched or anything, so I assume it's the normal human way."

He shook his head, sipping from his glass of dragon's blood. "I did not mean literally. A wyvern is born, not created. He has one dragon parent and one human. Wyverns ascend to their positions by right of tanistry, so they are not necessarily the direct descendant of a wyvern."

"You have a human parent?" I asked, stunned by that revelation. "You're only half-dragon?"

"No, I am completely a dragon," he answered, looking slightly annoyed. "Dragon blood is dominant, always."

"No surprise there. So . . . a wyvern is the most important person in the sept. Why don't the sept members want a full-blooded dragon at the helm?"

"Human blood is required for a wyvern because long ago it was proven that the mixture of dragon and human brought about the best attributes in both species, but most importantly, it heightened the dragon qualities so they stood out above others."

"So . . ." I sat back and allowed the waiter to place before me a plate of sesame chicken salad, waiting until he'd placed Drake's and Jim's lunches down and left the room before finishing up my thought. "Basically, you're saying that diversity strengthens the gene pool?"

"That is a gross oversimplification of a complicated genetic situation, but it is in effect true."

"Gotcha. What has this to do with me?"

Drake speared a piece of chilled marinated steak. "I am a wyvern. I have a human parent. You are a human. It is against the rules of nature for a wyvern to take a human mate."

"Why?" I asked, wondering if that was the rule Dmitri had referred to.

"Because too much human blood can dilute the dragon genes. Diversity is one thing—dilution to the extinction of dragonkin is another. Thus, for you to be my mate regardless of this fact indicates that we were intended to be together, no matter what the consequences."

"You're talking about children, aren't you?" I asked, setting down my fork, annoyed that even Drake would bring up this silliness. "Look, I don't know what Pál told you he overheard, but I'm not pregnant. I've never been set-your-calendar-by-it sort of reliable, so if everyone would lighten up about this, I'd be . . ." The words dried up on my lips at the sight of the emotions that passed over Drake's face: incomprehension, surprise, followed quickly by a fierce expression of utter and complete possessiveness that made me realize that until I'd opened my big mouth he hadn't the slightest inkling about that whole pregnancy business.

"You're pregnant," he finally said, a little wisp of smoke escaping from his nose.

I slapped my hands on the table on either side of my plate and stood up. "No, I'm not. I just said I'm not! Why does no one believe me?"

"We mated several weeks ago," Drake said, his eyes narrowing on me, but I had a feeling he wasn't really seeing me. I could almost hear his brain working as he cast his mind back over the last month. "We had unprotected sex. Frequently. If you were in the middle of your cycle . . . yes, it is possible."

"Possible is not the same thing as probable. Anything is possible, as Amelie is always telling me. But this is not happening, Drake. So wipe that pushy, going-to-tick-Aisling-off look right off your face. Yes, we didn't use birth control. But it was only for a few days, and since I was newly mated, my body probably hadn't changed over to mate yet."

Drake just looked at me, the only sound being Jim as it snored its way through its postlunch nap.

"It doesn't work like that?" I asked.

He shook his head.

I sighed. "Great. Now I have to go get an at-home pregnancy kit before the breakdown gets a good grip on me."

"That will not do you any good," Drake cautioned as I pushed my plate aside and grabbed my purse. My appetite was gone, shriveled into nothing in the sudden, gripping worry that everyone was right and I was wrong.

"Why? Jim, wake up. We have to find a pharmacy right away."

"Huh?" Jim asked, its voice sleepy as it shook itself awake. "What's up?"

"The chemicals that a human test uses to determine pregnancy are not relevant with a mate," Drake answered, standing when I headed for the door.

Jim's eyes opened wide as it whistled. "Oh, man. You told him, and you didn't let me hear? I miss all the good stuff!"

"Fine. I'll use a dragon one, then," I told Drake from the doorway. "Just point me to someplace that sells one."

Drake shook his head again. "That is not possible."

"They don't make them?"

"They do, in fact, but just as the chemicals in the human one wouldn't be applicable in your case, nor would those in a dragon test. You are a mate, Aisling. You are neither fully human nor fully dragon. You are something unique."

"Well . . . hell!" I swore, slamming my purse onto the table.

"Abaddon," Jim corrected.

"Whatever. Was your mother or father human?"

Drake's eyes burned with a bright light that I was familiar with. I'd seen it before, when he looked at anything that qualified in his dragon brain as treasure. "My mother, Doña Catalina de Elférez, was born in Seville, Spain, sometime around the year 1580."

It took me a couple of beats to get past that date. "So, what did she do when she thought she might be pregnant?"

Drake smiled fondly. "She tried to kill my father."

"I know just how she felt," I muttered.

"She succeeded thirty-five years later, after I was born," he added, handing me my purse. "If you are finished, I will drive you home."

"Wait a minute—your mother killed your father?" I

grabbed Drake's arm before he could leave the room.
"She *killed* him?"

"Yes." His eyes held mine for a moment, the emotions
in them too mixed to read. "Like you, she did not take
kindly to the idea of being a dragon's mate. My father
was less sympathetic than I am, however. He forced the
oath out of her by threatening to kill her family unless she
accepted her role. He slaughtered half her family before
she finally gave in."

He paused for a moment, ignoring my openmouthed,
silent, bug-eyed gawk of horror. "She's stubborn like you,
too. An unfortunate trait that I hope is not passed along to
our child."

"I am not pregnant!" I ground through my teeth as I
left the private room, forcing a smile on my face for
István and Pál, who were in the middle of their meal.
They immediately jumped up.

"No, please, sit down and finish your lunch. I'm just a
little"—I shot a look at where Drake stood next to me, his
hand possessively on the small of my back—"tired. It's
been a long day, what with Jim eating the imp king and
everything."

All three men looked at Jim with identical startled
expressions.

"It's a long story, one I'll have to tell another time.
Right now I'm going to go home. It was nice to see you
both. I'm sure I'll see you again soon."

Without waiting for Drake to start tossing around orders and commands that would be sure to infuriate me, I
hurried out of the restaurant. I half hoped Rene would

magically be waiting for me out front, but the street was strangely empty of taxis.

"I will take you home," Drake's voice announced from behind me.

"My home?" I asked, braced for the worst. "My home with Nora? I don't have anywhere else to go, but I'll keep her safe from the imps."

"Surely in view of this situation, you see that your place is with me?" he asked, doing the usual dragon trick of answering a question by asking one.

"There is no situation. I'd prove that to you if I could, but since I can't, you're just going to have to take my word for it until time proves me right," I said firmly, holding up a hand to stop his objections. We stood on the sidewalk, surrounded by people. This was not the time to discuss something so tangled as our relationship.

"We will discuss this when we get home," he said, acknowledging my thoughts. "I will take you to Nora's flat so you may gather your things. You may also tell me about the imp situation."

I got into the car that István pulled around a few minutes later, my heart heavy. This was the same old Drake, arrogant, stubborn, and seeing only his own way, with no sense of compromise. I couldn't live like that. I just couldn't. But could I live without him?

I gave him a brief summary of the imp events while I tried to sort out my conflicted emotions. He said nothing but looked a whole lot more worried than I was happy about.

Jim yacked nonstop all the way to Nora's, ignoring the fact that no one was really responding to it. Drake sat silent, his eyes on me as his fingers rubbed his chin. The gesture melted the stone wall I'd tried so hard to build around my heart. I loved the man; that was the bottom line. And since that didn't seem likely to change, it would be better for everyone if I stopped fighting that fact and focused on making it work.

I examined all the possibilities, decided that absolutes weren't going to get me anywhere, and came to the final conclusion that I was willing to give Drake another chance if he could learn to compromise. I'd stay at Nora's house until that time, dividing my day between Guardian training (or nontraining, given the order from the committee) and the dragons.

It was a sound plan. It was reasonable. It would allow Drake and me to explore our relationship without the usual stresses that happened when people moved in together. We would have time to get to know each other, to be comfortable with each other, and most important of all, to understand our respective roles. When the time was right, I'd move in with him, and we'd live happily ever after.

We arrived at Nora's street to find the way blocked with police cars, fire engines, ambulances, and at least a hundred people watching a fully engulfed building.

Nora's building.

"Do I get my own room?" Jim asked, turning to Drake. "One with a water bed? I've always wanted a water bed. And I hope you have satellite cable, because I get really cranky in the morning if I don't get my dose of Montel."

9

We found Nora ashen faced and shaken but safe as she stood behind the fire line giving information to a policewoman.

"Aisling!" she yelled as we pushed our way through the crowd toward her. "There she is. That's my roommate. Oh, thank god you're both all right. I didn't think you would be sleeping at this time of the day, but I worried."

"What happened?" I asked, embracing her in a swift hug. "You're not hurt? Paco is safe?"

"Yes, he is safe. We aren't hurt; we weren't home when the fire started. I got here just as the firemen arrived. As for how the fire started . . ." Her voice fizzled out to nothing.

"I didn't do it," I said quickly, knowing what she hesitated to say aloud. "I wasn't even here. I was with Drake all day."

Nora turned to greet him quickly. "Hello, Drake. It's a pleasure to see you again."

"The pleasure is all mine," he said, bowing over her hand in that Old World way the dragons had.

"Of course you didn't set the fire," Nora said, turning back to me. "I didn't mean to imply that. All the fires you've started have been small and easily put out . . . oh, dear. That didn't come out quite the way I meant it."

"You are still having difficulty controlling my fire?" Drake asked, giving me an unreadable look.

"Yes. No. Sometimes. Just when I'm under stress or emotional or angry about something," I answered.

"Which pretty much means all the time," Jim added. "Fires of Abaddon! I just thought of something. Is everything burned up? Even my collection of *Welsh Corgi Fancier* magazines?"

We all turned to look down the street at the building. It was a dark, sodden shell, the firemen having been able to keep the fire from spreading to other buildings. The roof had collapsed inward, leaving black, partially destroyed walls that still glowed with occasional embers.

"*Merde*," Jim said.

"Was anyone in the building?" I asked Nora. She shook her head, then introduced me when the policewoman who had been talking to her strolled over with a clipboard. I answered questions about what I'd last done in the apartment, where I'd been, and whether I'd noticed anything that could cause a fire.

"So you don't know how it started?" I asked the fire captain when he came over to join us.

"Not yet. We will be investigating," he said, giving me a close look. "You have no idea as to the source of the fire? You were the last person in the flat."

"I've no idea. Have you talked to the owner of the other apartment? Maybe something started there—"

The fire captain frowned. "No, the pattern of fire is consistent with the fire originating in Miss Charles's flat. Our investigation team will be contacting you later."

"Oh, Nora, I'm so sorry," I said once he had left, giving her another hug. "All your things! All your lovely things!"

"They are just possessions, Aisling," she answered, giving me a squeeze in return. "I am safe, as is Paco, and no one else was hurt. That's all that really matters. Things can be replaced."

"I know, but it's still awful to lose everything. And . . . I know I've been having problems with Drake's fire, but I swear to you this wasn't due to me. When I left the apartment earlier, it was just fine."

Drake interrupted both the conversation and my train of thought by putting an arm around me and pulling me up close. Nora's eyebrows rose a smidgen above the frame of her glasses at his possessive move. "We will have to work on your control of my fire before it becomes dangerous."

I edged my way out of his embrace, giving him a glare as I did so. "I am not dangerous! I do not burn down buildings!"

"I didn't say you did," he answered calmly. "But you yourself admit you can't control my fire. Whether you acknowledge the fact or not, you are a powerful woman. When you join my dragon fire with your own power, you hold a potential tool for great destruction."

"Just what we need in the world—another demon lord

with weapons of mass destruction," Jim grumbled. I glared at it. It grinned back at me.

"The likelihood is that the fire was a form of retaliation," Drake added thoughtfully, watching the firemen poke around the remains of the building.

"The imps?" I asked, my stomach going sour at the thought.

He nodded. "I do not believe that would be out of their scope of retribution. Do you agree, Nora?"

"Absolutely." She hugged Paco's carrier even tighter. "Fires are second nature to common European imps. It is one of their favorite weapons. Given the nature of that . . . er . . . blow against them, they would have lost no time in mobilizing a response that targeted Aisling."

"All the more reason for you to cease being stubborn," Drake told me. "Come, mate. You have been on your feet too long. The question of where you will live is now moot. You will live with me."

"No," I said, stepping back so he couldn't grab me. Two fire trucks and an ambulance left, the crowd of people watching the mopping-up process thinning as the excitement ended. "Nora and I are in this together. I'm not going to leave her, especially not now, after everything she owns has been destroyed because of me."

Drake sent a little smile Nora's way. "Naturally, Nora will have a place in my home, as well. I shall see that everything possible is replaced. It is not my intention to separate you, *kincsem*."

I looked at him, ignoring all the people and noise and general chaos around us. "It's not? In Budapest, you wanted us apart. You didn't want me to learn how to be a proper Guardian. You didn't want me signing up with a mentor."

Drake shrugged. "I changed my mind."

"You changed . . ." My look turned to a finely honed glare. I couldn't keep from whapping him on the arm as I hissed in a low voice, "You changed your mind and you didn't tell me? I left you because you betrayed me—you refused to support my Guardian training. You great big scaly, blue-clawed dragon! You could have mentioned that you'd finally seen the light."

"I was intending to, but you took the conversation in a direction I had not anticipated," he answered, glancing down to my stomach.

Nora stepped closer. "I'm sorry to interrupt you two, but I cannot accept your offer, Drake. Paris is a lovely city to visit, but it is out of the question for me to live there. My portal is here, in the city. I cannot leave it unguarded."

Drake put his hand on my back, gently pressuring me to walk forward, waving his hand for Nora to proceed. She clutched Paco's carrier to her chest. "I understand. Although it would have made things easier if you could move to Paris, what you ask is not impossible. You may move into my home here."

"You have a house here in England?" I asked, surprised. Drake didn't seem like the sort of person who would be happy in England. "In London?"

"Yes. It is a family house, one I seldom use. Fortunately, the family I was letting it to has left for the Middle East. We will take possession of it immediately."

I didn't fail to notice the slight inflection on the "we." "Just a minute—maybe Nora has different thoughts, or friends who can put us up until we find a place of our own. I appreciate you offering your house to us, but if it's a family home, it's probably too big and too expensive for the two of us."

Nora frowned. "None of my friends has room for both of us, I'm afraid."

"We could stay in a hotel," I said, aware that I was throwing out objections just because Drake's domineering manner irritated me. "Somewhere cheap."

"You are not being reasonable," Drake said, pushing me gently toward the car. "It would be foolish to spite yourself and Nora just because you have issues with me."

"But—"

"The house is empty. It is large enough to house all of us in comfort but not so large it will be a strain on my resources. Nora will live there as my honored guest for as long as she desires. You are my mate. My homes are now yours. Does that eliminate all of your objections?"

He held open the car door for us. I was about to get in when a tiny piece of mortar erupted from the building next to me. I looked at it curiously for a moment, touching the tiny little crater in the stone facade. Drake swore under his breath, shoving me backwards toward the sole remaining policeman, shouting for Pál and István.

The latter leaped out of the car.

"There!" Pál shouted and quickly followed István as he raced around the corner.

"What—hey!"

"Stay with Nora," Drake commanded, his eyes dark. He bolted after Pál and István before I could ask him what was up.

"What on earth is going . . ." I looked back at the damaged spot on the building, about two feet from my head. My spine stiffened as I realized I was looking at a bullet hole. Quickly I scanned the people across the street, but no one stood out as a potential sniper.

"Wow," Jim said, putting its front paws on the building to examine the bullet hole. "Someone shot at you. You're going up in the world. First a train, then a hit-and-run, now a sniper. I can't wait to see what the red dragons think up next."

"I can," I said grimly, my hands on my hips as I spun around trying to see what it was that Drake and the bodyguards had seen. "Nora?"

"It looks like a bullet hole to me, too," she said, peering over her glasses at the spot on the building. "What is this about the red dragons?"

"They're at war with us. Right, I'm not going to stand for this. Come on, we're going to find whoever shot at me and scare the crap out of them."

"We are?" Nora looked startled.

"Damn straight we are." I looked at Jim. "I don't suppose you'd care to do the dog thing and sniff the path the sniper took?"

Jim rolled its eyes. "Don't even go there."

"OK. Then it's up to me." I put my hand on the wall, closing my eyes to help me focus as I opened the door in my mind.

"Aisling? What exactly do you expect us to do? Guardians are protectors, watchers of portals. We disperse beings back to Abaddon—we're not meant to bring retribution to those who act against us."

"I refuse to be a victim," I told Nora, my eyes still closed as I tried to push out all the noise and distractions of the street. "We have power. We shouldn't be afraid to use it."

The magic door in my head opened wide, allowing me to see all the possibilities. I used my improved vision to look across the street but saw nothing that gave me any clues to who had shot at me. Turning, I swung my attention to the direction Drake and his men had run, but nothing there set off any warning bells, either. I spun around, figuring I'd call the quarters like I did when I summoned a demon, but the second I faced south, the hairs on the back of my neck stood on end. I focused, trying to pinpoint the sensation, but nothing came to me other than the strong belief that whoever had shot at me was located in that direction.

Who am I to quibble with a hunch?

"This way." I grabbed Jim's leash and weaved my way through the throng of people slowly passing the remains of our building. The people on the street faded slightly into the shadows, as if the something that drew my attention was casting darkness on everything else.

"Aisling? I'm not sure we should be doing this," Nora said slowly, following Jim and me as we dashed across a busy street. "Drake would probably not like you running off if the situation is dangerous—"

"He said to stay with you. I'm doing that. And don't worry, Drake has been around me enough to know I don't wait for someone else to rescue me. I'm perfectly capable of saving my own ass. Over here. We have to take the tube—I don't think it's terribly close."

Nora cast out a few more gentle protests and suggestions that we wait for Drake or one of his men to help us, but I nixed that idea. "No time. I don't know where Drake is, and since I keep forgetting to get his cell phone number, I can't call him up to chat about the situation. Besides, I don't intend to corner whoever shot at me—at least, not unless he or she is alone. I just want to find out who and where they are; then we'll go in with a beefed-up force and deal with things."

"All right, but I reserve the right to call for assistance if the situation becomes too difficult," Nora answered. We sat side by side on a short bench in the Underground train that whisked us to an outlying part of London. The feeling that had first caught my attention continued to grow. I still couldn't pin down any particular sensation other than a strong belief that I needed to go in that direction.

"Wait . . . I smell something," Jim said as we emerged from the station into Islington, a chic neighborhood in northern London.

"What? One of the red dragons? Which one, do you know?"

Jim spun around, its nose high in the air. "Not a red dragon."

"What then? A silver one? Blue?"

"Neither. Something better." Jim stopped, one paw lifted, its neck thrust forward as it tried to assume a position better suited to a pointer. "Indian take-out!"

"Oh for god's . . . I swear, demon, there are times when I seriously think I'd be better off without you."

Jim grinned at Nora as I snapped its leash and hurried

down the crowded sidewalk. "It ain't easy being the comic relief."

Nora made no comment, but every time I glanced back at her, her eyes were worried. A frown wrinkled her brow, and the closer we came to what I was sure was the location of the red dragon who'd shot me, the slower she walked.

"Is everything OK?" I asked when we reached the corner of a suburban street.

She shook her head. "I feel . . . there's something here, Aisling. Something big. Don't you feel it?"

I opened myself up for a few minutes but felt nothing out of the ordinary. "Nope. Something like what?"

"I'm not quite sure. It's nothing that I've ever felt before, but I think . . . I think it's very bad."

I looked across the street at the plain white building that stood on the end of a row of almost identical white houses. They were three stories tall, probably late Victorian row houses, now done up and home to yuppies. The house that interested me looked no different from any of the others: black railing out front, windows screened with white lace for privacy, little flower boxes at the windowsills. . . . It all looked perfectly mundane.

"Well, I can't just stand here and wait for one of Chuan Ren's people to show. I'm going to see if anyone is home."

"I don't think that's a good idea," Nora said slowly. I dashed across the street at a traffic break, marching up the stone stairs to the black lacquer front door. Just as I raised my hand to knock, she lunged at my arm, jerking me down a couple of steps. "No! Aisling, you must not!"

"Why?" I asked, confused by the terror I saw in her eyes. "Nora, what's going on?"

"I don't know," she admitted, pulling me down the rest of the stairs until we stood on the sidewalk. "I've never been what you would call psychic about places, but I do know that something big is in that house. Something . . . terrible. And you must not face it."

I glanced back at the house. I got nothing from it other than the sense of confidence that what I sought was in there. "I'm pretty sure that's the place we want. Jim? You get any weird emanations from the house?"

"Weird emanations? What, I'm a medium now?" Jim shook its head. "Feels perfectly straightforward to me."

"Hmm." I wasn't a fool. Much as I wanted to investigate whomever it was who was in that house, Nora was an experienced Guardian, and if she wasn't happy with a location, then I would heed her warning.

For now.

"OK, then," I said, slipping an arm around her shoulders as I gently steered her back toward the zebra crossing. "I won't go in by myself. We'll just make note of the address, and when Drake and his guys are available, we'll check it out together."

"No, you must not. In there is"—she cast a worried look over her shoulder at the house—"something truly evil."

We walked away in silence, returning to the remains of Nora's destroyed home, Nora breathing easier with each step we took, while I pondered who could possibly be behind the attack. We arrived to find Drake storming around shouting for me.

"Where have you been?" he snarled, marching up to me. "I distinctly remember telling you to stay here—"

"I'll tell you about it later," I said in a soft voice, watching Nora carefully. She flashed a smile to Pál, who hurried around to take Paco's carrier from her and help her into the car.

"I wish to be told now. I dislike being made to wait," Drake said crossly.

"You first. Did you find the shooter?"

"No." Irritation made his eyes bright green. I bit back a smile and the urge to kiss the tip of his nose. "We were unable to find him. Now, where have you been, and why did you leave when I told you to stay?"

I sighed, climbing into the car to sit between Nora and Drake. Even though I didn't believe Drake and I were ready to shack up, we needed a home, and if he really had changed his mind about supporting me in my Guardian training, then perhaps there was a future for us after all.

Maybe.

"We followed the trail of the person who shot at me, but when we got to the house the person was in, Nora said it was too dangerous to go in ourselves, so we came back. Happy?"

"No. I will investigate this house you found and determine if the person in it is a threat. You should not have gone without me to protect you. I do not like you rushing off in such a heedless manner."

"Well, tough. Just so you know"—I leaned over and spoke quietly next to his ear, telling my body to stop its celebrations that we were pressed so closely together—

"until we've had time to work out several things, I want my own room."

His eyes burned with answering heat. "*Kincsem*."

"What?"

He nodded toward my lap. My purse was on fire. I slapped out the flames, shooting him a little annoyed glance. He just smiled. My body threatened to melt under the effect of that smile.

This was going to be a long, long day.

10

"Now, this is what I call living. Wooo! Drinking fountain!"

I glanced into the elaborate bathroom as I passed the door. Jim stood with one furry paw on a handle. "Stop playing in the bidet. This is *not* our room."

"Drake said we could have it," Jim said, examining itself in the shiny gold faucet attached to a sunken marble bath. "Why can't we take it?"

"Let's just say I have issues with one of the fixtures in the room." I closed the door on Jim's bathroom ecstasy and crossed my arms to look at the fixture in question, lying with negligent grace on the biggest bed I'd ever seen.

"You don't like the room?"

I looked around it. "It's . . . big. Very big. This room alone is bigger than my entire apartment. And it's . . . old. I'm assuming these are very antique antiques?"

Drake propped himself up on one elbow and glanced around the room. "Yes. This was my mother's house for many years. She eventually tired of it and gave it to me. I haven't bothered redecorating because I'm in London so little. But now that you're here, and given your situation"— he paused to look meaningfully at my stomach—"perhaps you'd care to put your own mark on the house. You may redecorate to suit your taste."

I defy any woman to resist those sorts of words. I was speechless for a few moments, weighing my need for independence against the mouth-wateringly delicious thought of having carte blanche to redo a five-bedroom London house. I compromised with, "That's a thought. If we get things resolved between us so I know there's a future here, then I would be delighted to take charge of a bit of redecoration."

His hand stroked the embroidered bedspread. My entire body tightened at the sight of Drake on a bed, his long fingers moving rhythmically over the material. "You desire to speak to me about our relationship. I am amenable and willing to discuss the situation now."

I opened my mouth to tell Drake where he could stick his gracious permission but decided this was as good a time as any to get a few things worked out. I settled myself in an uncomfortable wingback chair next to an ornate marble table. "Very well. You mentioned negotiating earlier. Well, I have a few conditions to make if we are going to have a life together."

"Name your terms," he said, lolling back on a huge mound of silken pillows.

I spent a few minutes fighting with my body, which wanted to fling itself on the bed and have its wicked way with him. Several times. "First of all, there is the issue of my Guardian training."

He waved that away. "I told you I had changed my mind on that subject. I would prefer you to devote yourself solely to the sept, but I understand now that you would be extremely unhappy if I forced that upon you."

"Extremely unhappy doesn't even begin to touch it," I answered, ignoring his reference to forcing me to do anything. "Since that's a moot point, I'll simply say that I will require your help and full support to achieve my goals of Guardian education."

He was silent for a moment, then inclined his head. "You will have it."

"Oh, no; I'm not going to be caught on technicalities again. Say the words, Drake."

"I will support fully your wish to become a Guardian, including your training." Desire flared to life in his eyes. A little smile flickered across his lips. It took me a couple of moments to remember what it was we were talking about.

"Thank you," I said. "Next we have the issue of you telling me what to do all the time. I want autonomy."

A little frown pinched between his eyes. "That is not allowable."

"Hang on, I'm not talking about bailing on you. I will continue to support you and the sept. I will fulfill all the duties of a wyvern's mate. When it comes to things dragonish, I will follow your orders. But everything else in my life is opinion only."

His frown didn't lessen.

I sighed. "Look, Drake, I'm a big girl. I have a mind

of my own. You're more than a little bossy. I welcome advice, and I don't mind you offering your opinion, but if we are going to live together in relative peace, you have to give me some room to be myself."

"There are many things you do which are dangerous or which could bring trouble upon the sept. Many times you go headlong into situations at which a more knowledgeable person would hesitate. You have so much to learn about this world, Aisling—I cannot allow you to harm yourself or the sept in your desire to be independent."

"Nor would I want you to." I clutched the arms of the chair to keep my body from flinging itself on him. "I will modify that point to exclude times when I might be unaware of a dangerous situation, or one that would have political ramifications for the sept."

"We will try it your way," he said, his voice filled with suspicion. "But if it does not work out to my satisfaction, we will renegotiate this point."

"If it doesn't work out to our *mutual* satisfaction, then I'm willing to discuss the matter," I corrected him.

"Agreed," he said after thinking about it for a few minutes. "Your next condition?"

"It's something you just brought up—my cluelessness regarding dragons. You have to fill me in on exactly what the duties are of a wyvern's mate. Also, I want a list of my responsibilities with the sept and a detailed history of the dragons so I don't feel like such an idiot around you all."

"Granted," he said without pause.

"One last condition," I said, taking a deep breath. I was honestly surprised that he'd agreed to my conditions thus far. Maybe he *had* changed? Maybe the separation had done what I'd hoped it would—made him see I was serious about being a Guardian? Maybe we could live happily ever after, after all? "I want you to tell me what you're thinking."

He didn't move. Not even an eyelash trembled. "Why?"

"Because I never know what it is you're thinking or feeling unless you decide to spill, and that doesn't happen very often. I want to know what interests you. I want to know your pet peeves. I want to know what makes you giddy with delight, and what makes you sad. I want to know about your past, your hopes and dreams, the trials you've overcome, what you're proud of, what you want in life . . . everything. You're not a very forthcoming man, Drake. I respect the fact that you wish to have some privacy, but I feel like an outsider whose body is just conveniently handy for a little romping between the sheets. I want more than that. If I'm going to have you, I want every bit of you, dragon warts and all."

"I do not have warts," he said absently, mulling over my request. His green eyes sparked with inner fire that I could feel from across the room. "Will you do the same for me?"

I laughed. I couldn't help myself. Verbal reticence had never been one of my faults. "Sure. Consider yourself the recipient of all my thoughts and feelings."

"Very well. I accept that condition so long as you recognize there are some things I will not be at liberty to tell you."

"Things? What sort of things?" I asked suspiciously.

"Nothing about my hopes or dreams, as you put it. There are certain things wyverns swear to that I cannot discuss with anyone, not even my mate."

"All right. I can accept that some things are off limits. Everyone is entitled to a certain amount of privacy. I'm sure there is some supersecret Guardian stuff I won't be able to share, too. So long as you do as I've asked the rest of the time, I think we'll be OK."

"Where is Jim?"

"In the bathroom, with orders to stay there."

"Excellent. Let us make love."

I laughed again as Drake rolled backwards onto the bed, waggling his eyebrows and giving me the come-hitheriest of all come-hither looks. "You know, I don't think I've ever seen you be silly. Why don't you do it now, just to let me see a side of you that I doubt few get to see."

He stopped come-hithering. "You want me to be silly?"

"Yes. Just a little. A tiny bit of silliness. Something to give me a wee little peek into your psyche."

"I am a dragon. Dragons are not silly."

I tapped my lower lip. "OK, then, show me your dragon form. I've never seen one of you guys all scaly and winged and breathing fire. Why don't you show me that instead of being silly?"

Drake stood up, peeling off his shirt. "This is as silly as I know how to be."

As I stood there, blatantly ogling his bare chest, arms,

and every other bit of magnificent exposed flesh, he put his hands on his hips and breathed fire.

On me.

In the shape of a heart.

I burst into laughter a third time as the ring of fire wafted over to me, encircling me in dragon fire. "Very silly, and very romantic at the same time. Thank you."

"Now can we make love?"

I swear his toes tapped in exasperation as I spun around in the ring of fire, opening myself up to his unique form of passion.

"Oh, no, not yet. I have a lot more things to say." I stopped spinning and traced the sept brand that Drake bore on his collarbone in the same place mine was located.

"Very well," he said, his face resigned as he caught my fingers in his, flicking his tongue over the tips. "Proceed."

"For one, I want to apologize for leaving the sept in the lurch. I had no idea things hinged on me being present in Budapest. I honestly thought everyone would be just fine without me."

Drake gently bit one of my knuckles. I had to stiffen both my knees and my resolve to keep from jumping on him. "I accept your apology. I will admit that in hindsight, perhaps I might have explained the situation to you in a better fashion."

"Well, I'd make a comment about an understatement of the year, but that would be petty of me. I will content myself with accepting *your* apology."

"I didn't technically apologize," he murmured, turning

my hand over to nibble on my wrist, working his way up to my shoulder.

I shivered at the delicious feeling of heat licking up my arm. "I know. We're going to work on that, too. But since I don't expect miracles, I'm willing to be gracious. Um . . . Drake, there's something else. If we're going to do anything involving the application of your flesh against mine, we're going to have to use some sort of protection."

"That is unnecessary." He nibbled my shoulder. "You are pregnant."

"I'm not. Or at worst, we don't know that for certain."

"So?" His face was buried in my neck, nibbling all my little shivery spots. I arched against him, trying desperately to hang on to some sort of coherent thought.

"I'm not ready to deal with parenthood now. And I don't have any birth control pills with me, so it's going to be up to you until I get set up."

Drake pulled back a fraction to look at me with glittering eyes. He opened his mouth to say something. I bit his lip. "Please?"

He grunted something I took to be agreement, his head dipping back down as his tongue flicked over my lips, wordlessly asking for entrance. As his mouth took possession of mine, he breathed fire again, filling me with the heady, powerful rush of dragon fire. I welcomed it, embraced it, then turned it back on him, my body celebrating the act with a wanton little shimmy against his hard body.

"I want to do that," I said, moaning as he bit my shoulder, one hand sliding up to caress a breast, the other pulling my hips tighter against him. "I want to breathe fire."

"I will teach you," he rumbled, his lips demanding and mine answering. His kisses were so fiery, so potent, so filled with passion and desire, my legs melted away underneath me. Luckily, the bed was right behind me.

Drake pulled away for a moment, looking at me sprawled across his mammoth bed. I expected a slow, seductive strip, which was Drake's preference, but rather than him peeling my clothing off item by item, there was a flurry of hands and cloth, the sound of a heated growl, and suddenly the chilled air was teasing my exposed flesh.

All of it.

"No," I said, putting up a hand when he ripped off the remainder of his clothing, obviously intending to pounce on me.

His eyes spat green flame at me. "What?"

"Not until you hold by your part of the deal. I want to know what you're thinking, Drake. I want to know what you're feeling. You know what you do to me—lord knows I tell you everything, but I need to hear this. I need to know that I'm more to you than just a convenient body. I want to know what you really feel about me."

He looked down at his erection. "You don't know what I'm thinking?"

"Well, I know what *that's* thinking—it's the rest of you I want to hear about."

"You infuriate me," he said, sliding down until his mouth was poised over one extremely anticipatory breast.

"I know that," I said, hissing as he licked my breast

with fire, capturing my nipple and gently swirling his tongue over it. "Tell me something I don't know."

"I need you," he said, switching to the second breast. "You are my mate. You are necessary to me."

"No, tell me what you feel," I groaned, scraping my nails up his back. He moaned in pleasure, nudging my knees aside.

"Condom," I reminded him. "Please? It would make me feel better."

His eyes were bright with desire tinged with annoyance, but that melted into sheer passion as he applied the condom and rolled back onto me. "You matter to me, Aisling. A great deal."

"More than all your treasure?" I asked, teasing him as he sucked my belly button.

"Yes," he answered without hesitation, astonishing me. A treasure was all to a dragon. "You are beyond price. You are my mate. There is no other like you and there never will be."

"Oh, Drake," I said, squirming against him, trying to pull him down onto me where he belonged. "That's just about the nicest thing you've ever said. More!"

"I cannot wait, *kincsem*. I have missed you greatly these past weeks. You fill my thoughts. I crave your presence. I am not happy unless you are near me, around me, annoying and infuriating and fascinating me. I want to bury myself in your body and never leave." He pulled my hips up to meet his thrust.

I couldn't help the little yelp of surprise as he plunged into me, but it wasn't his actions that brought tears of love to my eyes . . . it was what he said. I knew that Drake was not a man who discussed his emotions easily, so for him, the admission that he needed me was tantamount to a declaration of love.

"I love you, too," I told him, my hands dancing down his sides. Our bodies moved together in a rhythm that was familiar and unknown at the same time. "Make me burn, Drake. Make us both burn."

The molten core of heat that had never left me since Drake kissed me the first time flared to life, answering his call. Flames erupted on the bed, dancing and leaping around us as Drake drove me to the point where I knew I would lose all control. My body tightened around him as his back arched, his head snapped back, the long, beautiful line of his neck and chest etched permanently into my brain. The fire between us exploded when he shouted his ecstasy to the heavens, flames licking along his back as his hips flexed twice. He thrust hard a third time before collapsing on me.

I opened my mouth to tell him what I felt at that moment, to tell him how much I loved him, and needed him, and how horrible our separation was, but the words that echoed in the big room were not mine.

"Drakeling, what are you doing in London? I thought you hated this city. *Madre de dios!* Who is that woman?"

It took a few seconds for the words—spoken by a strange woman—to sink into my sated, Drake-bemused mind, but in that time Drake rolled himself off me, yanking the side of the blanket up so it covered most of me. I lay like a stupefied log and stared at the well-dressed, gorgeous, dark-haired woman who glared at me from the doorway.

"You have the worst timing of anyone I know, Mother," Drake said with a sigh.

Mother?

11

"Yes. I understand."

"No, you don't. You say you do, but you can't possibly imagine the embarrassment I felt. Feel. Will continue to feel to the end of my days."

Drake's hand was warm on my hip as we walked down the hallway to the staircase that split midway down into two curving arms ending at the marble-floored entryway, which looked as big as a football field to my overwhelmed eyes. "You're being overly sensitive. I was covering you. All my mother could see was that I was lying on you in an intimate manner."

"Leaving aside the fact that anyone saw that, it was your mother! Why didn't you tell me you had a mother?"

Drake shot me an exasperated look. "I did."

"You know full well what I mean," I told the look. "Why didn't you mention that your mother was alive and well and prone to walking in on you at any moment?"

"I had no idea she was in this hemisphere, let alone in England. She loathes England. That's why she gave me this house. I doubt if she's been to this country more than three times in the last hundred years."

I took a deep breath as Drake paused outside the double doors I knew led to a formal library. I'd had a quick tour of the house when we arrived, just enough to see that it wasn't so much a house as a small mansion, but none of that mattered now. Inside that room was someone I'd never expected to have to meet, and certainly not in the circumstances I'd just found myself.

"Made it downstairs, did you? So many comments come to mind," Jim said, sitting up from where it was lying on the gray marble floor.

"You make just one of them, and it's back to limbo for you," I warned.

Jim evidently read with unusual accuracy the threat in my eyes. "Sheesh! Fine. Make a big deal about it. It's not like I haven't heard you two going at it before."

I narrowed my eyes and thought about a nifty curse Nora had told me about that turned the target into a slug.

"I'm really impressed with the flame-proof quality of your bedding," Jim said in a conversational tone to Drake as the latter swung open the double doors. "Think I can get a dog bed made up in something like that for when Ash gets pissed at me? The last time she got really annoyed, she singed my blanket."

"Behave yourself, or there won't be anything left of you to need a bed," I whispered, slapping a smile on my face that I felt far from feeling. The four people in the room—Nora, Pál, István, and Drake's mother—turned to look at us as Drake gently pushed me into the room.

"So. Here you are," the dark-haired, olive-skinned

woman said from a gold brocade couch. Nora was perched next to her, Paco at her feet. Pál and István sat in chairs opposite, both looking uncomfortable. They leaped to their feet as Drake entered the room.

"Yes, we are here. *Kincsem,* this is my mother, Doña Catalina de Elférez."

"It's a pleasure to meet you," I said pleasantly, lying through my teeth as I held out my hand for her.

She looked at it like it might contain toads.

"Mother," Drake said in a voice rife with warning.

I dropped my hand when she stood up, her dark eyes hard as she looked me over from feet to forehead. I felt hideously gawky and awkward despite wearing clothing Drake had purchased for me—a lovely pair of raw-silk black pants and a flowing fuchsia shirt that highlighted my assets. "Your woman is unacceptable."

"That's the second time today someone has said that." My nerves were clearly a bit on edge, but despite the desire to snap at her, I kept a pleasant expression on my face. "Your nephew shares that opinion, for which I'm very sorry."

"You look tired." Catalina ignored me completely, examining Drake's face for a moment. "You are unhappy."

"On the contrary, at the moment I am quite content," he answered, escorting me to a loveseat that sat at right angles to the couch. "You, however, are being unforgivably rude to my mate. Aisling has done nothing to justify such hostility and poor manners on your part."

"Mate!" she shrieked, sending me a look that could have dropped a horse.

My fingernails bit into my palms as I squelched back

any number of things I wanted to say. To my surprise, Jim marched over and sat next to me, leaning on my leg as if to offer support. I was touched by that, as well as by Drake's hand, which he kept on my shoulder as he stood on my other side. I felt oddly protected by the two of them, although why I needed to be protected from Drake's mother was beyond me.

"She is human!" Catalina accused, pointing a scarlet-tipped finger at me.

"Yes, she is," Drake answered calmly. His fingers tightened slightly on my shoulder. I took that as a sign that he appreciated my silence while he dealt with his mother.

"You cannot have a mate who is human! You are a wyvern!"

"I know what I am. I also know what Aisling is, what the rules governing the weyr are, and the history of the sept. Regardless of all three, Aisling is my mate. The sept has accepted her. You would be wise to do the same."

"Wise?" Her voice had a Spanish accent that became more noticeable as she shrieked. I had a few moments of trouble with the fact that she didn't look any older than Drake—or me, for that matter—but pushed that aside to cope with the important things happening before me. "You are as insolent as your father was! If I had known you would shame me in this way, I would never have allowed them to rip you from my belly!"

Pál and István sidled toward the door.

"I think I'll just take Paco for a walk," Nora said quietly, following the two men. She slid me a sympathetic glance as she left. I gave her a feeble smile and wished like the dickens I could escape with her.

"And you are being deliberately insulting," Drake answered as the door closed behind Nora. "If you are finished—"

"I have not yet begun to express myself," she snarled, storming toward me, her black eyes lit with an unholy glint.

Jim stood up, the hackles between its shoulders standing on end as it gave a low-pitched warning growl. I stared in surprise at Jim for a second. It had never growled before, not even when various people were trying to kill me.

Catalina stopped, waves of hostility rolling off her. I wondered what I had done that set her so against me. "The mortal has a demon. How fitting."

My hackles rose at the tone in her voice. I sat up straighter, aware that Drake moved closer until his leg was pressed against my arm. "Do not, Mother," Drake said, the note of warning back in his voice.

Her eyes narrowed on him. She spat out something that had me flinching, even though I didn't understand it. "You dare to criticize me? You made this choice, Drake. You cannot blame me or anyone else for having this response to your slap in the face of dragon tradition."

"Tradition has been broken in the past and survived," he said somewhat cryptically.

"*Cabrón!*"

I pursed my lips. I knew from watching Spanish-speaking TV that Drake's mother had just called him a bastard.

"A backhanded insult if ever there was one," he replied, releasing my shoulder to walk over to her. She was a tall woman, both taller and bigger than me, but not as tall as Drake. He loomed over her in a menacing fashion. "Are you finished, or is there a bit more bile you wish to work out?"

"You are as abominable as your father," she snarled, her face tight with fury. "The day I was cursed with you both I fell to my knees and begged the Virgin to take me! I would have rather had my heart ripped out from my chest than know that my son, flesh of my flesh, bone of my bone, would shame me in this way!"

Drake had evidently had enough. His face was almost as dark as his eyes. "For Christ's sake, Mother! I have mated with a mortal woman, not a goat! There is no disgrace in Aisling being human."

"Tradition—"

"Can go to hell as far as I'm concerned," Drake bellowed, startling everyone in the room.

It had an interesting effect on his mother. She stood still for a moment, then suddenly smiled, satisfaction positively dripping off her. "There is more of me in you than of your accursed father."

I watched in utter surprise as she leaned forward and kissed Drake on the cheek. She gave me a narrow-eyed look that was downright frightening, then turned on her heel and left the room without another word.

The silence that filled her absence was almost deafening.

Drake looked at me. "You are no doubt expecting an explanation."

"Oh, yes. About a whole lot of things, but foremost why your mother took such an instant and all-encompassing dislike to me. What did I do wrong?"

"Nothing. She has a volatile temper and is happiest when raging about something or other. She evidently decided to pick a minor point in dragon dogma to use as an outlet for her latest tantrum."

I allowed him to pull me to my feet. My legs were still a bit boneless after our romp in bed, the fire inside me banked but not quenched. I leaned up against him, inhaling the wonderfully Drake scent that never failed to make me shiver with delight. "You're talking about that thing where wyverns have one human parent, right? So she's upset that rather than take a dragon mate so one of your kids will be a wyvern, you picked me?"

"I didn't exactly pick you," he said, escorting me through the hall to a side passage. "It just turned out that way."

"Well, you know—" I started to say but stopped when my name was called. I hurried back into the main hall. Nora raced down the stairs from the upper floor, her bag of Guardian things in her hand.

"Pál, would you watch Paco for me? Normally I take him with me, but this time he might be considered a snack. Aisling—oh, there you are. Come quickly; there are blight hounds in the tube station."

"Blight hounds? Oh. Sure. Gotcha." I grabbed my purse and started after her. "Jim, heel!"

"I really hate it when you do that," my demon grumbled, shambling after me. "I may look like a fabulously handsome and intelligent dog, but that doesn't mean I'm going to act like one!"

"Pál will accompany you," Drake said in a bossy voice, standing in the middle of the hall with his hands on his hips.

Nora paused and sent me a curious look. I stopped at the door and looked back at Drake. Here we were just settled back together, and already the terms of our relationship were being tested. "Thank you, but we'll be fine."

"I would be happier if Pál—"

I interrupted him before he could continue. "This is our business, remember?"

"Yes, it is. However, you just agreed to allow me to protect you in situations where you might be in danger."

I took a deep breath and tried to phrase carefully what I needed to say. "Just as I trust you to not let me screw up dragon things, I trust Nora to keep me from a situation with beings I can't handle. I've read about blight hounds, and I'm prepared to help her with them. They aren't that dangerous, and I'll have Jim and Nora with me. So thank you for offering Pál's assistance, thank you for caring enough to want to shield me, but we'll be fine on our own."

An interesting parade of expressions passed across Drake's face.

I ran across the floor to him, putting my hands on his chest as I leaned into him. "Trust goes both ways, Drake. You have to learn to trust that I know what I'm doing."

"It's not your abilities I doubt," he said slowly, his eyes dark. "It is not easy to let you go in this manner."

"I know it's not. But it'll get easier. OK?"

The anger on his face faded into annoyance, which did a brief tango with stubbornness, and finally morphed into resignation.

I gave him a swift kiss. "That was a hell of a battle you fought, but I appreciate your faith in me."

"I have always had faith in you, *kincsem*. It is all others I distrust." His eyes were like molten emeralds.

I smiled. "We'll work on that, too. Don't worry, Nora and I will be back soon."

"You had better be," he grumbled, giving Nora a significant look.

"I never thought you'd be able to pull that off, but you know, you just may end up getting what you want with him," Jim said a few minutes later as we hurried down the cement steps into the belly of the Underground station located two blocks from Drake's house. It was commuter hour, which meant the station was swarming with people entering and leaving. The distant rumble of trains echoed down the long tile corridors, dimmed by the sounds of commuters.

Before I could answer Jim, in the distance a high-pitched howl rose above the din, making every hair on the back of my neck stand on end.

"That doesn't sound good," I muttered to myself, keeping a firm grip on both my purse and Jim's leash.

"Tell me what you know of blight hounds," Nora said in between apologies scattered left and right as she pushed her way through the crowd.

I rustled around in my memory for the snippets I'd read about them a few nights past. "They're small beasts resembling hyenas, often used as a familiar to cast a curse on a location or structure. They generally serve demons but can . . . ow! Pardon me, sir; would you mind moving your paddle? Thank you." I limped past a man who held a kayak paddle, rubbing my abused shin.

Nora sped around a corner, leaped a barrier intended to keep the public out of a transit employees–only area, and disappeared down a long, unlit hallway. I hurdled the barrier after her.

"Go on." Her voice called back eerily from the darkness.

I ran almost blind, one hand out to keep from smashing into something. "They can be summoned by a knowledgeable practitioner of the dark powers."

A dim yellow glow at the end of the disused hallway showed Nora's form as she paused in an archway.

I leaped over a pile of disused signs, running the last few feet to her. "They are not generally considered dangerous unless found in great numbers, which seldom happens since they tend to fight with each other."

Nora said nothing as she peered over the railing to the floor below. I stepped forward to look. We were on an overpass perched above two disused platforms, dusty and dirty and evidently now used for storage of miscellaneous office equipment. Over the broken chairs, scuffed and stained metal desks, and naked metal racks once used in administrative offices, a good hundred and fifty or so fox-sized red-and-black forms crawled, snarling and yipping at each other as they milled around. "Oh, dear."

"This may be a little bit more involved than I originally anticipated," Nora said slowly, her eyes on the seething mass of blight hounds.

"You want I should go back and get that guy's paddle?" Jim asked me.

"Huh?"

Its lips pulled back in a smile. "From where I'm sitting, we're up a creek without one."

"We'll start on the left side and work right," Nora said, trotting across the overpass. "Use your wards to slow down any of them who rush you. Remember the three steps of dispatching."

"Halt, bind, and destroy," I said, following her.

"Exactly. Stay behind me, but don't let any stragglers escape past you."

"Gotcha. Jim, what's the policy on a demon attacking demon minions?"

"We're go for launch," it panted as it ran after us.

"Great, so you don't have any issues with helping me wipe them out?"

We stopped short of the platform, the nearest blight hounds about ten feet away. "Not a one. I never liked blight hounds. They have no sense of humor to speak of."

"OK, but how will you dispatch them?"

"With lots of slobber?" Jim grinned at me as I drew a protective ward over myself. It gave a mock sigh as I narrowed my eyes. "They're demonic, Aisling. If I destroy their physical forms, they will be sent back to

Abaddon. I'll just do a little neck snapping, and back they go."

"Ew. No details; just do it." I slung my bag over my back and unsnapped Jim's leash, freeing up both my hands to draw wards.

Nora looked at me and cocked an eyebrow.

"Let's do it," I told her. "Effrijim, I command thee to wipe out the blight hounds!"

Jim gave a little battle cry as it ran forward into the mass of snarling bodies. Nora followed, her voice raised as she started clearing a path with a couple of high-level incantations.

The next hour and a half was grueling, exhausting, and draining on all levels—and I loved every minute of it.

"Now *this* is what I'm talking about!" I did a little victory dance as I dispatched the last blight hound, its body turning into a puff of nasty-smelling black smoke that hung heavily in the air. I twirled around to make sure that there were no more little nasties hiding anywhere, but Nora had rousted out the last of them. "Woohoo, we rock!"

Jim collapsed next to an overturned table, its tongue lolling to the ground as it panted, giving me an intolerant look. "Jeez, woman, get a grip. It was just a few blight hounds, not the princes of Abaddon themselves."

I jumped over a stack of boxes containing clunky dot-matrix printers, pausing to give Jim a well-deserved pat on the head. "Cut me a little slack, OK? It was my first official infestation, and I'm celebrating. How did I do, Nora? I felt good. I felt in control, and even when that big herd rushed me and I got a little frenzied with the binding wards—sorry about freezing you, Jim, that was totally unintentional—it didn't take me long to get the situation back under control."

Nora poked a stack of discarded furniture to make sure no blight hounds remained, straightening up to dust off her hands and smile. "You did very well, as a matter of fact. You kept your head despite overwhelming circumstances."

Even though I was filthy with dirt from the abandoned platform, and covered in demon smoke grit, I glowed with happiness from her praise.

"There is the little matter of the fire," she added, hesitating.

"I put that right out. As soon as I saw the furniture on fire, I doused the flame." A pang of guilt zinged through me as I glanced down the platform where the charred bits of rubble remained, the wall now stained black with smoke.

"Yes, you did." Nora continued to hesitate. I stood before her, anxious to know how my first outing as a Guardian trainee had gone, worried by her obvious reluctance to speak.

"But?" I prodded her, my heart sinking as her smile faded.

"That wasn't actually the fire I was speaking about." She looked uncomfortable for a moment, which made me feel even more uneasy. "Are you aware that when you draw a ward, you invoke dragon fire?"

I frowned, mentally going over the ward-drawing process. "No, I wasn't. I draw the pattern you showed me, add my own little bit, and imbue it with my belief in my powers and abilities, just as you told me. I don't see where it is I'm drawing on Drake's fire."

She pointed at rat that peeked out from under a stack of garbage. "Draw a binding ward on that rat."

"OK." I took a deep breath, focused, and drew a symbol in the air that would, when combined with my force of will, bind the rat to the spot.

The ward glowed red in the air for a second, then faded into nothing. The rat gave a squeak of surprise as it tried to scurry away. I started to turn away, but a slight flicker caught my eye. To my surprise, fire suddenly flared to life in the form of the ward I'd just drawn, sending the rat beneath it into a frenzy of horror.

"Oh, my god!" I ran over, ignoring my dislike of rodents to snatch the rat out of harm's way, swatting out the fire after I released the terrified rat. "I had no idea! I didn't see any fire with the blight hounds but the one on the furniture . . ."

"I believe it manifests itself when you cement the ward with your will," she mused, giving me a thoughtful look. "By the time you've done that and the fire manifests, you've moved on to the next being demanding your attention."

I glanced back at the charred wood. "Ugh. Now I'm a pyromaniac."

"Nothing so serious, although you will probably want to learn how to empower your wards without drawing on fire."

Jim snorted. "As if."

I didn't say anything as I followed Nora and Jim out of

the tube station. Jim's words echoed in my head with worrisome intensity. What if my demon was right? What if I couldn't draw a ward without pulling on Drake's fire? I struggled with the need to keep the Guardian part of myself separate from Drake.

If I couldn't do this on my own, what did that say about my abilities?

12

"*Salut.* You would like a ride, yes?"

We stopped at the top of the stairs that led down into the tube station. Next to us, blithely parked in a tow-away zone, a man sat smiling at us from the confines of a black taxi.

I wasn't surprised to see him any more than I was to see he'd acquired a new taxi. "Hi, Rene. We're only a couple of blocks from our new home, but sure, a ride would be nice. And maybe if you have the time, you can come in and say hi to Drake and his men."

Nora greeted Rene and happily climbed into the taxi after Jim.

"It would be my pleasure, but is that not one of Drake's men there? Perhaps he would like to join you?" Rene nodded toward the doorway of a small art gallery.

I turned to look. I didn't see Pál or István. "One of Drake's men?"

"I cannot be certain, not having met all of them, but I

did see a dragon slip into the gallery. I assumed he was watching you."

"Dammit, Drake agreed to trust me. . . . I'll be right back. Just let me go tell whichever of them it is that the jig's up, and we'll go home." I marched into the gallery, mentally rehearsing the righteously indignant lecture I would give Drake. A quick scan of the main room showed it dragonless. I hurried through the other three, smaller, rooms, but none of them held anything but browsing artists and patrons.

It really wasn't worth pursuing Pál or István just to tell them I knew they were following me, but my pride was irked. Probably they'd seen me come into the gallery and were hiding from me . . . which irked me even more. After checking to make sure no one was around to see me, I slipped through a door marked PRIVATE and found myself in an apparently empty office.

I walked into the room, my hands on my hips. "All right, I know you're in here; you can stop . . . oh, god."

An odd whooshing noise interrupted me, but it was the sharp blow of pain in my back and odd burning feeling in my stomach that had me looking down.

The long, curved blade of a sword emerged from my front.

"Holy shit," I swore, my brain shocked into numbness as I tried to absorb the fact that there was a sword sticking through me.

A voice behind me snarled something in a guttural language. I spun around and was knocked backwards by a blow to the face. I managed to twist and land on my side rather than my back, some instinct of preservation keeping me from driving the sword any farther through my body.

Above me stood a dragon, all right. But it wasn't one of Drake's men. This dragon was Chinese and wore a black leather jacket with a red bandanna tied around his face. In his left hand he held a starlike spiky weapon that he aimed at my heart.

"No!" I shrieked at the red dragon, frantically trying to roll out of the way. The blade sticking through me made it difficult to move. My mind was shrieking all sorts of warnings and orders, all of them conflicting and sending me quickly toward a full-fledged panic attack. With a desperation born of frenzy, I opened the door in my head, pulling on Drake's fire to give me strength. A fireball the likes of which I had never seen formed in front of me and hurled at the red dragon.

It was then I realized my mistake. Fighting a dragon with fire was like adding gasoline to a blaze. The dragon laughed for a moment, then absorbed the fire and lifted his hand to throw the weapon at me. I cursed my foolishness, hurling a chair at him as I dragged my wounded self behind the safety of the desk. The dragon said something in Chinese, destroying the chair with a couple of deft moves.

I started drawing a binding ward on him, hoping to slow him down so I could get out of the room and get some help, but I didn't finish it before he grabbed me by my hair and yanked me up next to him.

"You die now," he snarled, his eyes glowing reddish brown as he spun the throwing star in the air, snatching it back to press against my jugular.

"I'm immortal," I gasped, my right hand trying to finish the ward.

"You can die," he answered. A moment later, the door burst open . . . but it wasn't help that swarmed into the room in a violent yellow wave.

"Oh, god, it's the imps," I moaned, wondering which of them—the red dragon or the imps—would finish me off first.

As soon as that morbid thought formed in my head, self-preservation kicked in and I slammed another bolt of fire into the red dragon, sending him flying back onto the mass of imps. Imps being what they are, they stopped to attack the dragon rather than continue past him for me. I'll always be grateful for that fact, because it gave me time to scramble over the desk, using another chair to break the window that led to a small service alley behind the gallery.

The dragon was screaming out curses as he beat the imps off him, but more were pouring in through the door. I didn't wait around to see what happened. Careful of the sword still jutting from my belly, I got out the window and dropped to the ground. The impact sent me to my knees, but it took me only a couple of seconds before I was racing down the alley, praying Rene would still be out in front of the building. I hurled myself around the corner into the mass of people streaming out of the tube station, ignoring the cries of surprise around me as people noticed the sword. Ahead of me sat a black taxi with an open door. I lunged to it, half falling inside it with a sob of gratitude on my lips.

"Oh, thank god. You have no idea how grateful I am to

see you. A red dragon tried to kill me, and the imps found me, and I have a sword sticking out of me!"

I allowed helpful hands to pull me off the floor of the taxi to the seat, turning as the taxi shot forward.

The eyes I met as I pushed my hair out of my face were not the ones I was expecting.

"Who are you?" I asked the blond woman who sat next to me.

"My name is Obedama. I am servant of the lord Ariton. You are summoned before him, Guardian."

"Ariton? The demon lord Ariton?" I ripped the bottom of my shirt to carefully wad around where the sword protruded. Part of my mind was still coping with the fact that I'd been skewered (and survived), but the rest of it had moved on without anything but a passing thought that it was odd I wasn't feeling more pain. The wound bled, but not copiously so. It hurt, but not to the exclusion of thought.

"Aye. We will go there now."

"Wait a second." I waved a hand around vaguely as the woman nodded to the taxi driver. "You'll have to forgive me, but I'm a bit woozy from loss of blood, not to mention having just barely survived an attack by a warring dragon and homicidal imps. Why on earth does a demon lord want to see me?"

The female demon—for that's what the woman had to be—looked at me for the count of three, then turned its head.

I was reminded that demons don't have to answer questions asked by anyone but those to whom they owed allegiance or who summoned them. I toyed with the idea of summoning this one but discarded that plan for two reasons—first, I didn't have the tools on me to call up a demon, and second, I had a vague memory of Jim telling me it couldn't nark on its demon lord to anyone.

Jim! Why hadn't I thought of my furry little demon? "Effrijim, I summon thee."

Obedama's head snapped around to face me as Jim's black shape took form at my feet.

"Wow. Do you know you've got a herkin' big sword sticking out your front?" Jim asked, peering around me to look behind.

Obedama hissed something under its breath.

Jim turned to look at the other demon. "Oh. Hi there, Obi-Wan. Long time no see. I see you're going for a female form now. Nice."

"My name," the demon snarled back at Jim with deliberate pronunciation, "is Obedama. You will remember that, Effrijim!"

"Man, no sense of humor!" Jim dismissed Obedama and turned back to me.

I gave it a look I thought it well deserved. "Do you honestly think I haven't noticed this sword?"

The demon shrugged. "I never know with humans. So . . . is it the newest in fashion accessories? Or do you just enjoy the skewered look?"

"God in heaven," I swore to myself. "I can't reach the handle to take it out, you boob!"

"OK. Lean forward and I'll get a grip on it with my teeth . . ."

"No!" I shoved the demon back onto the floor. "You'll do more damage yanking it out! I need medical attention!

It's not bleeding much now, and so long as I'm careful how I move, it doesn't seem to be getting worse."

Jim rolled its eyes. "You're immortal, Ash. A little sword through your gut isn't going to do any permanent damage."

"I'm not taking any chances. So, Obedama," I said, turning back to the demon who was studiously ignoring us. "What exactly does your demon lord wish to see me about?"

It didn't even look at me. "You are summoned before him. Anything else you will have to learn from Ariton himself."

"Fair enough. The problem is that I'm a bit busy at the moment, what with the impalement and all, so I think I'll take a rain check on visiting with your boss." I leaned forward to talk to the taxi driver. "If you could let me out at the nearest available stopping point, I'd be grateful."

The driver didn't answer.

"Um . . . sir?"

"It will do you no good. You have been summoned," Obedama told me. "The driver will not assist you to escape."

"Look, I appreciate that you've been sent to bring me to your boss, but right now is not convenient. So I'll just be leaving, with or without your permission." I had noticed we were coming up to a stoplight. By the time I had finished my statement, we were stopped.

"Uh . . . Ash . . . that may not be a good idea . . ."

Jim's concerned face was the last thing I saw. The instant my hand touched the door handle, Obedama raised her hands. A brilliant white light burst behind my eyeballs, sending me spiraling down into oblivion.

A cold, moist, soft something pressed against my cheek. "Aisling? You there?"

I cracked open one eye to find myself staring up Jim's nose. "Maybe. It depends. Am I still alive?"

"Yep. All in one piece, two if you include the sword."

Gingerly, I pushed myself up from the soft surface that rubbed against my face, blinking to clear my vision. I had been lying on my side on an old-fashioned dark maroon velvet fainting couch, tucked away in a dark corner of a room that seemed to my bemused eyes to be something taken directly from the set of the movie *Gaslight*. Flames flickered in art deco gas jets that bedecked heavily flocked gold-and-black wallpaper. Big rubber plants sat in the four corners of the room. A huge marble fireplace bearing ornate brass figures twisted in torment squatted across from me, but my attention skimmed past all that to settle on the man sitting behind a massive ebony desk.

"You are awake? Excellent. You have my apologies for the methods my minion was forced to employ in order to ensure your attendance at this most important meeting, but I assure you such extreme methods were necessary."

The man who rose from the desk and walked toward me could have doubled for Charles Boyer in *Gaslight*. He was of medium height, had slicked-back black hair and a pleasant face, and wore a black satin smoking jacket that would have looked silly on anyone else but seemed to fit this room to a T.

"Um . . . you have to forgive my stupidity, but this has been a heck of an afternoon. I assume you are Ariton, the demon lord?" Carefully, so as not to jostle the sword, I got to my feet. I was rumpled and dirty, dripped blood, and had a sword poking out of me, but by god, I was a professional.

"I am," the man said, stopping before me. He hesitated for a moment, his eyes on the sword. "And you are Aisling Grey, demon lord and wyvern's mate."

"Yes. You'll have to excuse my appearance." I waved a nonchalant hand toward my middle. "A dragon from another sept attempted to kill me earlier, and I haven't yet had time to have the sword removed."

"Ah," he said, considering it for a moment. "Then this is not part of your normal appearance?"

I shuddered to think about the sort of people he must deal with on a daily basis. "No, it isn't."

"Would you care for me to remove it?"

I was about to accept when some wild wiggling of Jim's eyebrows warned me to think carefully. The polite, well-dressed, and well-spoken man in front of me might appear perfectly normal, but he was in fact a demon lord, one of the eight princes of Hell, and commander of legions of demons . . . *not* the sort of person I wanted removing a sharp, potentially lethal if mishandled, object from my body.

"You know, it's not really hurting that bad, so I think I'll just leave it where it is for now." I offered the demon lord a bright, cheerful smile.

He gave me a bland "you're quite, quite insane" look. "Indeed. Well, shall we get to business?"

I headed toward the elegant Victorian armchair covered in petit point that he indicated, pausing as I considered best how to sit without moving the sword.

"Ah. You are having difficulties? Allow me."

Ariton took ahold of the chair by the back. I assumed he was going to remove the chair and give me a footstool or something to sit on but stared in surprise as he simply ripped the back off the antique chair, tossing the ruined part into the fireplace before returning to his own seat. I stared openmouthed for a moment at the now-backless chair, boggling just a little at how easily he had destroyed it, then snapped my mouth shut and took my seat without comment.

"As a fellow demon lord, you are no doubt aware of the lamentable recent events in Abaddon," Ariton said, playing with a polished bone letter opener. I wondered whose bone it was.

"Well . . ."

Jim sent me a pregnant glance.

"I am to the best of my ability, naturally. But you know, given the circumstances, I really don't consider myself much of an expert in the whole demon lord business."

Ariton frowned as he set down the letter opener. "Circumstances? Of what circumstances are you speaking?"

I crossed my legs and tried to look as if it was a perfectly natural thing for me to be sitting in the den of a demon lord, a sword piercing my midsection.

"Well, I have only the one demon."

We both looked at Jim, who was, come to think of it, being unusually quiet. Jim looked back at me, its eyes wary. "The number and . . . er . . . quality of your minions is not of importance at this moment. You are a demon lord. You are a wyvern's mate. Although I have heard a rumor you have been seen in the company of a Guardian, I'm sure there is a reasonable explanation for that. The fact remains that you will naturally be interested in the recent happenings, and weighing the evidence of which prince you wish to rule Abaddon."

Jim coughed.

"I am never hasty in my decisions," I said firmly, ignoring the fact that I hadn't been exactly truthful. "I need lots and lots of evidence before I make such an important decision."

"As I suspected." Ariton leaned back in his chair, his fingers steepled. "The reason I have brought you here is to seek an agreement between us."

I badly wanted to ask what the hell he was talking about, but Jim had sent me enough warning looks to keep me bluffing my way through the situation. I couldn't imagine what a demon lord wanted from me, but I knew that without a doubt, it wasn't going to be anything good. "What sort of an agreement did you have in mind?"

"A simple one by which we both benefit." His eyelids dropped until he was giving me a veiled glance that sent shivers of uneasiness down my back and arms. "You support me against Asmodeus's attempt for the throne of Abaddon, and I will rid you of any and all enemies."

"I don't have any enemies," I protested, then glanced at the sword. "Well, none that deserve being rid of by a demon lord!"

Jim stepped on my foot. Ariton's eyelids drooped even more. "Do you not? I was under the impression that the imp kingdom has sworn to have your head in exchange for the murder of their monarch."

"That was a mistake, and . . . oh, it doesn't matter." I stood up carefully, wondering where I was, praying it wasn't too far from London. "I appreciate your offer, but it's just not going to work for me."

"Do you mind telling me why you so abruptly spurn my offer of friendship?" Ariton asked, his voice rich with menace. Jim scooted over until its body was leaning against mine.

"I haven't spurned anything, and I'm sorry if it seems to you that I have," I said slowly, trying to pick my way through a path that seemed to be fraught with nothing but potential peril. "The truth is, I've got one little demon. I'm not a big, powerful demon lord. My support can't mean squat when compared to all the other demon lords you could be rallying."

"The six other princes have their own interests at heart," Ariton answered. "The seventh, Bael, will be leaving his throne. So you see, you *are* important."

There was an undertone that raised goose bumps on my arms. I badly wanted out of there, not just so I could have the blasted sword removed, but to get away from Ariton himself. There was a subtle, almost intangible miasma of evil around him, like darkness gathered, little snaky tendrils of it reaching out to tease me.

"I'm not talking about you guys. I mean all the other demon lords like me."

"Like you?" One eyebrow rose.

"Kind of part-time demon lords, if you get my meaning."

He was silent for a moment, then stood up and walked to a curtained window. "There is no other like you, Aisling Grey."

A little skitter of pain shot through me at the invocation of my name. I took hold of Jim's leash and wrapped one arm around myself, wondering if I made a break for the door, whether I'd make it out alive. "Surely there must be other demon lords—"

"No. There are the eight princes of Abaddon, of which I am one, and then there is you."

"Wait a minute . . ." I shook my head, hoping it would clear my confusion. "Are you saying that other than you guys, the big demon lords, the ones who rule Abaddon, I'm the only other demon lord around?"

"Your pretense bores me," Ariton drawled. "Your disrespect and insults I find less acceptable, but given the serious times in which we find ourselves, I will overlook them both. You have the cycle of one day to come to your senses and acquiesce to my generous offer."

He turned his back on me, as if dismissing me. Jim hurried for the door next to the fainting couch. "And if I don't acquiesce?" I asked, dreading the response but unable to keep from asking the question.

"Asmodeus poses the only serious threat to the throne. If you refuse me, I will assume you desire him in power and will treat you accordingly."

My blood curdled at the unspoken intent behind his words. I walked slowly out the door, down a wood-paneled hallway to what I assumed was a front door, wondering how my life had gone so wrong in such a short amount of time.

Ariton followed me to the door.

"Be warned. Aisling Grey." Ariton's voice stopped me as I reached for the doorknob. I fought the unspoken command he had issued me but decided after a brief battle that it would do me more damage to fight his compulsion. "I intend to rule Abaddon. Heed my warning if you wish to survive."

"Good luck with that," was all I said as I opened to the door and walked out . . . until I got a good look around me. The line of white stone houses, the black wrought-iron fences, the intersection were horribly familiar—goose bumps marched up and down my arms as I spun around to face the demon lord.

"You know, you might get a little more cooperation from people if you didn't try to shoot them first!"

Ariton's eyes narrowed. "You try my patience, human. You have been warned."

The black lacquered door shut with a solid click, leaving me to stare at the house and wonder whether my eyes had been deceiving me. I was willing to swear that the expression that flashed in the demon lord's eyes was blank confusion.

Was he working with the red dragons? He had to be . . . because if neither of them was responsible for shooting at me, who was?

13

"Hi. Do you think you can pay off the taxi guy? He seems to be a bit leery of me getting too close to him."

Pál, who answered the bell to Drake's house, stared in wordless horror at the sword that still stuck out of my stomach.

I stumbled past him into the hall, relief at being safe again causing my muscles to go all rubbery. "Thank god."

"Aisling? Is that you? What happened to you—oh, merciful heaven!"

"*Mon dieu!*" Rene appeared behind Nora, the two of them frozen in identical expressions of horror.

"Yeah, it's us. You wouldn't believe where we've been," Jim said, sauntering around me. "I stubbed a toe. Did we miss dinner?"

"What . . ." Nora took one step forward, stopping to gawk at the sword. It took her a couple of seconds to pull herself together. "Dear heaven. I'll call a paramedic."

"That won't be necessary," a familiar deep voice rumbled down the staircase. Drake stood at the top, his face impassive as I turned toward him. A shadow emerged from behind him and resolved itself into the hotheaded Dmitri.

I had been about to run screaming for comfort to Drake, but the sight of the other dragon had me stiffening my back instead. I might be willing to appear weak and needy in front of Drake and my friends, but a troublesome sept member was another matter.

"Hello, Dmitri. Hi, Drake. It would seem the red dragons are quite serious about war."

"Indeed." Drake sauntered down the stairs just as if the sword gutting me was nothing out of the ordinary. "István?"

The bodyguard nodded and headed for the phone. Nora hurried over next to me, carefully putting an arm around my shoulders. "You should sit. Or lie down. Or . . ." She stopped and looked at Drake. "Aren't you going to *do* anything?"

"Of course I am." Drake's voice was as smooth as his face was expressionless. I wondered what sort of trouble Dmitri had been stirring up to cause Drake to go so stony. "I am seeing Dmitri to the door."

The situation was so ludicrous, I almost laughed. I had to struggle to keep my lips in a relatively straight line. I knew Drake wasn't being callous. He could see for himself that I wasn't in any imminent danger of corking off. I was certain he'd had István call for medical aid, so I was quite content to stand around and act the brave, skewered Aisling.

Dmitri stopped in front of me, eyeing the sword. "This changes nothing. I will not accept your mate as my own."

"You what?"

Drake ignored my outraged squawk, keeping his eyes on Dmitri much as one would a dangerous asp poised to strike. "Such a situation would require you to be wyvern, and as you have not beaten me in a challenge, the point is moot."

"Yeah," I said, moving to stand next to Drake in a wholly supportive manner. "And for the record, I do not go with the job."

Dmitri gave me a scornful look before turning toward the door, tossing over his shoulder, "She is ignorant, this so-called mate of yours."

I knew I shouldn't do it; I knew I should let Drake handle anything related to dragon politics, but I'd had a trying day, and Dmitri seemed to be intent on insulting me. I'd had more than I could take.

"Hey," I snapped, grabbing his arm to stop him. He turned back to me with a surprised look on his face. "I've tried to be nice, but you know what? Surviving a murder attempt and a kidnapping makes me a bit testy. Now, I am the first person to admit that I don't know all the ins and outs of dragondom, but I'm trying to learn. And it would help if people like you would share information rather than just tell me I'm ignorant."

"Aisling, release the challenger." Drake moved around to my other side.

"No. Not until he explains what he meant. I may be a tiny bit clueless, but I'm not ignorant."

"Mate—"

Dmitri sneered. "You really don't know, do you? What you said before was wrong. A wyvern's mate, a *real* wyvern's mate, does go with the job."

I blinked a couple of times and opened and closed my mouth twice before looking at Drake, who stood frowning at me. "Is that true?"

"Yes."

"Do you dare call me a liar?" Dmitri asked, anger flaring up in his mossy green eyes.

"Does that mean if someone else gets your job—not that I believe anyone can beat you, because you're just about unbeatable—but if someone did, does that mean I would suddenly be their mate?"

"We can talk about this later," Drake answered, opening the door.

I closed my lips on the obvious comment, figuring I'd wait for Dmitri to leave before peppering Drake with questions.

"Afraid she'll find out too much?" Dmitri asked, his fingers flexing. His smile turned positively gleeful. "She doesn't know the truth about you, does she?"

"If you have nothing more to say about the terms of the challenge, you may leave." Drake's voice was so chilly, it sent little shivers skittering down my arms.

"I'm not interested in hearing any of your gossip about Drake," I said firmly. Dmitri clearly had issues with Drake. His idea of truth would no doubt be yet another groundless personal attack.

"You will leave *now*." Drake started toward Dmitri. Pál and István, who had been standing in formation behind Drake, also stepped forward, their intentions obvious.

Dmitri wasn't intimidated. He stood directly in front of me, his eyes filled with derision as he held my gaze.

"No? It doesn't matter to you that the man who wrongly claimed the position of wyvern to this sept isn't even a green dragon?"

That was the last thing in the world I expected Dmitri to say.

"But no, why should you care when you are as false as he is?"

"Are you insane?" I shook my head. He had to be.

"That is enough!" Drake roared, grabbing Dmitri and literally throwing him out the door before the latter could say another word. Pál and István followed him, standing with arms folded on the stairs to the house as Dmitri got to his feet, snarling with rage.

"Ask the man you've mated yourself to who his father was," Dmitri yelled, turning quickly when Pál and István started down the stairs after him.

I waited until he was out of sight before looking at Drake.

He held out his hand for me. "Come. We will see to the removal of the sword."

"You know," Jim said, following us up the curved staircase. Nora and Rene, both with faces filled with questions, trailed behind us. "My life used to be boring. A damnation here, a curse there, with an occasional blight or two to break routine. Now I have Aisling."

I glared over my shoulder at the demon.

It grinned back. "She's better than reality TV, Internet porn sites, and the trashloids all put together."

* * *

"Hmm. It doesn't look too bad. There was some minor bleeding, but judging by the clean entrance and exit points, there should be no permanent damage."

Gentle fingers probed carefully around the entrance wound on my back. I tried to look over my shoulder at it, but a head was in my way. A head with long black cornrows, smooth, latte-colored skin, and bright silver eyes. The eyes glanced up at me now, dancing with some inner merriment. "Do I want to know how this happened?"

"It was a red dragon assassin." Drake's voice rumbled above me. I slumped down again on my side, resting against his warm thigh, dreading what was coming despite the fact that he was holding me.

"Aisling, would you prefer to be knocked out for this?" Gabriel asked.

I opened my mouth to say I'd like to be drugged from here to eternity, but once again, Drake's voice answered for me. "Just get it over with."

"Hey, now!" I said, craning my neck painfully in order to glare at Drake. "The next time you get impaled, you can pick the method of healing. Until then . . . aiiiiii!"

Before I could rally a really quality scream, Gabriel put his hand on my shoulder and pulled the sword out backwards. "There," he said, his voice as warm and soothing as I'd remembered it. "All done. Now, let's see about aiding the healing of these wounds."

I stayed on my side, a few tears of self-pity welling up and spilling over my lashes to splotch Drake's nice pants. I didn't have time to get more than a couple out, though, before Gabriel had covered the wounds with healing ointment and soft linen bandages, quickly pronouncing me almost as good as new.

"Thank you so much," I said afterwards, pulling down the now-damaged-beyond-repair shirt. I gave an experimental stretch but, other than a slight pulling from the bandages, didn't feel any discomfort. "Wow. That dragon spit of yours sure is fabulous."

Gabriel smiled and put away the tube of ointment he had used on me. "It would have been better had I applied it directly, but . . ." His amused gaze flicked to Drake.

I smothered a little smile. Gabriel had politely asked Drake for permission to apply his mouth to my wound—silver dragons having a natural healing property to their saliva—but Drake refused, pointing out that the ointment based on the saliva was just as good.

"Well, I'm just grateful you were around to help me out. Have you been here long? The last time I saw you was in Paris."

"Yes, right before you fell in front of the train. I came directly to London."

"Ah, the train. I do not believe a satisfactory explanation has been given regarding those events. Perhaps Gabriel can shed some light on the situation?" Drake said in a mildly curious tone.

Gabriel shrugged and began repacking his first aid kit. "I doubt it. I saw Aisling fall forward, but before I could move, Fiat snatched her up. She seemed unharmed and safe in Fiat's care. I had pressing business in London, so I left once I saw that she was all right."

Hmm. Why did I feel like he was leaving something out?

"I am unharmed and safe, so I guess all's well that ends well," I said with a pleasant smile. "Would you guys mind if I changed? I didn't bleed a lot, but it's still making me feel itchy. Are there any special instructions, Gabriel?"

"None. The wound has closed, as you can see. It should be healed completely in the next few hours."

I waited until the two men left before opening the door to the bathroom that Jim had adopted as its room. "Jim, what do you know about . . . what on earth are you doing?"

Jim looked up from where it was paddling around the mammoth sunken tub, filled to the rim with expensive-smelling bubbles. "I'm a Newfoundland. Water dog, remember? Besides, Pál bought me a devil ducky toy and I wanted to see if it stained the water red the way a real devil does."

I peeled off my shirt and, with a damp washcloth, wiped up the dried blood that had dribbled down my belly. "What on earth are you talking about? You've never stained the water red."

"That's because I'm a demon, not a devil. Sheesh. Do you see cloven feet? Honestly, Ash, you really need to read that book Nora gave you. It gives the classifications of all beings with origins in Abaddon, devils included."

A few seconds passed in which I debated pointing out yet again that it was unfair to expect me to learn everything in the short span of time I'd been in the Otherworld, but I decided there were more important things upon which I could expend energy. "What do you know about Gabriel?"

Jim paddled to the other end of the tub, disappearing into a pyramid of bubbles. "Gabriel the silver wyvern?"

"Yes. I want you to tell me everything you know about him. And yes, that's an order."

A martyred doggie sigh emerged from a Jim-shaped bubbly figure. "He's the wyvern of the silver dragons. He's a healer. He makes goo-goo eyes at you when you're not looking. He's been wyvern since 1947 and was born in French Polynesia."

I sat on a marble bench and frowned. "That's it? That's all you know?"

"Yes, that's all I know," Jim said, its black face peering out of the bubbles. "What's with the quiz? Do I get bonus points if I tell you what color socks he's wearing?"

"No bonus points; they're gray." I sat staring at the murky shape I made in the steamed-up mirror. "Is there any reason you know of that Gabriel would want Drake dead?"

Jim jumped out of the tub, its body going into overdrive as it shook off the water. I screamed and leaped back, snatching up a bath sheet to throw over the wet dog.

I used another to mop up the splattered water and bubbles that dripped off me. "Thank you so much! Now I have to change my pants, as well!"

"You said you wanted to get clean. I'm just doing my demon lord's orders."

"Answer my question!"

"No. There's no reason I know of that would leave Gabriel wanting to off Drake."

"Hrmph." I ordered Jim to remain in the bathroom

until it was presentable, marching to the bedroom to change into something dry and lacking in bloodstains.

"You going to tell me why you suddenly think Gabriel is the Terminator?" Jim asked, poking its head out of the bathroom as I ran a brush through my hair. "Last I saw, you were all happy-happy around him, sighing over his dreamy silver eyes and dimples."

I threw the brush at Jim. It ducked. "I just want to know why he pushed me in front of the train."

"Why do you think he did that? He's your friend."

"Yes, he is, but he's the only one who was standing next to me on the platform. Not to mention the fact that he didn't try to save me once I fell. His bit about seeing me safe with Fiat is just a little too much. In fact, it pretty much points a finger right at him. And why is he in London now? Is that a coincidence? Are all the accidents I've had lately a coincidence? I figured it was the red dragons after me, but now I'm not so sure."

"What, being shish kebabbed wasn't enough proof for you that the red dragons have a contract out on you?" Jim shook its head. "Talk about paranoid."

"On the contrary, if anything, it makes me more suspicious of the other accidents. Those were subtle. Shoving a sword through me was a whole different level of attack."

"You're nuts, lady."

"So I've been told." I blew Jim a kiss and went to the door, pausing to look back at my demon. "Why didn't you say anything when we were visiting Ariton?"

"The day you read the demon rule book is the day the world will learn what real fear is. I'm a demon, right?"

"For the moment. I'd be happy to turn you into an ex-demon," I warned.

"Heh. Not as easy as you'd think. Demons are servants of demon lords. Ever hear the old adage 'seen and not heard?' That applies to demons as well as kids. When we're around other demon lords, we're all hush-hush."

"Ah. Don't forget to clean up the bathtub."

"What do I look like, a maid? I'm a dog! I don't clean anything but my own package!"

"And if you want to keep that package, you'll make sure that bathroom is as spotless as when you found it."

I went through the door, Jim's exasperated, "Sheesh. No wonder Ariton wants your support. You're downright mean," following me down the hall.

"Am I interrupting?" I asked a minute later, poking my head through the door to Drake's library.

"No," he said, waving me to a spot on the couch next to him. "We were discussing the war. Gabriel has offered to act as mediator between Chuan Ren and myself."

"Oh, that's nice of you." Gabriel rose to his feet, taking my hand and pressing a kiss to the back of it. Say what you will about the dragon boys, they sure had the niceties down pat.

Gabriel kept a hold of my hand, his silver eyes smiling at me. I clicked on my super-Guardian vision and gave him the once over, wondering whether I'd see any sign that he had tried to kill me by shoving me in front of a train. There was nothing other than a handsome, smiling dragon, his fingers warm on mine as he gently caressed my hand.

I struggled with my dark thoughts. If it wasn't Gabriel

who pushed me, then who had? And why had Gabriel let Fiat rescue me?

"Yes, it is, isn't it?" Drake stood up to retrieve my hand, pulling me beside him as he took his seat again.

"Jealous?" I asked Drake, rubbing my thumb across his palm.

"I am a wyvern, mate. Wyverns do not get jealous."

"No, we get even." Gabriel winked at me as he sat down.

I made a face. "Yeah, but evidently you don't know how to hang on to a mate once you've found one. What was all that business about mates going along with the job, not with the wyvern?"

"Oh-ho," Gabriel said, laughing. "You told her about that? You're a braver man than I thought, Drake."

"He didn't tell me. A green dragon said something about it earlier. I am having major problems believing something so sexist and archaic is actually true."

"Believe it; it's true. It's not really that big of a deal. There is lusus naturae, after all. It's not like a mate can't be taken away from a wyvern through a direct challenge for him or her."

"Yeah, but at least in that case it's the mate who is wanted, not the job. In the first case, it's more of an after-thought. 'Won a wyvern's position? Here's your sept credit card, your key to the wyvern's washroom, and your complimentary mate.' Well, sorry, guys, this girl doesn't go in for wyvern swapping."

"No one is asking you to," Drake said dryly, his fingers stroking mine. "Nor am I in any danger of losing the po-sition of wyvern."

"You could still be challenged for her," Gabriel said, a mischievous look on his face.

"Why are you doing that?" I asked him, leaning into Drake's side. The events of the day had finally started to sink in, and I was left feeling boneless with exhaustion.

"Doing what?"

"Teasing Drake like that."

"Who says I'm teasing?" Gabriel asked, taking a sip of the dragon's blood Drake had evidently poured out earlier. I nudged Drake for a sip from his goblet, needing the strength the fire of the drink brought me.

I frowned at Gabriel. "I say you are. We all know you're not going to challenge him for me. For better or worse, I'm in love with him. I've accepted him as my mate. I'm committed to the sept."

"Nothing says you couldn't change your mind."

"I'm saying." Drake was silent while I spoke, contently sipping from a silver goblet. I transferred my frown to him. He gave a martyred little sigh and got up to get me a glass of my own.

"Besides, you wouldn't want a secondhand mate, would you? I thought wyverns had more pride than that."

The teasing smile faded from Gabriel's eyes. Drake handed me a glass and sat down beside me, wrapping one arm around me.

"Unfortunately, I don't have much of a choice. My sept is cursed. Mates are not born to silver wyverns—they must be taken by some other method."

"Some other method being . . . ?"

"Lusus naturae is the most common," he answered, his eyes flat.

I said nothing but took a big swig of my dragon's blood . . . only to find that it wasn't dragon's blood at all. "What is this?" I asked Drake.

"Grapefruit juice. You like it."

"Yes, I do, but that doesn't mean I want to drink it all the time. I wanted some dragon's blood."

"You can't have it," Drake said matter-of-factly. He set down his glass and gave Gabriel a long, cool look. "We are agreed, then, that you will maintain a position of neutrality?"

"What is wrong with you? Why can't I have it?" I asked.

Drake flashed me an impatient look. "It has alcohol in it."

"So? It's not like I'm on the wag— Oh, you are *not* talking about that ridiculous business again." I clenched my glass of juice and thought about how lovely it would look dripping off his head. "Drake, it's not happening."

"We won't know for sure one way or another for at least a month or so," he said mildly.

Gabriel's eyes, which had been interested before, just about popped out of his head. "You're pregnant?"

"No! Drake's insane, nothing more," I snapped, setting down my glass. "And I'm tired. So if you'll forgive me, gentleman and irritating wyvern, I'm going to take my skewered belly to bed. Thank you again for the medical care, Gabriel, and I'm very happy to see you again."

I marched out of the room and up the stairs and was almost to my room when Nora emerged from the bathroom.

"Oh, Nora, I'm glad to see you. . . . Yes, thanks, it's

much better. Gabriel looked at it, and you know what a wonder he is with healing."

"That is his talent, yes," she said, tightening the belt to a bathrobe she'd borrowed from the things Drake had bought me.

"I wanted to talk to you about the imps." I paused to rub my head. I was so tired, I could hardly think. "What can we do about them?"

"Tonight? Nothing other than what we have done. I've warded the windows, and Drake assures me his alarm system is sensitive enough to pick up even imps. You look like you need some sleep."

I laughed an exhausted laugh. "It's been a long day. If you're sure there's nothing else I need to be doing about them, I'm going to hit the hay."

"Nothing more. Jim had its evening walkies with Paco, so you shouldn't need to bother with that. I believe it's already gone to bed."

"Yeah, the digital cable TV package Drake gets should keep it busy for a long time. Night."

"Good night. Sleep well."

I toddled off to our room, not seeing anyone else. Less than five minutes later I was asleep, but I dreamt of flames and destruction, and a river of ice that slowly wrapped itself around me, consuming all until there was nothing left but a frigid core of despair.

14

"Brrr. Drake?" I murmured sleepily as the bed dipped behind me. I cracked my eyes open to squint up at the man barely visible in the dim light. "What time is it?"

"Late. Do you wish to sleep?"

His voice was deep, rich with desire and promise, but it wasn't that which sent a little shiver of cold down my body. It was the ice cube he rubbed in tiny little circles on my shoulder. "That depends. Did you see *Nine and a Half Weeks*, too?"

"I do not often see films," he answered, using the ice cube to trace a path down my arm, pausing to swirl it around the suddenly sensitive flesh of my inner arm. I shivered again.

"Who needs sleep when there are a lusty dragon's urges to sate?"

He leaned forward, his hair brushing my breast as he licked the path the ice cube had taken, his tongue as hot as his fire. "I have a great many urges, and it takes a lot to sate me. Are you sure you're up to it?"

I pushed down the blankets and propped myself up to look at my belly. The wound had closed and healed over, but there was still a jagged red welt to mark the injury. Gently Drake pressed the area around it. "It doesn't hurt, if that's what you're asking. In fact, it's kind of numb there. I can barely feel you touching me."

"I believe I can change that," Drake said with a smile that never failed to melt me. He rolled over for a minute, returning to my side with a small crystal bowl filled with ice cubes. I couldn't help but notice that he was naked, and while not fully aroused, was definitely anticipatory.

I reached for the bowl, but he pushed it out of reach. "No."

"No? Why don't I get an ice cube?"

The smile that graced his lips was pure sin. "Oh, you will have many ice cubes, *kincsem*. As many as you can stand; that I promise. But tonight is for you. Once I have my pleasure of you, then perhaps we will discuss other situations."

"You know, normally you getting all dominant and bossy like that would rile me up, but since I know your pleasure and mine are intertwined, I'll let it pass," I said, watching with interest as Drake took his time selecting an ice cube from the bowl. He was on his side, his head propped up on his hand. He finally found an ice cube he liked, his gaze lifting to mine as he brought the ice to his lips, his tongue flickering out to taste it.

The look in his eyes was enough to kindle the always-smoldering burn within me. I licked my lips, my body tingling with the nearness of him. He touched the ice cube to my lips for a moment before popping it in his mouth. Before my lips had lost the chill of the ice, he kissed me, the burn of his mouth on mine sending goose bumps down my arms. My nipples went into overdrive, turning into two wanton knots demanding attention, little streaks of fire radiating from them as his arm brushed them when he leaned over me.

His tongue invaded my mouth, a cold shock that twined around my tongue, encouraging me to taste him as he was tasting me. I writhed on the bed, my arms going up to pull him down onto me, but he remained rock solid, his head bent over me while the rest of his body was just far enough from me that we weren't actually touching. I clutched his head instead, wanting to rub myself against him as he continued to kiss me. Inside, the familiar fires burst into being, consuming my entire body until I was one raging inferno of love, desire, and passion.

The touch of ice against my collarbone took me by surprise. Drake's mouth continued to ravage mine while the ice cube made little swirls downward, between my breasts. My breasts pleaded with me to put them into his hands, but it was no good. My brain had shut down at the touch of his mouth on mine and gone into the Drake Zone, where all I could do was feel, touch, and love.

"You taste like sleepy woman," he said into my mouth, allowing me to get some much-needed air. "*My* sleepy woman."

"Pushy dragon," I murmured, pulling his head back into place. I sucked his tongue hard before giving it a gentle little bite, squirming when the ice cube wandered down toward my belly.

"You know, my boobs really would like some attention."

My back arched as if to prove the point, presenting the now-close-to-hurting breasts to him. "They're hurt because you're not touching them. They think you don't love them anymore."

"Silly breasts," he said, touching my lips again with the now-mostly-melted ice cube before putting it in his own mouth. "Your nipples are hard?"

"Serious understatement. Near implosion is more like it." I arched again, tugging on his shoulders to pull him down, but the dratted man had other ideas.

"Would you like to wager I can make them harder?" Drake asked. Before I could answer, his head dipped and he took the aching tip of one breast in his mouth, the combination of the melting ice cube and the heat of his mouth causing every muscle in my body to tighten up. It was an exquisite pleasure, so great it almost hurt, but before I could put the sensation into words, Drake's now-icy tongue laved my tight nipple, and all words were lost to me.

"Yes," he said a moment later, eyeing my rosy nipple with satisfaction. He picked up the sliver of an ice cube and placed it on his tongue. "I believe I win that wager, but if you would like to try it again, to be sure . . ."

"Best to be certain," I gasped as his icy mouth enveloped the tip of my other breast. I swear I saw stars. I clutched at his shoulders, twisting and turning with the sweet torment of his mouth. Every muscle, every sinew was wound tight, leaving me feeling as if I was about to explode in a million pieces. Drake kissed a steaming path down to my belly, making me squirm even more at the combination of fire and ice. I was sure I couldn't take any more of it, but just as Drake's tongue swept in a circle around my belly button, a burning cold touched the very center of me.

"Drake, that's cold!" I shrieked, unsure whether I liked the sensation of the ice cube on such sensitive flesh.

"Shall I warm you up?" He didn't wait for an answer, breathing fire on the part of me that was still tingling with cold. I went into sensory overload as he alternated flicks of his hot tongue, the ice, and little blasts of dragon fire on my quivering parts. The muscles in my legs were tense as he spread them further, settling down between my thighs to attend to the business at hand. I whimpered a little as his fingers joined in the fun, clutching the blanket in an attempt to keep myself from leaping off the bed.

I thought I would cry with pleasure when Drake crunched a few ice cubes and tormented my burning flesh. I wanted to scream when he brought me time and time again to the very edge of a climax, only to stop and focus his attention on a nonerogenous zone, tracing intricate designs on my skin with the ice cubes. I figured I was as good as dead when he simultaneously tortured a breast with gentle nibbles and touches of ice, and let his fingers do an icy dance in regions south. But I knew I was in heaven when, with a particularly fiery flash of his emerald eyes, he slid a small piece of ice he'd been using on my belly into my body, the sensation of the cold on parts that were literally on fire almost too much for me. Heaven became nirvana when he lifted my legs onto his shoulders, his penis a burning brand that pushed its way into my chilled depths, the feel of both together pushing me over the edge and into a climax that triggered his.

Even as we rode it out together, his body shifted, the skin pressed against me changing from that of a man to yellow-green glittery scales. The hands next to my head arched, stretching into blue claws. As Drake yelled my name, his form shimmered into an elongated version of his human self, the breadth of his chest filling my vision. My brain shut down at the thought that I was making love to a dragon, a real dragon, not just one in human form, and I drifted into a sated, happy cloud of oblivion.

It was probably only a few minutes later that I came back to my senses. I was lying on top of Drake, supported on one of his thighs. I kissed the ear that was next to my mouth and pushed myself up so I could look down at him. "We have to talk."

"Now?" His eyes had a drowsy look to them that read satisfied man. I took a moment of pride in that fact, but there was something I had to know.

"Yes, it's called pillow talk."

"Why do women always want to talk after lovemaking?" he asked, wrapping an arm around my waist when I tried to slide off him.

"Because afterwards we feel all warm and fuzzy and intimate, and we like to share our feelings and thoughts, and I've got to be heavy. Let me go."

"No. The bed is wet."

I looked at the bed. "Oh, man, we forgot a condom. And . . . er . . . is that all me?"

"No, it was the ice cube melting." He laughed at the no-doubt horrified look on my face that faded with the as-surance that I wouldn't need to be visiting my gynecologist in the very near future. "You're not heavy. If you insist on talking, you have to stay here."

I allowed myself to fall back onto his chest, rolling onto my belly, resting my chin on my stacked hands.

"Deal. I have a couple of things I want to know, but first, you get a big gold star and an A for the semester for the ice cube idea, although the next time it's my turn."

"I look forward to that," he said, a smile in his eyes. I kissed his eyelids. "What else did you wish to say? If you want to know what I'm thinking, I'm afraid it's beyond me to describe the rapture our lovemaking generates."

"No, I'm not going to ask you that," I said smugly, drawing a protection ward on his chest. It burst into flames as soon as I gave it a bit of power. I frowned, patted it out, and rested my chin on my hands again. "I want to know what Dmitri meant by saying you were more human than dragon. Why did he call you Drake Fekete, and why on earth did he say I should ask you about your father?"

Drake's chest rose and fell in a sigh I felt down to my toes. He was silent for a moment, his hands warm on my behind. "I suppose you should know my history."

"That would be nice. And just so you know, this falls under the sharing category, so you get bonus points for doing it."

He didn't respond when I nibbled on his chin, but his fingers tightened on my butt. "Fekete was my father's surname."

"OK. So that was your original name before you took over the sept and got to use Vireo as your name?"

"No, my name has always been Vireo." His eyes were

a dark green, the irises so narrow, they were mere slits of black. I wondered at that telling reaction—Drake's eyes only went dragon when he was highly aroused or under the influence of a strong emotion.

"Sweetie, if you don't want to tell me this, you don't have to," I said, aware that beneath me, he was tense. "I'm not going to push you into telling me anything, Drake. If it's something that you don't feel ready to tell me yet, I can wait."

His hands slid up my back, wrapping around to hold me close. I felt cherished, protected, safe . . . and as if he was clinging to me like a lifeline. I snuggled my face into his neck and kissed his pulse point.

"It's not that I'm unwilling to share this. I'm just not sure how I can do so without dealing with a lot of history that would probably bore you."

"Doubtful. Try me."

He sighed again. "*Fekete* in Hungarian means *black*."

"Black?" I pushed up for a moment to look at him. "Black as in black dragons?"

"Yes. My father was a black dragon." He pulled me back down onto his chest. I traced the line of his collarbone as I thought about that.

"But your mother is human. So how did you end up wyvern of the green dragons if you're a black dragon?"

"It's complicated. Dragons take their lineage from their father's family, but in special circumstances, the paternal grandmother provides the bloodline."

"And you were one of those special circumstances?"

"Yes. My grandmother was a green dragon. When I was born, she had no male descendants in the green sept.

She claimed me even though my father belonged to the black sept."

"Hmm." Drake pulled the blankets over us as I snuggled closer into him, breathing in his usual spicy scent, and the faint residual odor our lovemaking had left. "Wait . . . I'm confused. Dmitri's your cousin, right?"

"Yes."

"That means you guys share a grandmother. But if your dad was a black dragon, that means his father must have been, as well."

"Yes. But my grandmother mated twice—first to my grandfather, who was beheaded by the French in the late fourteenth century, and later to a green dragon."

I pinched his waist. "You told me dragons mated for life!"

"They do under normal circumstances, but my grandmother's life was anything but normal. She was a reeve."

"What's that?"

"The closest mortal approximation would be princess."

I pushed back on his chest so I could look at him. "Your grandma was a princess? A dragon princess?"

"I just said that." His eyes were just barely glowing green. I smiled at the disgruntled look on his face, kissed the tip of his nose, and resumed a snuggling position. "That doesn't make you a prince or anything, does it?"

"No. I am a wyvern—there can be no greater honor for me. Reeves are a special class of dragon. Their bloodlines are purest, and they are much sought after by families as mates since their children have exceptionally pure blood."

"If Dmitri is an example of what exceptionally pure

blood can do, I'd rather have a mutt like you." I kissed his neck just to prove that point.

"I am not a mutt!" he said, outrage dripping from his voice, his hands tight on my waist.

I giggled, and his hands relaxed.

"You have much to learn about genetics."

"I have a lot more to learn about dragons," I answered, relaxing against him, a feeling of happiness swelling over me. Yeah, we had problems, and yes, my life wasn't all I wanted it to be, but all in all, things were settling down. I began to hope our future together wasn't going to be as stressful as the last few days had led me to believe.

Boy, do I need to be whomped upside the head with a premonition stick.

15

"How's the lady of the manor doing?"

I set down the *Field Guide to Imps, Kobolds, Pixies, and Demonic Minions* and gave my own little demon a glare. "One interview. One interview with a potential staff member does not a lady of the manor make. Besides, Drake asked me to check out potential domestic staff. I was just doing as he asked."

Jim rolled its eyes and sauntered into the small sitting room where I'd curled up to do a little studying. "Don't tell me you're not loving the thought of having servants waiting hand and foot on you. You were all Lady Bountiful to that woman."

"I was not. I was being polite, yet professional. What are you doing here? I thought you were going with Nora and Paco to Oxford."

"Changed my mind. I thought she wanted to go shopping and eat—turns out she just wants to visit a friend. A *vegan* friend. No sense in wasting my time there. What are you doing?"

"Just killing time." I glanced at the clock on the green marble table next to the door. "Drake is off doing things to transfer his business stuff to England. Nora's visiting her friend. Rene ran home to Paris for the day. I've been forbidden by both Drake and Nora to tackle the imps or the person who shot me on my own, so I'm pretty much stuck here with nothing to do but read."

"Geesh. You shack up with Drake and turn into a big ole lazy lump of nothing." Jim shook its head and strolled over to the window, looking out at the street below. "My previous boss would never have just sat around on her duff waiting for life to happen to her."

I sat up straight and gave my demon another glare. "Hey! I think I'm entitled to a little downtime now and again. And what do you mean 'her'? I thought your demon lord was Amaymon?"

"He was."

"OK, you're being mysterious now, and you know how I hate that. You said you haven't had any other demon lord."

"What do you think I am—a three-time loser? The only way you can be bound to a demon lord is if you've been cast out. That's only been done once, thank you very much."

"So you worked for someone *before* you were bound to Amaymon?"

Jim sauntered to the couch opposite, shooting me a look.

"Absolutely not. This is not my house with its old, crappy furniture. Drake's things are nice, and I'd like them to stay that way. I bought you a dog bed—use it."

The sigh Jim heaved was rife with martyrdom as the demon plopped down on the comfy dog bed I'd set next to the couch, but I ignored it. "Yes, I worked for someone else."

"Who?"

"No one you'd know."

My lips thinned. "That's not an answer. Who did you work for before Amaymon?"

"I believe 'whom' is the correct grammatical—"

"For whom did you work before Amaymon?" I said in a loud voice.

"Clio."

I frowned as I tried to place the name, but it didn't ring any bells. "Who was she?"

Jim rolled over onto its back. "Man, what is this, a third degree? If you're going to interrogate me, the least you can do is scratch my belly while you do it."

"I'm not interrogating you. I'm just curious about your life before Amaymon. You're the one who brought this other employer up."

"Only as an example of why it looks so bad for me now to have a boss who just lazes around and waits for everyone to take care of her problems for her."

"Oh, now that is patently untrue!" I got to my feet and grabbed my purse, marching over to prod Jim's shoulder with the tip of my shoe. "I am very proactive! I always solve my own problems—or at least I try to. Come on, demon. If you're so hot and bothered to see a little action, you'll get it."

"That's more like it." Jim trotted after me as I headed

for the front door, pausing to write a quick note for Drake. "Where are we going?"

"The British Museum."

"Huh? Why there?"

The pleasant late summer days we'd been having in London had fizzled into a gray, overcast dampness. I hurried through the drizzle to the closest tube station. I consulted the big chart of tube routes, trying to figure out which line would take me to the museum. "Because they have the best collection of books detailing the history of the Otherworld. Nora told me I should be hitting the special collection there as much as possible. OK. I think we just need to make one transfer. Shouldn't take us long."

"What are you looking for at the BM?" Jim asked, obediently dropping the volume of its voice when I tweaked its ear. "Ow. Meanie."

"I want to see if there's anything about a mage named Peter Burke."

"Who's that?"

"Amelie and I talked about him at G and T."

"Oh. Like I was paying attention. Who is he?"

I gave Jim a brief, under-the-breath explanation of who Peter was on the tube ride. The British being what they are, no one looked twice at me as I carried on a conversation with my dog. By the time we got to the museum, Jim was asking questions about what his role would be when I became Venediger.

"Nothing, because I'm never going to be the Venediger. I'm only just coping with demon lord, wyvern's mate, and Guardian, thank you."

"I think you're making a mistake. You could be someone if you were Venediger! Think of the fame! Think of the glory! Think of all the free food!"

"We can do quite well without any of that, thank you. Now zip thy demonic lips, or a museum guard will hear you."

It took me a bit of fast talking (and the slightest bit of a mind push) to get Jim and me access to a collection of texts normally reserved for those with the proper academic qualifications, but eventually I found myself tucked away in a corner with a list of books about the otherworld.

Fat lot of good it did. "You can speak now," I told Jim a couple of hours later as we exited the museum.

"I really hate it when you order me to silence," Jim grumbled. "A simple 'hush' wouldn't suffice for you, oh, no. With you it's all bossy orders to do whatever catches your fancy."

I pointed my finger at the demon. "Do you want to talk to Cecile tonight?"

Its lips twitched. "I hate it even more when you threaten me with revoking my phone privileges. Fine. Have it your way, oh mighty and fearsome demon lord. What did you find out about this Peter dude?"

"Nothing. Which is significant, don't you think?" The drizzle had turned into an outright downpour, sending everyone who didn't possess an umbrella scurrying down the wet road. I, being a true Oregon girl, had no idea where my umbrella was, or even whether I had brought it with me to London, so I turned up the collar of my coat and ran for the busiest street corner, hoping for a taxi rank.

"Significant how?"

"In the absence of information. This guy is a mage, right? Assumedly a big, powerful mage if he's shooting for Venediger. And you don't get to be big and powerful without someone taking notice of you. So if he's been around the block a few times—dammit, that cab should have been ours! Damned pushy tourists. If he's been around for a while, why hasn't he made it into any of the books or magazines that detail Otherworld history and society?"

"Maybe because he's not as big and powerful as he says he is?"

I joined the queue at a taxi stand and thought about that. "Doubtful. Amelie said the other contenders to Venediger weren't as powerful as him, and they ended up killing each other. So it's pretty much a granted that this guy is all that."

"Maybe. Or maybe he's just been in the Far East like he said he was."

"Even so—" An awareness of someone behind me caused me to turn as I was speaking. My body changed position just far enough so that the dart that was intended to pierce my neck zipped past me and embedded itself in the taxi sign.

"Whoa," Jim said, its eyes big as it looked at the two-inch thin metal dart tipped with a plastic cone. "You don't see one of those every day."

I didn't waste time examining the dart. I spun ninety degrees, caught sight of an Asian man turning away as he tucked a long, thin metal pipe into his jacket, and flung myself forward in a leap that would do a long jumper proud. "Jim, attack the dragon," I yelled as the man sprinted away. He crashed into two elderly ladies emerging from a shop. Jim's dark form raced past me as I paused to help the ladies up and make sure they weren't hurt.

Jim's muffled woofs clued me in to its location, a fact I was grateful for, because the red dragon had managed to find a way behind the row of shops, into a narrow access alley devoid of anything but crates, garbage cans, and the usual detritus of city life. I caught sight of them next to a large square metal garbage can, the red dragon trying to climb a fire escape, but Jim, bless its demon heart, threw itself at the dragon. The two of them went down with a loud crash. I snatched up a half-empty can of paint and ran over to where the dragon was bashing Jim's head into the wall.

"You son of a bitch," I snarled, swinging the paint can at his head. Words from my self-defense instructor regarding the best way to disable someone echoed in my memory, causing me to switch targets. The can slammed into the dragon's left knee, connecting with a sickening crunching noise. The dragon screamed and went down again, both hands on his leg. Jim shook its head, a long line of bloody slobber flying from its mouth.

"Stay back," I warned Jim, in case it had thoughts of attacking.

"No problemo," it croaked, making an odd face as it ran its tongue over its teeth.

"All right, you bastard," I said, raising the paint can (which now had a big dent in the side). "If you don't want your other kneecap smashed to hell and back again, you'll hand over that blowgun and any other weapons you have stashed on you."

The dragon said something in Chinese. Judging by the face he made as he did so, I assumed it wasn't "I surrender."

"Have it your way," I said, swinging the can again, praying the threat would be enough to make the dragon talk. I have no issues with defending myself and those I love, but I was not really a fighter. The fact that I'd already disabled his knee was enough to live with—I didn't want to be responsible for crippling him.

"No!" he shouted, pulling his body into a fetal shape as he rocked back and forth with pain. "I give you gun."

"Jim, how's your head?"

"It hurths. I think he knocketh a tooth looth. I thay we kill him."

"It's a thought," I answered, hoping to scare the dragon into believing I was callous and cold. "You're Shing, aren't you? One of Chuan Ren's bodyguards?"

The dragon refused to answer me. It didn't matter—I remembered him. "Look, it's not going to do you any good to cop an attitude. You're at our mercy here, so if you don't want to die, you'd better start telling me what I want to know."

"Kill me," Shing said, his face grim. "There is only honor in death at the hands of an enemy."

I thought for three seconds before snatching the two-foot-long plastic blowgun that peeked out of his jacket. "I've got a better idea." He glared at me. I smiled. "One that just reeks of dishonor."

Fifteen minutes later Jim (drooling excessively) and I grimly marched up the stairs to a nondescript hotel while I maintained a firm grip on the collar of the dragon. Shing had adopted a hunched over, half-shuffle, half-limp, shooting me periodic glares of outright loathing, but most of the fight had gone out of him once he realized that he was in a vulnerable position. "Chuan Ren will repay you for shaming me!" he managed to snarl as I dragged him into the hotel.

"Uh-huh."

"You will die the Death of Ten Thousand Screams!"

"Only ten thousand? I thought she was good for at least eleven."

Shing tried to straighten up, but the pain of his dislocated kneecap was too much even for his stoic self. "Followed by the Dismemberment of a Thousand Slashes."

"Yeah, you mentioned that one in the cab. Jim?"

"Right behind you."

"I myself will participate in the Ceremonial Rending of the Flesh!"

"Good for you. Hi. I'd like the room number for Lung Tik Chuan Ren," I told the reception clerk, who was looking somewhat flustered at our sudden, unkempt appearance into polite company. "I have something of hers I think she'd like returned, but he doesn't seem to be inclined to tell me what room she's in."

"Never will I talk! I will die before I reveal anything to you!"

"For thomeone whothe not talking, you thure are blabbing a lot," Jim said in a low voice.

Shing's face went red.

"I will ring the room and announce you," the woman said, glancing at the dragon nervously.

I leaned across the reception desk and put my free hand on the phone, my eyes on hers as I opened the door in my mind and focused my attention. "You just need to tell me the room number. I'll find her on my own." I gave a little push as I spoke. Her eyes went blank as her hand fell limply to her side.

"Room number?" I asked, a tiny bit nervous about using the mind push without proper supervision.

"Six oh four," she answered, looking over my shoulder at nothing.

"Thank you. Have a nice day. Oh, and forget about seeing us, OK?"

"As you wish."

I smiled cheerily, gave Shing's collar a jerk as he tried to twist out of my grip, and trundled my little gang toward the elevator.

"Your head will be severed from your body," Shing promised in as mean a voice as he could rally. The whimpers of pain kind of took away the threatening effect, however.

"Aw. I wath hoping we could take the thtairth," Jim lisped, narrowing its eyes on Shing. The dragon growled at it. Jim growled back, deliberately slobbering on his foot.

"Stop it, you two. Honestly, it's gotten so I just can't take them anywhere," I told the woman who was about to get on the elevator. She wisely chose to wait for the next one.

"Thithy," Jim said.

"We are not here to judge others. And please remember your party manners," I reminded Jim. "The red dragons may have declared war on us, but that doesn't mean we have to descend to their level and be rude."

"I will rip out your heart and eat it before your eyes," Shing moaned, clutching his knee.

I doubt I'll forget the look on Sying's—Shing's buddy and Chuan Ren's second bodyguard—face for a long, long time. The disbelief that chased horror when he saw his compatriot crumpled on the floor in front of the door (Jim had "accidentally" managed to trip Shing) was priceless, and definitely worth the aggravation of being the victim of yet another assassination attempt.

"Hi. We're here to see Chuan Ren," I said, pushing past the stunned Sying to enter the suite. "I'd appreciate it if you could tell her I'm here, and I'd like to have a couple of words."

"Your death will be one that lasts a thousand years," Shing whimpered as I half dragged him into the room. "Our poets will write many songs detailing just how horrible it will be."

"Oh," I said as Sying continued to stand openmouthed at the door. I pulled out the small gun that I had taken from Shing and pointed it at the second bodyguard. "Just . . . uh . . . in case you had thoughts of saying no, or something. Would you mind removing any guns or other weapons you happen to have stashed on yourself?"

Sying closed the door, hesitated for the count of four, then reached into his suit jacket and pulled out a gun, which he laid on the table next to him.

"Thanks. Jim?"

"On it." Jim brought the gun to me, then returned to check over Sying. "He'th clean."

"Excellent. Now, where is Chuan Ren?"

Sying's eyes flickered for the briefest of moments to

the double doors across the room. He said nothing, though, clearly unsure of whether he should try to attack me or help his friend.

"I wouldn't," I advised as I grabbed a handful of Shing's hair and prodded him into moving forward. "I've got your guns, Shing is in poor shape, and Jim's really annoyed at having a tooth knocked loose. Why don't you just open the doors for us, and we'll get out of your hair."

I don't know quite what I was expecting Chuan Ren to be doing—maybe torturing an innocent child or plotting the overthrow of Western civilization—but standing in the middle of a small living room kissing someone was not it.

"Hi. I don't know if you remember me, but I'm Aisling Grey, and I'm sick and tired of having your guys on me."

Chuan Ren spun around, her long black hair flying out behind her, caressing the chest of the man she'd been kissing.

I took one look at that man—the broad, broad chest, long legs, and dark emerald green eyes, and fire literally burst forth in a ring around me. "Just what the hell is going on here!" I yelled as I stormed forward. Shing squawked as he was dragged along with me. I released his hair and marched over to where Drake stood with an extremely irritated look on his face, trailing fire with every step. "You are in so much trouble, buster! I cannot begin to tell you how much trouble you are in, but I will say this—it is trouble like you have never seen before!"

"Would it appease you at all to know that she kissed me?" he asked.

"Barely."

"What are you doing here?" Chuan Ren demanded to know. "Shing, why are you on the ground? Did I not send you out to kill her? Can you not accomplish even the simplest of tasks? Where is Sying?"

I stopped glaring at Drake long enough to take two steps over to Chuan Ren. Without thinking about it, I pulled hard on Drake's fire and slammed it into her, sending her flying backwards three feet. "Don't think I'm not holding you responsible for this, either, you witch!"

"I think you lefth the *R* off that word," Jim said.

"Witch!" Chuan Ren screamed, lunging forward for me, her long nails clawlike. I'm willing to admit that I would have been a goner if Drake hadn't been there. I might have caught Chuan Ren by surprise the first time, but she was first and foremost a warrior, and had been for over a thousand years. I really didn't stand a chance with her.

"Cease!" Drake bellowed, suddenly in front of me, his body shielding me from Chuan Ren's attack. She snarled something at him but sheathed her claws, her dark brown eyes glittering with a deep red light that did not bode well.

"Mate." He turned his head slightly to look at me.

"What?"

One eyebrow rose. I followed his gaze and cleared my throat. "Is there a fire extinguisher in this room?"

Chuan Ren spat something in Chinese. I lifted my chin, gave her a look that let her know I wouldn't dignify whatever insult she had hurled at me with a response, and fetched the small extinguisher from where it hung next to the door. By the time I put out the fire on the couch, coffee table, two chairs, and Shing, Drake had managed to get her to the other side of the room. She stood with her feet slightly apart, her eyes burning, looking every inch a dragon lady.

"I am willing to admit I might have been a bit hasty with the first interpretation of what I saw," I told Drake as I set the extinguisher down and stepped over the slightly smoking, still-moaning Shing. "But the fact remains that you"—I pointed at Chuan Ren—"just declared war on him." I stopped next to Drake and leaned into him in a way that I hope screamed possession. "And as odd as dragon politics are, surely lip wrestling the person you just declared war on is not standard operating procedure."

"I was supposed to meet Gabriel here to discuss a cease-fire," Drake said calmly, putting his arm around me and pulling me even closer. "He did not show up."

"OK. That explains why you are here. Now would you like to tell me why you were kissing him?" I asked Chuan Ren.

She turned her back on me, shaking her long black hair so it hung in a perfectly straight line down her back.

"She was attempting to seduce me again, that's all." Drake's voice might be placid, but I could feel the angry fire within him.

"Thome guyth get all the breakth," Jim said, walking over to drool on the top of Shing's head.

"*Again*?" I asked, twisting around to look at Drake. "As in, she's seduced you other times?"

His jaw worked for a second, his eyes wary. "We have a somewhat complicated history," was all he said.

"Complicated in that she's another ex-girlfriend?" He

said nothing but didn't dispute it. I sighed. "I seem to be running into them with increasing frequency. Can you warn me when the next one pops up, so I'll know that she's likely to try to kill me or get me sent to prison?"

One side of Drake's mouth twitched. "I will try," he said gravely.

"Thanks." I turned back to Chuan Ren, who was now poking around a desk. "So, I take it peace is out of the question."

She looked down her nose at me. "We will not rest until the green dragons are destroyed."

I forbore to comment on her sleeping-with-the-enemy tactic and simply said, "OK. It's on now. Just so you know—you're going down. Drake did it before, and I have every confidence he can do it again."

We left her sputtering and slamming things around the room. Sying raced in when she hurled a vase through the window.

"We're going thraight to a dentitht, right?" Jim asked as we walked through the lobby.

"I'll get you an emergency appointment with a vet who specializes in dentistry," I promised. "I'm sure Nora must know of a good vet."

"Can I get a gold thooth to replathe thith one?"

"No."

"How abouth an enamel thathoo? I heard they're all the rage."

"No."

"Meanie," Jim muttered, sucking on its loose tooth.

"What you said to Chuan Ren was not, perhaps, the wisest way to end a conversation," Drake told me as he beckoned the hotel doorman. "Her temper was difficult enough without you reminding her of her past failures."

I raised my eyebrow at him. "Do you honestly think you're getting off this easily?"

"No." He grinned as I followed Jim into a waiting cab. "I have every confidence you're going to have much to say on the subject. But I anticipate the making-up process will be most enjoyable to both of us. In fact, I'm looking forward to it."

The little smile I tried to hide curled my lips. I knew that Drake wouldn't betray me, but it wouldn't hurt him to wish to placate me.

Drake wasn't the only one looking forward to our discussion.

16

I woke up the following morning to find my breasts on fire.

Literally.

"Oooh," I purred, shivering a little with excitement despite the flames that licked up my body . . . right next to Drake's tongue, which was licking a suddenly aching breast. "We haven't spent enough time together for me to be certain if you are the type of man who wakes up in the mood to frolic, but I see you are."

"*Kincsem*, where you are concerned, I'm always in the mood to . . . *frolic*. Did you get enough sleep?"

"Oh, yes," I said, although whether I was answering his question or responding to his touch was unclear. Pleasure, sweet and pure, started at the touch of his mouth to my flesh, rippling out to all points on my body, turning me into one gigantic quivering erogenous zone. My hands slid up his chest, around his ribs, then down his back. I flexed my fingers and dragged my nails gently up his spine, something I knew he liked. His head rose from the sweet torment he was laving up my breast, the fire in his eyes so bright it made his eyes glow.

I traced the line of muscles around his hips to the front, my fingers wrapping around the heavy, hot part of him, marveling yet again that such a simple bit of flesh and muscle could bring so much pleasure.

"You were right, yesterday."

"I am always right," he growled, his entire body stiffening for a moment as I caressed him.

"Not even close. But you were right about the making-up part being enjoyable."

His mouth was busy with a sensitive patch of my flesh, but I heard him mumble something about my ire being worth tolerating just for the resolution of our differences.

"You promised me you'd teach me to breathe fire," I reminded him, licking his lips as he groaned when my fingers found sensitive skin. I bit his shoulder, releasing one hand to push him over onto his back. "I think it would be an extremely handy skill to have, and what better time than the present to learn it?"

"What better time, indeed?" he agreed, watching with interest as I flicked my tongue over two little pert nipples peeking through the dark hair of his chest.

"Let me have it, Drake."

"It is all yours, *kincsem*."

I bit gently on his nipple, enjoying the little shiver of pleasure that shook his chest. "Not that. I want your fire. Let me have it."

Dragon fire roared up within him, spilling over into me. I allowed it to fill me, embracing and welcoming it.

"Focus it," Drake said in a tight voice as I moved over

to nibble on the other nipple before using my tongue to trace the glossy trail of hair that led down his belly to points south. "Make it take the form you want, then release it."

A thick, abrupt burp of fire escaped me.

"Focus more. You're allowing yourself to be distracted."

I looked down at his penis, standing so patiently yet proudly, waiting for me to make my way to it. "There's a lot to be distracted by. I had a thought about this shape-shifting issue—you shift when you have an orgasm, did you know that? I figured maybe if we make love a whole lot, it'll ease up your shifting muscles, or whatever it is that's holding you back. Um. I don't seem to be able to breathe the fire, do I?"

"You must exercise control, Aisling. Without it, you'll never be able to harness the fire. It is a tool for you to use. Make it into what you want."

I flicked my tongue across the tip of his penis, savoring the salty drop of moisture collected there. I gathered the fire within me, holding a mental picture of just what I wanted to do with it. As I opened my mouth to take him in, fire blazed out, setting the lower half of his body ablaze. I concentrated until the fire was in a fine stream, and licked a fiery path along the length of his shaft, sending a blast of it at the sensitive underside of the head.

Drake shouted and just about came off the bed. I laughed. "You can't tell me you don't like that."

"Christos, *like* doesn't even come close to it."

"What does it feel like?" I prompted, using both hands

with my mouth to set up a rhythm that had his hips thrusting upward.

"It's an agony of ecstasy," he groaned, his fingers tangled in my hair. I glanced upward to see his eyes closed, his jaw tight as his fire and my mouth worked their magic. *Agony of ecstasy* was a good description, so I decided to let him off the sharing hook, and concentrate on bringing him to the very edge of rapture.

Our bodies were coated in flame, Drake groaning nonstop and begging me to climb on him and end the torment, when a cool breeze whispered along my back. Dragon fire being what it is—formed from the originating dragon's well of emotions—it had never yet harmed me, or left me feeling anything but empowered and usually aroused. But for some reason, this time I was left slick with sweat, as if the fire was impure.

Just as Drake had had enough and was hauling me over himself, his penis poised to impale me, I caught the flash of something yellow from the corner of my eye.

That's when I realized that what I had thought was sweat was really water . . . coming from the overhead sprinklers.

"Imps," I yelled, sliding off Drake to point at the nasty little yellow creature bolting for the opened window. Although Drake's bedding had been fireproofed, the rest of the room hadn't been so treated, and everything from the drapes to the wardrobe, uncomfortable Louis XIV chairs, and a squat, ugly desk in the corner was aflame.

As the word left my mouth, a smoke detector near the door went off, sounding a piercing siren that seemed to cut through the thick black smoke that was filling the room.

Drake snarled an oath and was across the room before I could blink, the imp in his hands for a second before he hurled it out the window to the ground three stories below. He slammed open a second window.

"Not again," I cried, grabbing up his discarded shirt to slip on as urgent voices sounded in the hall. Pál and István burst into the room, both bearing fire extinguishers. Drake snatched a third out of the bathroom, and mindless of his nudity (thankfully, he no longer exhibited visual evidence of his ardor), stood with the other two men to put out the fire.

"What is going on here? What is that appalling noise at such an unholy hour?" Drake's mother stood in the doorway, clad in an elegant rose-colored silk negligee, her scowl enough to douse any flame. Her eyes pierced me, narrowing at the sight of me standing in nothing but Drake's shirt. "You! It is all your doing, this unpleasantness!"

The smoke billowed out around her as Nora appeared, peering over Catalina's shoulder, her eyes owlish as she watched the three men quell the last of the flames. "Imps again?"

"Yes. Drake caught one as it was trying to leave."

"Aisling, I am prepared to be tolerant of many things, but this situation with the imp kingdom must come to an end," Drake said, coughing a little as the last blaze died under the white chemical foam. "My house is well prepared to deal with the commonality of dragon fire, but it is not built to withstand fires set by murderous arsonists."

"I know. I'm so sorry." I wrung my hands, feeling utterly helpless as I surveyed the damage caused by the fire. It hadn't had long to burn, and yet the furniture was destroyed, the walls stained black by the smoke. "I'll take care of it. I promise."

"I knew it was her doing. All those lovely antiques destroyed," Catalina said, shooting me another scathing look before sweeping past Nora and returning to her room.

My shoulders sagged.

Outside, in the stillness of an early London morning, sirens sounded. Drake's security system must have kicked in and alerted the fire authorities.

"I'll tell them it's controlled," István said, clad in only a pair of pants. He, too, gave me a look as he walked past, although it wasn't nearly as daunting as Catalina's.

My spirits took a nosedive.

"I'll get a cart to start clearing this mess away," Pál murmured, avoiding looking at me altogether as he, barefoot and also wearing only a pair of hastily donned pants, scooted around me.

Guilt, despair, and a frustrating sense of impotence filled me.

Drake eyed me closely. "You are all right? You did not breathe in too much smoke?"

"No, I'm fine," I said miserably, unable to meet his gaze. "Drake, I'm really, really sorry about this. The fire and . . . everything."

"I dislike having any of my possessions taken from me, but I would rather lose a few pieces of furniture than you," was all he said, and despite the misery swelling within me, his words formed a solid little core of happiness.

That happiness died with his next words. "You have twenty-four hours to take care of the imp situation, or I will do it for you." He grabbed a pair of pants and shoes from a second wardrobe and retired to the bathroom.

I thought about crumpling up into a little ball and wishing the world away.

Jim burst out the moment the door was opened. "Fires of Abaddon, what's going on in here? You guys having an orgy or . . . oh, man."

With lips pursed, Jim surveyed the mess. Slowly, the demon turned to look at me. "You had a barbeque and you didn't invite me?"

Two fat tears of self-pity rolled down my cheeks.

"Come, Aisling. No one was hurt, and not much destroyed." Nora put her arm around me and escorted me out of the room. "Let's have some breakfast, then put our heads together about how we're going to placate the imp kingdom."

"Breakfast! Great idea, Nora. I could really go for a couple of grilled imps right about now," Jim said, following us out of the room.

I just wanted to rewind the last couple of days and do them over.

A few hours later Nora, Jim, and I left just as a cleaning crew arrived to muck out, repair, dry, and de-smoke Drake's bedroom. The last sight I had of Drake was a smoldering look he sent me before he left for Paris to deal with an issue that arose with his French businesses. He was as unsatisfied as I was with the lack of culmination of our morning's activities, but I knew Drake—his passion matched mine, so I was confident we'd find a way to get together before the sun had time to set.

"What is it they say about the weather on a wedding day?" Jim asked as it stepped out of the house, glancing up at the sky, filled with gray, sodden clouds.

"It is *not* my wedding day," I said firmly, giving Jim's leash a snap to pull it away from smelling a passerby's butt. Rene pulled up in front of the house, the windshield wipers of his taxi making slow passes across the wet windshield. "Morning, Rene."

"Good morning."

"Hey, don't kill the messenger. You wanted a bloodless solution to the imp situation, and I suggested you marrying the current monarch. End of problem. It's not like it would be a real marriage or anything. Hi, Rene. I'll arm wrestle you for the best-man position."

I sighed as I followed Jim into the taxi. Nora climbed into the front seat next to Rene, settling the carrier with Paco on her lap. "Good morning, Rene. We've had a bit of an upset this morning."

"Best man?" Rene asked, craning to look back at us. "Upset?"

"It's a long story. Can we tell you en route? We've got to get Nora to a meeting with the committee in twenty minutes, then we're off to sacrifice Jim in order to make peace with the imps."

"Hey, hey, hey! I distinctly remember saying no to that whole sacrifice-Jim idea!"

Rene gunned the engine and pulled out into traffic,

narrowly missing a bus, two elderly pedestrians, and a suicidal squirrel. "Do not leave out a single word. I want to hear about it all."

It didn't take long to bring Rene up to date with the latest happenings, which is good because it turned out that the London headquarters of the International Guardians' Guild was a short ride from Drake's house.

"I believe I understand," he said, turning in an underground parking garage. "You must settle the imps most strenuously. And Nora must convince this committee that she has done nothing to be punished for, *hein?*"

"Right. And I have"—I checked my watch—"oh, man. Where did the day go? I have less than fifteen minutes to come up with a plan to get Ariton the demon lord off my back. Lovely. Oh, well, I'll have to do it after the Guardian meeting."

I thought Nora's head was going to come off her neck, so fast did she swivel her head around to look at me. "What is that about Ariton? What dealings do you have with him?"

We pulled into a parking spot. "We are here. I, too, am interested in hearing about this demon lord," Rene said.

"There's not much to tell, guys, honest." I made a little gesture of innocence. "Evidently because I'm technically a demon lord, there's some sort of etiquette that says I'm eligible to vote on stuff to do with Abaddon, or something like that. And before anyone starts freaking, I'm not going to get involved in any petty squabbles between demon lords."

Rene stared at me in the rearview mirror. Nora gazed at me with a mixture of horror, concern, and sympathy.

Jim groaned, laid its head on the seat, and covered its eyes with two big, hairy paws.

"What?" I asked everyone, wondering why they were making such a big deal out of it.

"Aisling, I can't believe you don't know about the Vexamen. I was sure you had heard of it."

I sighed. "You know, I don't want to always be so clueless, but it's a bit difficult when I'm new and everyone assumes I know stuff. What's a Vexamen, and what does it have to do with Ariton and all the surprised faces you're making at me?"

Rene shook his head as he got out of the car, opening my door, then going around to take Paco from Nora and help her out.

"Vexamen is the event that happens every six hundred years. It falls on the autumnal equinox, which is in three days. Vexamen is an upheaval in Abaddon, when one demon lord rises to supremacy and rules over the others. Surely you've heard of it?"

I shook my head as I got out of the car, snapping a leash on Jim's collar. "Nope. Jim, why didn't you tell me after we left Ariton's place?"

"You didn't ask me," my annoying demon said.

Nora stumbled, grabbing my arm to stop me as we crossed the parking garage. "You went . . . you *visited* a demon lord in his abode?"

Rene sucked his teeth and looked thoughtful.

"It's not like I had any choice," I told them both. "I was pretty much kidnapped, and I had just been skewered, if you'll remember. What's the big deal about me going to Ariton's digs? It was that house in Islington that gave you the willies, so bonus points to you for sensing Ariton's presence. Although, I have to admit . . . I am having doubts that he shot at me."

Nora's hands fluttered around with distress. "Aisling, this just isn't done! No one I know—no one I've ever heard of has visited a demon lord in his home. To do so would imply that one is . . ."

I straightened my shoulders, lifting my chin. "Go ahead. I'm strong; I can take it. What am I? Damned?"

"Unclean," she said after wrestling with the word for a moment.

"Unclean as in impure? Tainted? Dabbling in dark powers?" I asked, my heart dropping. It seemed like I just couldn't catch a break lately.

"That's as apt a description as any," Nora said slowly. She hesitated for a moment, then started toward the stairs that led to the building above us. "I know you are innocent and not at all influenced by this demon lord you met, but it's vitally important now that you not have anything further to do with him. As it is, I am not sure how we are going to explain to the guild this latest, but we will cross that bridge when we come to it."

"I'm sorry to be giving you more trouble," I said miserably as we climbed to the lobby of a busy building filled with professional offices. "I had no idea this Vexamen thing was going on. I never intended to become involved."

"But surely you must have noticed the increase this past week in outbreaks? First the kobold scare, then imps, then blight hounds." Nora punched a floor number on the elevator panel, giving me a curious look.

Rene blew out a breath. I didn't spend longer than a second wondering why he was coming along with us. He seemed so much a part of my little gang, I was just grateful to have one more head to consult. "*Mon dieu*. Three in a week?"

Nora nodded. "And three last week, at Salvaticus."

"That being . . . ?" I asked.

"The start of Vexamen. It's the date when the ruling prince of Abaddon begins to lose his powers." Nora stepped onto the thankfully empty elevator. We all filed in with her, including a woman with short blond hair who was carrying a coffee mug and a portfolio.

"I thought the . . . er . . . situation was normal," I said, mindful of the stranger in our midst. "To be honest, I thought it was due to the dr—to Drake and his kind. I had gathered that things like those outbreaks happen whenever they disagree."

"Not this sort of thing," Nora said, shaking her head.

I mused on that for the few seconds it took to get to the seventh floor, following Rene and Nora as they walked down a long hallway to an office in the rear. Nora paused with her hand on the doorknob. "Rene, the guild has very strict rules about who is allowed into their offices. I know you do not present any threat, but I want to warn you that you may be refused admittance."

He gave one of his effective Gallic shrugs. "We will see, *hein*? You do not mind if I come with you?"

"No, certainly not. I'd be grateful for a friendly face." Nora gave him a bright smile that made me feel ashamed of my self-absorption. Here she was facing an investigation into her professional capabilities, and I was too busy worrying about my own problems to be supportive and helpful.

"Don't worry; we won't let them mess with you," I said with a little hug. "If it's me causing the guild concerns, I'll formally de-mentor you, and we'll just go on in an unofficial capacity."

Nora laughed, hugging me back. "I wish it was that easy, but let us not borrow trouble. Brave hearts, everyone."

She opened the door and stepped through it, Rene following. I started to go through the door but found myself held back as if by an invisible webbing. The door had been warded with a powerful protection ward, no doubt to keep dark beings out.

"Uh . . . that's not happening," Jim said. "Ward. Big one."

"There's nothing I love more than a little challenge," I muttered to myself as I opened the door in my mind, gathered up some dragon fire, shaped it, and focused it on the ward. The pattern glowed purple in the air for a moment. I grabbed Jim by the collar and forcefully shoved it through the doorway, bullying my way through the ward. I thought for a moment that I wasn't going to be able to pass it, but I broke through just as the purple ward turned silver, then evaporated. "Whew. That was a toughie. You OK, Jim?"

"I feel like I've been brushed backwards, but yeah, OK otherwise." The demon licked a few rumpled patches of fur.

I turned to see where Nora had gone and found myself facing a room full of people all staring at me with disbelief, Nora included.

Rene smiled.

A tall, balding man built like one of the dragon bodyguards stepped forward, obviously a security person. "Guardian. Mortal. Identification?"

Nora brought out her wallet and showed him a card.

"Member number 1112," he read to another guard behind a computer, who promptly tapped the information onto the keyboard. The second man nodded at the first.

"You may pass," the guard told her. She walked forward a few feet, stopping to chat with one of the men sitting behind a desk.

The guard turned to Rene. "Daimon. Immortal. Identification?"

"I have my passport," Rene said pleasantly. "But beyond that . . ." He gave another shrug.

"You may pass."

I sent a little triumphant smile to Rene, who winked at me. At last, confirmation of what I'd suspected—he wasn't mortal! Now, if I just knew what a daimon was.

"Guardian. Wyvern's mate." The guard frowned at me, speaking loudly so everyone in the room—people waiting in a waiting area, others bustling around doing office work—could hear. "Demon lord. Immortal. Identification?"

I smiled pleasantly. "All I have is my passport, too. I'm not a member of the Guardian Guild yet."

"Name?"

"Aisling Grey."

At least two people in the room sucked in their breath. One woman at a desk dropped a stack of papers and went running out of the room.

"I'm beginning to feel like either a rock star or Typhoid Mary," I whispered to Jim.

"Go with rock star. You get groupies that way."

"You may pass," the guard said after a brief consultation with his partner.

"Thank you. Er . . . have a nice day." I spread my smile out to everyone who was still staring at me and followed Nora and Rene as they left the reception area.

"Some are born to greatness, others aspire to it; some have it thrust upon them," Rene misquoted as Nora took us to a conference room.

"Shakespeare didn't know the half of it," I grumbled softly as we entered the room.

17

Three people stood at one end of the room, chatting as they poured themselves coffee. All three stopped talking to turn around at our entrance. I recognized one of the men as Mark Sullivan, the guy who had left the injunction with me, but the woman and other man were strangers.

"Nora Charles?" Mark asked, setting his coffee down at the head of the table.

Nora nodded.

"I see you have brought . . . what? Witnesses?"

"Friends," I said quickly, immediately going into defensive mode at the snarky tone in his voice. "Naturally, if you do not wish to allow Nora any form of moral support, we will leave. I assume, however, that you have no problem with her facing this inquisition with a few friends at her side."

"Well done," Rene said under his breath. I shot him an appreciative glance.

"I can assure you this interview is far from the inquisition you seem to imagine, Aisling Grey." Mark waved a hand toward the end of the table closest to us. "By all means, stay if that is what you desire."

The other two people were introduced. "This is Eirene Mathers, the head of the mentor program, and Greg Gillion, of the internal investigative committee."

We took our seats at the opposite end of the table. I bent down to whisper a warning to Jim to be quiet unless I indicated it could speak.

"All this power is going to your head," Jim grumbled. "I had more fun with Amaymon. He wasn't always forbidding me to talk just when things got juicy."

"I would be happy to send you back to him," I said in an undertone, then sat up and tried to look supportive and forthright.

"As you know from the injunction I left with Aisling Grey earlier, a complaint has been lodged regarding certain inconsistencies with your training program," Mark said, shuffling through a couple of papers until he found what he was looking for. He gave it a quick once-over, then slid it to the side to the internal investigations guy. "Although we are not at liberty to reveal the name of the individual making the complaint, I can assure you that the complaint itself was investigated thoroughly to determine if it was valid. Once that was deemed so, the injunction was issued and an investigation commenced to examine the subject of the complaint—that is you, Miss Charles."

Nora inclined her head, her hands clasped in front of her on the table. She looked interested but relaxed. I gave her full points for style—although she presented a brave front, I knew she was worried about this slap in the face from an organization she had long served.

"The investigation was carried out by a three-person committee headed by myself," Greg Gillion said, evidently taking the floor. He didn't look like the sort of person who should be investigating anything—he looked like a Santa Claus who had been on the South Beach diet for the past ten months. Balding, with white hair and a beard, and clothing that hung off him as if it had been meant for a much larger person, this man looked like anything but a take-charge sort of person.

Which just shows why you should never trust first impressions.

"This interview is the final part of that investigation. It is your opportunity to answer the investigating team's questions and to make a statement in your defense. Do you understand what has been said thus far?"

Nora didn't so much as bat an eyelash. "Yes, I do."

"Excellent. The nature of the complaint itself is as follows," Greg said, consulting a leather portfolio. "First, that you offered apprentice testing to an individual despite the fact that the period of testing had passed, and subsequently gave approval for the individual mentioned to receive official recognition as an apprentice. Second, that you maligned and otherwise ridiculed a member of the guild in public at the recent GOTDAM convention. Third, that you aided and abetted a murderer in his attempt to escape."

My jaw just about hit the table at the ridiculous allegations. I sneaked a peek at Nora out of the corner of my eye. She was sitting just as still and attentive as she had been when the interview started. My admiration for her restraint and self-control was boundless—if someone had lobbed those absolutely ridiculous accusations at me, I

would have been ranting by now. As it was, I had to remind myself that I was there on forbearance, and my silence was more helpful to Nora than any protestations of
her innocence.

"Those three allegations, I am pleased to say, were dismissed as groundless and based on the accuser's somewhat biased interpretation of recent events," Santa Greg
said, peering over the top of his gold-rimmed glasses to
see how Nora would take that news.

She smiled slightly and inclined her head in acknowl-
edgment.

"However . . ."

"Somehow, I just knew there was a *however* coming,"
I whispered to Jim. It nodded.

". . . the fourth and final accusation was not so easily
dismissed. That is simply that you have taken into your
home a servant of dark powers."

I frowned, not sure whether he was referring to Jim or
me. "Er . . . pardon me for interrupting, but are you talking about me? Because if you are, I need to set the record
straight on a few things."

"No, Miss Grey, I am not referring to you," Santa Greg
told me with a slight look of admonishment. "The investigation team thoroughly checked the bylaws of the
Guardians' Guild and could find no mention of a rule regarding the possible apprenticeship of a demon lord or
wyvern's mate. Neither situation has come up before."

"However, amendments will be added at the earliest
possible date," Eirene Mathers piped up. I'd almost forgotten she was there, so quiet had she been. "You may be
interested to know that any existing members of the

guild who are demon lords or wyvern's mates will be allowed to retain their membership once the new laws go into effect."

"That's very nice of you." I worked hard to keep my voice level and sarcasm free, even though it was making my mouth sour.

She gave me a weak little smile. "The guild is interested in the welfare of all its members, even those of an . . . untraditional mien."

"The being in question is the demon known as Effrijim," Santa Greg said, taking control of the conversation again.

Jim's head shot up.

"It is true that Jim lives in the same house as I do," Nora agreed. "But it is not my servant, nor do I have control over it any more than it has control over me. It does not have the least amount of influence over me, and I do not receive power or abilities from it."

Everyone looked at Jim.

"You can speak if it's something helpful," I whispered.

"Yeah, what she said. Nora takes me on walkies with Paco and feeds me sometimes, and if she's really in a good mood, she'll scratch my belly, but other than that, we're just roomies. There's no favoritism or anything. She even yells at me when I get busy with the furniture or take a dump too close to Paco."

Santa Greg looked confused. I wanted to throttle my demon. "Paco is . . . ?"

Nora lifted the carrier off the floor and set it on the table. Visible in the wire door was the figure of a small Chihuahua curled up asleep. "Paco is my dog."

"Just so. Regardless of the lack of contact with the demon Effrijim, it is the opinion of the investigating team that having such a being in constant close contact provides too much of a temptation. A recommendation has been made to restore your mentorship should the demon be removed from your residence."

"Wait a minute," I interrupted, giving Nora's hand an apologetic squeeze. "I'm sorry to break in again, but this is just silly. Jim is my demon. It responds only to my commands. It can't give Nora power, or corrupt her, or do whatever it is you seem to think will happen with us living in the same house. Even if Jim wanted to—and you have to admit, as demons go, Jim is not exactly a prime specimen—it couldn't. Not without my command."

"Exactly," Mark said, an oddly satisfied look on his face.

A little light began to dawn in the back of my head.

"Oh, I see now," I said, goose bumps marching down my arms and legs as the truth hit me. "This is a witch hunt, isn't it? You don't want to ban Nora from the mentor program—you're after me."

"I can assure you that your name was not mentioned in the complaints," Santa Greg said, sliding a paper toward me. "There is a copy, if you'd care to examine it."

"I don't need to," I said, trying to imitate Nora's calm exterior. Rene was trying to signal me something with an odd form of eyebrow semaphore, but I didn't have time to translate it. "It's quite clear where this is heading. You are going to use the utterly ridiculous and completely groundless idea that Nora could go through me to influence my demon solely to give us grief."

"On the contrary," Mark answered. "We fear just the opposite."

Next to me, Nora gasped. Rene's eyes widened.

"I am one of the good guys," I said, stunned by the unspoken accusation. "I'm a Guardian! I *protect* people, not harm them!"

"You are also a demon lord, have control of a demon, and are high in the powers of a dragon sept. Although your own powers have not been tested by the guild, it is evident that they are beyond the scope of an apprentice."

Nora's hand grabbed my wrist. I bit back the smart-assed reply I wanted to make.

"Is the guild now punishing Guardians who show exceptional talent by deeming them dangerous?" she asked. "I can assure you that I weighed the pros and cons of taking on Aisling as an apprentice. I am aware of the limitations she has regarding her apprenticeship, but I was convinced then—and remain so—that her dedication, her abilities, and her commitment to the guild are sufficient to overcome any obstacles her other roles may present."

"Aisling is not bad," Rene said suddenly. "She is different, yes, but that does not make her bad."

"We have strayed from the purpose of this interview," Mark said, tapping a pen on his portfolio.

I had to speak or burst. "I think I should be allowed to defend myself just as Nora is allowed. And to be perfectly frank, I'm insulted by the idea that you'd call into question my dedication, not to mention Nora's judgment and ability to pick an apprentice. I am not a bad person. Jim was an accident—I never sought to become a demon

lord and don't have anything to do with the rest of them.
In fact, I don't have anything to do with anyone who dabbles in the dark powers. None whatsoever!"

There was a ripple in the air behind Mark's chair. Outside the room, a distant alarm sounded.

"In fact, I don't even know anyone who . . . er . . .
does . . ."

The air thickened, twisted, and formed into Obedama. The demon stepped forward, its hands on its hips
as it ignored everyone to glare at me. "The lord Ariton
has waited for you, but you have not responded. The
hour of your appointment with him has passed, and Vexamen is near. You are summoned now to make your
fealty to him."

"Other than Ariton and his minion Obedama, of
course," I said, my stomach wadding up into a little ball
as three men burst into the room, each bearing a demon-
banishing silver dagger. I slumped back in my chair. My
goose was really cooked now . . . and I suspected Nora's
was as well.

"Well, that went well," Jim said a couple hours later,
as we emerged into the exhaust-laden parking garage.
"*Not!*"

"We're free, aren't we?" I pinched Jim's ear.

"Ow. Demon abuse!"

"Stop complaining. It's not like you were grilled,
anyway. Or had to put off a demon lord. I just hope Ariton isn't going to be pissed that the Guardians sent his
minion to Abaddon when I told it I couldn't talk to him
right then."

"I'm sure she gets hazard pay." Jim paused, an odd, abstracted look on its face. "Oh, boy, I should have gone with Nora when she took Paco to the park. Emergency walkies! Like, right now!"

"What are you going to do with the demon lord?" Rene asked just as Jim bolted toward the exit. "Aisling?"

I had stopped when I spied a familiar man standing at the elevator. With one eye on Jim racing toward the street and the other on the man behind us, I shoved the leash at Rene. "Would you mind taking Jim to the square? Nora's probably still there walking Paco. Here are two plastic bags. . . . They should take care of things. I see someone I know and just want to find out what he's doing here."

"What person? Who?" Rene asked.

"A man who may just possibly be stalking me, and if he is, I'm going to put an end to it here and now."

Rene looked curious as I turned back the way we came and hurried over to where Peter Burke stood patiently waiting for the elevator. "Hi. Er . . . this is going to sound really rude, I know, but would you mind telling me what you're doing here?"

"I don't think the question is particularly rude," he answered, his eyes just as curiously flat as I remembered them. Either he had an incredible amount of self-control or he was not what he seemed. I decided to try another look at his true self using my super-Guardian vision. "As a matter of fact, I was following you."

His answer startled me right out of opening the mental door to my powers. "You . . . you admit you're stalking me?"

"Not so much stalking—just trying to find the opportunity to speak with you once more before I return to Paris," he laughed, but the laughter did not reflect on his face. It was as if he wore a mask, shielding his thoughts and feelings from humanity.

"I'm glad to hear it's not a stalking, because my boyfriend is rather possessive, and I don't think you want to tangle with him. What is it you wanted to talk to me about?" I asked, knowing it was probably the same thing he'd wanted last time.

"You need not look so wary—this is merely a courtesy, not a plea for your help again. My contacts in Paris inform me that since no serious contenders for the position of Venediger have come forward in the duly allotted time, and as you are determined to refuse any nomination should that eventuality materialize, I am assured of victory. I wanted you to know that I appreciate you stepping aside in order to allow me to take the role for which I was intended."

I opened my mouth to tell him I was not stepping aside in order to help him when it occurred to me that he was just too pat, too slick. I had the distinct feeling that for some bizarre reason, he was manipulating me into opposing him. "Good luck with the job," I said, biting back all the responses I had wanted to make. I swung open the door in my mind and took a good long look at him before saying good-bye and walking out to the park across the square.

Peter Burke looked exactly the same as when I had seen him in Paris—utterly the same, in fact. It finally dawned on me what was wrong with that.

"I don't understand what the problem is," Rene said

five minutes later as he returned from the garbage can where he'd dumped Jim's offerings. "Why is something bad with this mage?"

"Everyone looks different somehow with Guardian vision," I said slowly as we headed back to the parking garage. Nora walked alongside me, frowning slightly. "Everyone, with no exceptions. Usually it's just an aura, but sometimes you can see hidden features or entities tied to a person."

"I, for instance, look a hundred times more handsome, especially now that I have this tooth fixed," Jim said, charging forward at a lull in the traffic. We followed.

"How do I look different?" Rene asked as we turned in the parking garage.

I smiled. "You've got a slightly golden aura around you. I never thought much about it before, but now . . . well, now I know."

He winked to let me know he understood what I wasn't saying. I had no idea whether Nora had heard the guard at the Guardians' Guild say that Rene was immortal, but I wasn't about to spill his secret if she hadn't. "Nora has a rose-colored aura. Drake and the other wyverns are surrounded by coronas of dragon's fire."

"So when this man, this mage who would be Venediger, does not look different at all . . ." Rene cocked an eyebrow at me.

"It means something is up with him. I just wish I knew what."

"Does it really matter, if you have no intention of interfering with matters in Paris?" Nora asked as we approached the car.

"I suppose not. It's just something odd, and I have enough oddness in my life right now. I'd like a little normalcy for a change."

"Speaking of the oddness—you did not tell me what you intend to do with the demon lord who wishes you to join him." Rene unlocked the car doors for us.

"Ugh. Him. Keep stalling, I guess. I'm great at stalling. I'll just keep putting him off until he gives up on me and goes on to something else."

Nora looked worried. "If he has gone to the trouble of locating you twice, he probably is serious in his desire for you to join your power to his."

"Well, that's not going to happen. Trust me, I know people. If you stall them enough, eventually they give up. Since demon lords were once human, he's bound to be the same."

"Hmm." Nora didn't look convinced. My attention, however, was on other things.

"I'd say I'm sorry again about everything, but you're probably sick of hearing it." I gave a decidedly wry smile. "But as it is, I am really sorry about everything. What do you think the chances are of an appeal?"

"I'm not sure. No one has ever had to appeal this sort of thing before."

"At least you were not pushed out from the guild, eh?" Rene said, obviously trying to look on the bright side of things. He held the door open for Nora and Paco. "And Aisling, she was not forbidden from joining?"

"No, but only because they can't refuse admittance because my application was accepted before they had any anti–demon lord rules in place. Oy. What a nightmare."

"It's not as bad as it seems." Nora patted my hand as I climbed into the taxi and sat next to her. "Yes, I've had my mentor status stripped from me, but as Rene said, I wasn't kicked out of the guild, and there is always the appeal process. I have no doubt that once I have made my case, the guild will have no choice but to reinstate my title."

"I hope so. I think it's pretty evident to everyone that I need as much training as I can get. How long do you think the appeal process will take?"

"Up to two years," she said calmly as Jim jumped into the front seat next to Rene.

"Two years!"

Her smile was surprisingly calm and without a shred of accusation or disapproval. "Don't look so appalled. We will continue as we are, Aisling."

"But . . . you could get kicked out of the guild."

"Perhaps. But that's a chance I'm willing to take."

"But . . ."

"No, no *buts*." She laughed at the look on my face. "Aisling, I'm paying you the highest compliment I know, and you're looking at me as if I've asked you to suck lemons. Stop worrying about things beyond your control, and focus on the job you must do."

I wanted to argue with her that I wasn't going to let her take a fall for me but reminded myself in time that I was there to learn from her. She was a big girl. If she didn't think there was a problem with continuing to teach me, then I needed to trust that she was right. I took a couple of deep breaths to calm my agitated brain. "OK. I'll let that go for now. And you're right; I need to focus. I can do this. I'm a professional."

"You're good enough, you're smart enough, and dog-gone it, people like you!" Jim said in its best Stuart Smalley impression.

"Only the fact that I'm going to ritually sacrifice you in a half hour is saving your butt," I told it.

"Can we reopen that topic of discussion?" Jim asked. "'Cause I'm really not comfortable with the whole idea. It's like something Lucy on crack would think up. The only thing missing is the demented chocolate-making assembly line."

Nora and I ignored Jim to go over once again our plans for the imps.

"You're sure this ward is going to be enough to protect me against a mass attack?" I asked a short while later as we tromped over a partially wooded field on Hampstead Heath and headed for a culvert that led to an underground lair. I stood in front of the opening, which was about four feet high, and fretted. A lot was riding on this—not just an end to the imp attacks, but I needed to prove that I could handle myself in a situation where Nora would not be available to back me up.

She shook her head at me. "Aisling, Aisling, Aisling . . . I've told you—it's your belief in the ward that creates the magic, not mine. You must believe in your power to protect yourself."

Well, that I had no trouble with. I was a relatively tough chick. I'd kissed a wyvern and lived to tell the tale. I'd breathed fire. And I'd been skewered and still managed to carry on as usual. It was just all the other things out of my control I worried about.

"OK. I can do this." I drew the protection ward across my chest, satisfied when it glowed silver in the air for a few seconds before melting away.

"Are you sure you do not want us with you?" Rene asked, squatting on his heels to peer into the culvert. Dirt and debris had been washed out of it, but it looked relatively clear. An occasional flicker of movement indicated rodents, but those didn't cause me any grief. "I will watch your back. As you said, I am the sidekick extraordinaire."

"I'd love for you to come along, but Nora says it would never work. The imps are bound to be touchy about this whole thing, and they won't negotiate if anyone else is there. So wish me luck, and if I'm not out in an hour, send in a whole platoon of Drakes, please."

Nora gave me a thumbs-up as I stepped into the culvert. Rene wished me *bonne chance*. Jim peed in three different spots, tried to convince me it was going to throw up a hairball, and finally, reluctantly, shambled after me as I hunched over and crab walked my way into the belly of the imp kingdom.

The last bit of daylight winked out as the big drainage pipe turned a corner. Before I could switch on the flashlight Nora had thoughtfully provided, a small herd of imps bearing tiny, little torches descended upon us.

"Stop!" I yelled in my most forceful voice, putting my belief of my power behind it as Nora had warned. The imps swarmed around me, some of their torches coming dangerously close to my clothing. The ward glowed brightly in the air for a moment, though, causing the tiny little beasties to pause in their attack. "I am Aisling Grey! I am here to negotiate with your monarch. I bring to him the true slayer of"—I had to stop to take a quick glance at the name I'd written on my hand so I wouldn't forget it—"Mehigenous the Fourth. Behold, the imp-killing demon Effrijim!"

"You're loving every minute of this, aren't you?" Jim muttered as the imps held their collective breaths for a moment, then with a bunch of high-pitched squeaks, ran over to surround Jim. It bared its teeth and snapped at a couple who got too close.

"Do not touch the demon!" I bellowed in the same pushy voice. "I am here to negotiate the sacrifice of it with your monarch. Take us to him!"

Jim rolled its eyes as the imps gathered together in a clutch for a moment, their squeaky yip-yips making my teeth itch. "You couldn't think up a more original version of 'take me to your leader'?"

"No. And hush. You're supposed to be repentant, remember?"

"Yeah, right, and imps could fly out my ass. Hey! There's an idea!"

"I'll make it a command if you can't keep your lips zipped," I whispered.

Evidently I had done the demanding bit right, because the imps turned en masse and escorted us deeper into the culvert. It took another five minutes of crab walking, sometimes almost crawling, to get through to their main living area, but with the imps on one side pulling, and me behind shoving, we managed to get Jim's bulky body through a very narrow opening and into a large, open area.

"Welcome to imp central," Jim said, licking a patch of dirt off its shoulder.

I don't know what I was expecting—some sort of cavern with grubs and rats—but the imps' main headquarters wasn't anything like my expectations. The walls were curved, like a tunnel, but tiled. The floor was cement and relatively clean, although awash in imps. Forerunners from our escort had warned the main assembly that we were coming, for they had a path cleared for us to walk up to a small pedestal with a stone garden bench, upon which sat a blue imp slightly larger than the others.

It held up two of its four hands, and the yip-yips that had broken out at our appearance silenced.

Mindful of Nora's advice, I made a show of bowing before the monarch. *Do not show weakness,* she had said, *but be respectful.* I decided a little buttering up wouldn't hurt, either. "Greetings, oh mighty imp king. I am Aisling Grey, Guardian, wyvern's mate, and demon lord. I come to you in the spirit of cooperation to make amends for the death of Mehigenous the Fourth."

The imp king's eyes narrowed. It squeaked something at me.

"Um. I didn't quite catch that." Oh, great. Why had none of us thought about the fact that I didn't speak imp?

The imp king gestured, and from behind his stone throne a small green being emerged. It was the size of a small child, but horribly malformed. "His Majestic Majesty, Mehigenous the Fifth, sovereign of all imps, bids you to

explain why you insult him by bringing the slayer Effrijim into his presence."

"I am here to negotiate the cessation of hostilities between the imps and myself. I am no enemy to imps."

The king stood up and shouted at me—at least I assume the aggressive noises it made were shouts. I know
it shook three fists at me in a menacing fashion. The imps
surrounding us leaped up and down and yipped their
opinions as well.

"You are demon lord to the slayer! You must be destroyed as well as it."

"I am no enemy to imps," I said firmly, looking the
king in the eyes. "I have much power. I could wage a war
the likes of which you have not seen for many millennia.
Instead, I come in peace to bring the demon, and offer to
sacrifice it myself to appease the heinous crime it has
committed."

"You should be on a soap opera; you really should,"
Jim said almost inaudibly over the noise of a couple of
thousand yipping imps.

"Silence," I roared, startling Jim as well as the imps. I
lifted my hand in a dramatic manner and pinned back the
imp king with a firm gaze. "See within my hand the silver dagger of death? I will destroy this demon once and
for all before your very eyes. With its death, there will be
peace between your kingdom and me. Is that agreed?"

The king thought for a moment, consulted with a couple of what were probably advisers, then gestured for the
green being.

"What is that?" I asked Jim in a whisper.

"The translator? That's a boggart. Sort of the poor

relation to the imp world. Nasty little things. Don't turn your back on it."

I hadn't planned on it. The boggart fixed its cold black eyes on me, gesturing toward the imp king. "His Benevolent Majesty, Mehigenous the Fifth, graciously accepts your offer of peace. You may proceed with the sacrifice."

I knelt before the king, dragging Jim down onto its side at the foot of the throne.

"If this doesn't work, you'd better find me a body just as good as this one, or I'm going to make your life a living Abaddon," it warned me as it scrunched its eyes closed, its face in a grimace of imagined pain.

"What makes you think you haven't already?" I pressed Jim's paw quickly before lifting the dagger overhead with both hands, opening up the doorway in my mind.

"By this act, I avenge the death of Mehigenous the Fourth. By my hand, I sacrifice this demon to its origins in Abaddon. By my voice, I command thee to leave this existence and return to that where I send you!"

I plunged the dagger into Jim's inert body just as the last words were spoken, throwing down at the same time a little ball of dragon fire. The flames hit the stone floor and burst upward, then back down in an impressive shower of sparks that had the imps within a thirty-foot radius screaming and slapping at themselves.

When the smoke cleared, I bowed again to the king, held up the dagger to show the blood on it, and made my way out of there as quickly as possible.

Rene was perched on a rock smoking a cigarette, staring up at a few clouds dotting the sky. Nora paced past the opening, Paco trotting obediently at her heels. She spun around when she saw me. "How did it go?"

I tipped my head toward the culvert. I wasn't certain the imp patrol hadn't followed me, but I didn't want to take any chances. "I destroyed Jim before them all. Come on, I need a bandage. I forgot to get one before we left, and this dagger is sharper than I thought. My hand is stinging like a son of a gun."

18

"Murderous imps down, murderous red dragons and equally homicidal demon lords to go," I announced as we returned to the house.

Drake walked out of the library to where we stood in the hall, looking from me to Rene, Nora, and Jim. One of his delicious eyebrows rose in the way that never failed to make my legs go all melty. "I am delighted to hear of your success. How did you achieve it?"

"I sacrificed Jim. Is there any lunch left? I know it's late, but I'm starving, and I know Nora and Rene must be just as hungry."

Drake considered the very real form of Jim for a moment. "I'm sure we can appease your hunger in some manner. If I could have a word with you for a moment, first?"

"Of course," I said, noting the fire visible in his eyes. Either he was annoyed with me about something or aroused. Either way, it was better to have no witnesses to whatever it was he wanted. I entered the library and leaned against the desk, watching as he moved toward me. Drake didn't so much walk as prowl, almost stalking like a big cat. It was a fabulous interplay of muscles and sinew, and I had the worst desire to ask him to take off all his clothes so I could watch his body move as he walked, but I knew full well that if he took his clothes off, I'd pounce on him.

"Looks like Ash is going to get her hunger appeased, all right," Jim said before the door closed behind Drake.

I tipped my head a little and did my best to bat my lashes as the light of my life approached. "You wanted to see me?"

"I have a challenge tonight." He stopped in front of me, not touching me, but close enough that I could feel the heat of his body. I leaned toward him, intending on kissing the breath right out of his mouth, but the meaning of his words sank through the miasma of passion.

"The challenge from Dmitri? I thought you settled that. Isn't that why he was here yesterday?"

The irises in his eyes narrowed a bit, making him look even dragonier. "He was here yesterday to settle the terms of the challenge, not to dismiss it."

"Hmm." I perched on the edge of the desk and considered the gorgeous hunk of dragon in front of me, a little glow of happiness that he was mine warming my insides. "You know, I like this whole I-ask-a-question-and-you-actually-answer-it thing. I could get used to it."

He grimaced. "I assume this counts as sharing my thoughts. I expect extra credit for being so accommodating." As he spoke, his hands slid up my knees, parting my legs so he stood between them.

"This isn't a contest, you know. It's not like you accrue a certain number of intimacy points, and then you can stop telling me things. It's called sharing, and I'm going to expect you to do it for the rest of your life. Now, about this challenge . . ." My breath came shorter and shorter as his hands returned to my knees, this time his long fingers sliding under the silk material of my skirt, tracing an intricate and arousing pattern up my bare thighs.

"Yes?" He leaned forward, his mouth brushing the sweet spot behind my ear. Within me, passion, desire, and love all roared to life at his nearness, answering his silent call.

"I . . . you . . . Drake, everyone is waiting for us. They saw us go in here. If we stay to make love—which I admit sounds like heaven right about now—they're going to know exactly what we're doing. And while I don't care that they know we're mated, I really hate to flaunt illicit sex in their faces."

He nibbled the edge of my ear, his hands sliding up to the apex of my thighs, stroking the satin of my underwear. I squirmed against his fingers, suddenly feeling that we both had far too many items of clothing on, clothing that constricted and bound and was just plain old in the way. "What we're doing is not illicit, *kincsem*. It is recognized and sanctioned by the sept."

My knees tightened around his hips as his fingers struck pay dirt, sliding beneath the now-damp satin to torment me further.

"Yes, by the sept, but not by the rest of the world," I said on a half-sob, yanking his shirt of out of his pants so I could stroke the delicious planes of his chest beneath it.

His fingers froze in their beautiful dance of pleasure, his mouth ceasing the delicious nuzzling. He frowned slightly. "You are speaking of human marriage. You wish for me to marry you?"

Now, that is a question that a few short days ago would have had me rolling on the floor in hysterical laughter. But life had changed since Drake and I had resolved (most of) our problems. Now it didn't look nearly so ridiculous.

"My family is going to have a collective heart attack if they find out I'm shacked up with you for any length of time without marrying you. So although I don't want to run out today and get married, I think that ultimately, we're going to have to talk it over."

"You understand that being a mate is much more binding than a human legal convenience which can be unmade so easily?"

"Yes, I understand, although I'd like to point out that you yourself mentioned I can be . . . er . . . de-mated, I guess."

I swear flames flickered in the depths of his lovely green eyes. "Not easily," he growled, his fingers sharp against my flesh. With a polished move, he whipped my underwear off my body without unseating me, grabbing my hips and pulling me forward to the very edge of the desk. I was pressed so tightly against him, I could feel the thud of his heart. "You are mine, and you will stay mine."

I melted against him, my fingers dancing along the swells of his chest as I nibbled on his sweet lower lip. "Sounds good to me. Only"—I sighed and released his lip—"we can't now, Drake. Oh, don't look at me like that; I want to just as badly as you do." I squirmed against his fingers. "As you can tell for yourself. But we can't. Everyone is waiting for us."

As if on cue, the door to the library opened. "There you are. You are engaging in intercourse again? Has the woman been tested for diseases?"

Drake sighed into my mouth, gave me a little taste of his fire that had me mentally damning any circumspection, and reluctantly pulled himself away from me to face his mother.

"In the future, you will knock before entering this room."

"Don't be ridiculous. This house was mine. I do not knock in my own home." Catalina swept into the room, pausing a moment to frown at my underwear lying on the floor at my feet. "That is obscene. Tell your woman to remove it from my view."

I started to slide off the desk to retrieve my undies— not because she ordered me to, but because I wasn't comfortable having them lying around as an objet d'art—but Drake wrapped an arm around me and pulled me close.

"This house is *mine* now, and you *will* knock when you enter my private rooms. In addition, you will address Aisling by her name and refrain from giving her orders."

Catalina smiled and sank gracefully into the nearest chair, crossing one leg over the other to show off a pair of elegant and no doubt extremely pricey shoes. "I am thirsty. Have your woman bring me wine. Spanish, not French."

Drake's face darkened with anger, his eyes flashing a warning. "Mother, I have just told you—"

"You know what? I'm going to let you two argue this out in private while I go grab a late lunch." I kissed the tip of Drake's nose just because I knew it would annoy Catalina, and picked up my underwear. "We can finish this discussion later, Drake. Maybe while you're showing me the pool?"

"Yes. Later," he said, his eyes filled with desire.

I smiled to myself as I left the room. Water was the green dragons' element, and they had a special affinity for baths and pools. A large sunken bathtub filled with warm, scented water was one of Drake's favorite places to make love, and I had to admit that I was very much looking forward to seeing the lap pool he'd told me was located in the basement of the house.

"Aisling? Telephone." Pál handed me a cordless phone as I left the library.

"Thanks. Hello?"

"Bonjour, Aisling, it is Amelie here."

The tense tone in her voice, so different from her cheery self when I had called her earlier, signaled that all was not well. I leaned against the wall and idly watched the people walk by on the street below. "I'd say it's nice to hear from you, but I have a horrible feeling I'm not going to like what you have to say."

"*Non.* You are not. The situation here is very bad; very bad indeed. It is without a doubt that Peter Burke has his origins in the dark powers. No one knows where he has come from. No one knows who he is. He simply showed up after the Venediger's death and stated his intentions to take the position. We cannot tolerate such a being as he in control of the L'au-delà."

My spirits fell. "Dammit. Any idea why he's trying to get me in the position of Venediger?"

"No, but I must tell you—the feeling here is very warm toward you. People are saying that you are a Guardian, thus you will be able to control him. Banish him, even."

I banged my head a couple of times on the wall. Pál, sitting in the next room, leaned sideways to look at me. I waved and walked to the other end of the hall. "Did you tell them I'm not interested? That there's no way whatsoever I can do the job?"

"Yes, but they do not care. Aisling, I must tell you—I know you do not wish for this to be thrust upon you, but I, too, will vote for you over this dark one."

I groaned. "This is not happening. This is just not happening."

"Perhaps if you could agree to be Venediger as a temporary situation only," Amelie suggested. "Only until another person, one more suitable, could take the job?"

"No. Not happening. I'm sorry, but it's just not going to happen."

"Then we are all doomed," Amelie said sadly, and after a few more minutes of discussion, she hung up. I struggled with a vague sense of guilt that I should be doing something to help, but I honestly didn't see what I could do without taking on yet another massive responsibility.

I straightened my shoulders, put the problem on my mental back burner, and went to get some lunch.

"Wow," Jim said, glancing from its plate to the clock

as I entered a small, sunny dining room. "That was fast. Drake losing his touch?"

"Drake will never lose his touch, not that it's any of your business." I stopped in front of the demon, my hands on my hips. "What on earth is that?"

"Your panties, I think," it answered, squinting at my hip. "Doesn't it look like panties to you, Rene?"

"*Oui.* Very much so. Satin?"

I stuffed the undies I held in one hand into my top, giving Jim a good glare. "Less observation and more explaining. What is all that food on your plate? You're not allowed to eat that much! You're on a diet, remember?"

"Yeah, but—"

"Have you eaten any of it?" I interrupted.

"I was just about to. Hey!"

"No excuses, buster." I scraped half the mound of chicken salad, one hardboiled egg, and several small pieces of garlic-toasted French bread onto another plate, returning a diminished portion to the demon.

Nora sat down next to me as I took a fork from the sideboard and with a meaningful look removed a small plate of chocolate cake from Jim's possession.

"Cake thief!" it muttered, managing to look sullen even while eating chicken salad. "You owe me after I put up with being disemboweled and stuff."

I rolled my eyes at the disemboweled accusation, and ate the confiscated portion of its lunch.

"I never asked because you were bleeding, but your fire, it worked?" Rene asked, munching on bread and thin-sliced steak.

"Yeah, it worked fine. It hit just as I plunged the knife

down, hiding the fact that Jim's body had disappeared when I spoke the words sending it to Akasha."

"Ah. You have learned to control the fire, then. This is good."

"Definitely."

"Aisling?" Pál stuck his head into the room. "There is a demon at the door for you. It demands you go with it to meet with the demon lord Ariton."

I waved a fork of chicken salad at him. "Would you tell Obedama that I'm busy for the next couple of days, but as soon as I have a free hour, I'll pop in to visit Ariton."

Pál blinked twice. "Very well."

I smiled at everyone in the room as he left. "There's something to be said for living with a dragon who knows how to keep demons out."

"*Mais oui*," Rene said, helping himself to another hunk of bread.

We spent a few minutes talking about what I'd done with the imps, Nora suggesting we spend some time going over the more common attributes of several recently spotted beings.

I begged off for a quick nap, feeling drained by the events of the last couple of days. En route to the room, however, I heard Drake's voice saying something to Pál about the swimming pool. I raced down the back stairs as quietly as possible, my libido shifting into high gear.

The pool wasn't hard to find, and, thankfully, had a door with a lock on it for privacy. I smiled at it as I sat on a cedar bench and kicked off my shoes, removed my underwear from where I'd stuffed it into my bra, and peeled off the rest of my clothes in record time.

Drake liked his water warm rather than cool, so I wasn't surprised to find the temperature of the lap pool a little warmer than normal. I didn't mind it and swam a few lazy laps while I waited for him.

"I thought you were tired."

I swam to the end of the pool and admired the man who stood leaning against the door.

"I thought I was. Then I remembered this pool and figured a little gentle exercise would do my gore spot good."

Drake walked to the end of the pool, squatting next to me. "Is it bothering you? There was no redness this morning. Let me see."

I swam backwards, smiling. "You'll have to come in here if you want to examine my belly."

His eyes, which had been exhibiting a subtle green smolder, lit from deep in their depths. He glanced at his watch. "I have a *chevauchée* shortly."

"A what?" I reached the steps, lolling around in the water like a seductive sea nymph, flashing signals with my eyes that I was sure he couldn't miss. He pulled off his shirt, carefully placing it on a cedar bench, sitting briefly to remove his shoes and socks.

I smiled and undulated at him.

"Technically it means a horseback raid, but in this instance, it is a ritual performed by those about to undergo a challenge." His eyes narrowed when I ran a hand down my breastbone, the irises in his eyes all but disappearing as my back arched, exposing my breasts.

"I've been meaning to talk to you about that challenge.

What exactly is going to happen? And what do I need to do? And why aren't you naked and inside me yet?"

A splash was all the answer he needed to make. Before I could wipe the water from my eyes, I was in his arms, my nipples rubbing against his now-slick chest. I squirmed a happy little squirm that had as much of me touching him as possible, licking a couple of drops of water off his chin.

"Dmitri has chosen trial by combat for the challenge. In specific, swords. You need do nothing other than be present. And believe me, *kincsem*, being inside you is all I can think about. We have been parted too many times today. I have been hungry for you."

My hands slid around his hips to the proof of his hunger. "Good, because I'm positively famished."

His hands closed around mine, gently prying them off his penis. "Aisling, right now I do not think I can bear your touch for long."

I rubbed my hips against him. He groaned and grabbed my butt to stop me from moving.

"In the mood for a quickie, eh? That's fine with me. My pot has been simmering all day. It's not going to take much to make me boil."

"I'm afraid that's all I have time for." His breath was hot on my mouth as he backed me up against the wall of the pool. The water was just over breast height on me, high enough to give me sufficient buoyancy to wrap my legs around his hips while I kissed the fire right out of him.

His body was hot and hard against me as I all but purred, squirming against him to feel as much of him as possible. My body ached for him, waited with every muscle clenched for the familiar invasion, needing him the way I needed to breathe.

"Drake, are you here? We will be late for the . . . ah."

Pál's voice echoed slightly in the room. Drake swore into my mouth. I made embarrassed eeking noises and sank into the water until I was submerged to my neck, my arms over my breasts.

Pál had his back to us, evidently examining a water pipe that ran across the ceiling. "I'm sorry to disturb you, but the *chevauchée* is to commence in fifteen minutes. Shall I tell Dmitri that you will be delayed?"

Drake swore again, his lips hot on mine as he gave me a quick, hard kiss that promised almost as much as the look in his eyes. "That would give him the opportunity to claim I defaulted on the challenge. I am ready."

I cocked an eyebrow at his naked butt as he strode over to his clothing, snatching up a towel from a nearby stack. "OK. It'll take me a few minutes to get ready, but I can put on makeup in the car."

"You cannot attend the *chevauchée, kincsem*. It is a ritual cleansing for the combatants only. There is no need for you to hurry—István will remain behind to bring you to the fencing club."

"You're holding a challenge in a fencing club?"

"Yes. Is there something wrong with that?" He pulled on his black pants and the heavy silk green shirt I loved for him to wear because the material seemed to caress his skin.

"No, it's just kind of an incongruous place to hold something so serious as a challenge, isn't it?"

He finished with his shoes, grabbed another towel, and shook it out for me. I made sure Pál still had his back to me, hurrying out of the pool to clasp the towel around me.

"It is no less incongruous than holding a challenge in a bar."

I smiled. "Yes, but my challenge to you wasn't serious. I hope you'll notice that I'm not freaking out about this at all. I haven't even asked you how good you are with a sword."

"I noticed." His mouth burned on mine for a moment, his fire being shared between us as his tongue twined around mine in a fiery—albeit brief—dance. "You are learning to have faith in me as is proper between a mate and her wyvern."

"No, I am learning to ask around. Pál told me earlier today that Dmitri had picked swords and that you were pleased because you were some sort of master swords-man a few centuries ago. You'd better not have forgotten anything."

Pál peeked at me out of the corner of his eye, his grin not too obvious. Drake pinched my bare behind as pun-ishment for my saucy tone. "I never forget. István will drive you when you are ready. The challenge is not for an hour. Do not be late."

"Happy *chevauchée*-ing," I called, feeling remarkably happy.

Pál hesitated at the door. "There was another phone call for you, but I thought you were resting."

"Phone? Who was it?" Just about everyone I knew on this side of the world was in the same house as me.

"Apparently it was the demon lord Ariton."

I sighed. "Him again. What a pest. Did you take a message?"

"Yes. He said if you will not come to him, he will come to you." Pál's eyes were dark as he considered me. "You are not in some sort of trouble?"

"Just the usual stuff."

"Ah. Should I inform Drake?"

"Naw. I've got Nora to help me if Ariton gets bossy. Thanks for covering for me, though."

Pál left with a cheery smile that I wholeheartedly shared. Life was finally starting to come together for me. Oh, there were trouble spots, but nothing I couldn't handle. I just had a demon lord to placate, and a dragon war to end, and the Guardians' Guild to convince. "No big deal, really," I said aloud as I walked over to the bench.

Behind me, glass tinkled to the stone floor. Before I could turn to look, something stung my back, right between my shoulder blades.

I was out even before I hit the floor.

19

The voices around me were not speaking English. For some reason, that grated on my nerves. "It's very rude to speak in a language that people can't understand," my voice said.

I frowned at the sound. I wasn't aware I'd given my mouth the order to speak, but then, I didn't quite understand why I was drifting somewhere on a gently rolling dark cloud of oblivion, or who was standing near me talking in a lyrical foreign language.

The voices stopped.

"*Cara*, you are with us again?"

I frowned again. That voice was familiar, as was the brush of cool fingers across my neck. My shoulder twitched in response. "Goddamn it, Fiat. What have you done to me? Why can't I see? Do I have a blindfold on? Did you cast some sort of blinding spell on me?"

His voice was filled with dry humor. "Nothing quite so drastic. Your eyes are closed, *cara*. You will see again if you open them."

"Oh." I thought about that for a moment, wondering why something so simple seemed to take such an exaggerated amount of time to be processed in my brain. The answer came a few seconds later. The sting on my back! He'd shot me, and I was in shock!

"Do you need help?"

The cool fingers were back, this time gently pulling one of my eyelids upward. My eye rolled up and took its time focusing on the blurry figure in front of me.

"And now the other one."

"I can do it myself," I grumbled, slapping at his hand. I got my other eyelid opened, and my gaze focused, but it took far longer than it should have. "You drugged me or something."

"I regret that is so. There was no other way to get you out of Drake's house."

That filtered through the drug-induced haze in my mind. A thought formed right after that, a good thought, a welcome thought. I opened my mouth to give voice to it. "Effrijim, I summ—"

A hand slapped over my mouth. "I do not believe we need your demon along for the evening's events," Fiat said. I realized then that I was lying on my side along the seat of a car, which explained the rolling motion. I propped my head up to glare at Fiat, but it swam so badly, I let it fall back to the seat.

"You will feel the effects of the drug for a short while yet, I'm afraid. If I have your assurance that you will not try to summon your minion, I will release you."

I was very aware of Fiat's cool fingers on my mouth. It was not a pleasant sensation. I thought about what he was saying, tried to figure out any reason he had for kidnapping me from Drake's house, and decided there wasn't much I could do in the current circumstances. I gave a sharp nod of agreement.

"Excellent. Now, you no doubt—"

"EffrijimIsummonthee," I said at warp speed the second his fingers left my lips.

Fiat sighed as the familiar furry black shape of Jim formed and solidified in front of me.

"Wow. You're naked, Ash. Hi, Fiat. Hi, Renaldo. We're going for a ride?"

Carefully, so as not to dislodge the towel I still wore wrapped around my torso—and, more important, to give my head time to cope with movement—I sat upright in the seat, glaring at both Fiat and Renaldo, his bodyguard, who sat next to him blatantly ogling me.

"Eyes up *here!*" I told the latter, pointing to my face, one hand making sure the towel was securely tucked into itself. Fortunately, it was long enough that it went almost to my knees, so there wasn't too much of me exposed . . . if you can call being kidnapped while clad in a towel not too exposed.

"Nice car," Jim said, looking around. "Does it run to snacks?"

For a moment, a chink showed in Fiat's armor. "*Cara,* I must insist that you control your demon."

"What? I haven't done anything! I didn't point out that your limo isn't as big as Drake's, or that you've got a nasty scuff on one of your shoes, or even that someone stuck a wad of gum under your seat. I've been good."

I smiled at Jim, both relieved and somewhat reassured

by its presence. Jim may not be much protection, but we had made it out of some sticky situations together.

A flash of true anger showed in Fiat's clear blue eyes. "If you do not subdue your demon, I will do it for you."

"You and what army?"

"Hey, now!" I pulled on Jim's collar as the demon bared its teeth. "Jim, stop being rude. Fiat, stop picking on Jim. It hasn't done anything."

"Its mere existence offends me."

I was a bit surprised by the vehemence in his voice. Fiat showed even less emotion than Drake, but this time the naked anger was visible for a moment before his usual polite, handsome, Greek-god mask settled into place.

"I am —"

"Going to be quiet," I finished for Jim. "Until I say otherwise."

Jim shot me a look, but I ignored it to level a quelling glare at Fiat. "I don't have time for your odd games. I have no idea what you think you're proving by kidnapping me, but I don't have time to find out. I have to go to a challenge."

"That is where I am taking you, *cara*. Do not get your"—his gaze dropped to the bare lower half of my thigh—"panties in a twist."

Jim bared its teeth again, silently this time. I put a warning hand on its head, gently stroking its ears. I knew when I was deliberately being baited, and I wasn't going to lose my cool with Fiat. "Speaking of that, you couldn't have kidnapped my clothing along with me?"

Fiat smiled. "Unfortunately, I told Renaldo to acquire

you. I did not think to specify that you should be clothed first. Not that it is difficult to look upon you as you are."

I tugged the towel down my thigh a smidgen. "Let's start this whole conversation over again. Why are you kidnapping me?"

"*Cara, cara, cara*," he said, tsking and shaking his head at me in mock sorrow. "So demanding. So forceful. If I did not know better, I would think you were a dragon."

"Where are we going? Why did you kidnap me?" I asked again, keeping firmly to the subject that mattered. Fiat was notorious for banter, but I didn't have time for that any more than I had time for an impromptu kidnapping.

He spread his hands wide. "Such antagonism. Do you not trust me to keep you safe?"

"Trust you?" I goggled at him. He had to be insane.

"And yet, I am the one who saved you recently from certain death. I understand the red dragons have dealt a death sentence upon you. Surely you cannot fear one who has saved you from their wrath?"

"I don't fear you, Fiat. I'm annoyed by you and these games you insist on playing, nothing more. And stop trying to get into my mind. The NO TRESPASSING sign is up, if you haven't noticed." Ever since I'd woken up, I was aware of the brush of his mind against mine, trying to get into the inner sanctum to read my thoughts. But one of the first things I'd learned when entering the Otherworld was how to close out my thoughts from Fiat and his sept of mind readers.

He sighed, an exaggerated, martyred sound. "Very well. I can see you are in no mood for polite talk. You are coming with me to the challenge of your mate because there is something I wish to do there, and you are vital to my success."

"Fiat, so help me, if this is another one of your attempts to cause trouble between Drake and the other wyverns, I'll . . ."

A smile flirted with his lips, his eyes mirroring the amusement. "You are naked and in my power, surrounded by my men. What exactly do you think you have to threaten me with?"

I sat up a little straighter. "I am a Guardian. I have resources."

"Perhaps. But in this instance, you are helpless. And if you attempt to escape me, as you have done in the past"—he leaned forward and placed a hand on my knee; I tried to brush it off, but his fingers tightened. Jim's lips pulled back in a silent growl—"I will be forced to subdue you. And that, *cara*, I can assure you will not be pleasant. If you cooperate, all will be well."

"Define *well*."

He let go of my knee and sat back. "You will be with your mate."

"What is it you want me to do?"

"Very simple." He brushed off an infinitesimal bit of dirt from his pants. "I want you to—"

The car slammed to a stop with a horrible shriek of brakes applied to tires. The back end of the limo fishtailed out to the side, sending the occupants of the back flying to the opposite side, bodies colliding, limbs entangled, and in my case, my head crashing painfully into the door handle.

I touched the top of my head, my fingers coming away red. "Holy . . . ow! I'm bleeding! . . . cow. What happened?"

Fiat and Jim were tangled together on the floor, each trying to rise by using the other as leverage. Beneath them both was Renaldo. Before anyone could answer me, the door I was slumped against opened, and I tumbled out to the ground, striking my head again.

"Right. That's it. I officially call an end to today. I'm going home and going to bed until it's over." I rolled over onto my side and propped myself up on one hand. A pair of shoes appeared next to me, attached to a woman's legs. I followed the legs up to the rest of the person.

"The lord Ariton wishes to see you. *Now!*"

"Oh, hi, Obedama." I grabbed Jim's collar in an attempt to help me to my feet. "Sorry about those Guardians sending you back to Abaaaaaaaaaaa—!"

Before I could finish the sentence, Obedama wrapped both hands around my neck and yanked me backwards, wrenching me with a horrible, sickening feeling right through the fabric of time and space.

It was such a nauseating experience that when I was released, I fell to my knees and vomited right on the middle of Ariton's plush Victorian rug, one of my hands still wrapped around Jim's collar. The demon didn't say anything, but its cold nose pressed against my cheek in sympathy as I clutched myself and tried to keep from barfing a second time.

"You come at last," Ariton said, rising from behind his desk, his eyes narrowing as I wiped a tendril of saliva off my lips. "Do you think I am such a fool that I do not see through your idiotic scheme to put me off? Who are you working with?"

Ariton grabbed me by my hair and brutally yanked me to my feet. I squawked with pain and outrage.

"What are you talking about? I'm not working with anyone! I'm sorry I've been too busy to see you, but—"

"Silence!" he bellowed, power crackling off him as he backhanded me. I flew across the room, slamming against a thankfully bare spot on the wall, my head whacking painfully against the solid wood paneling. The room spun before my eyes for a moment as I tried to regain my wits. "You will cease this deception!"

"I am not deceiving you," I snarled back at him, pain chasing fear enough that it kept me on my feet. I have never been one to take abuse, and I wasn't about to let Ariton be the first. "And you can stop with the rough treatment! I am a fellow demon lord! You can't treat me like that!"

He laughed, a horrible sound that made my soul weep. "Do you seriously believe I cannot destroy you where you stand?"

I rubbed the back of my head as he walked around me. Obedama stood next to the door, a sentinel of silence. Jim sat a few feet away, its eyes dark and unfathomable as it watched us. I could order Jim to attack Ariton, but there was no way it had the power to defeat a demon lord.

"Do you know what it would take to destroy you, Guardian?" Ariton stopped in front of me, his face hard.

I lifted my chin on the principle that offense was the best defense. "I am immortal. You can't destroy me."

A slow, blood-chilling smile slid across his face. "Not

kill, no. But there are other forms of death. There are ways to destroy your mind but leave your body intact."

Horror skittered down my back at the depth of evil in his eyes.

"You cannot kill a demon lord. But you can destroy one. Once you have the soul, you can render the physical form inert, and banish the essence of what remains to the Akashic plain, where it will be trapped, powerless, for an eternity."

"Demons don't have souls," I said, my voice a croak.

The power that surrounded him in a dark aura snapped around me, sending little frissons of pain deep into my being. "But demon lords do. It is what gives us our power. Would you like to see how that power can destroy you, Guardian?"

I licked my lips. I knew as I did it, Ariton could smell the fear on me, but I was struggling as it was to keep a grip on myself in the face of sheer, utter, almost incomprehensible evil. "I think I'll pass on that."

He turned away, his voice as smooth and polished as it had been the first time I'd met him. "You will tell me with whom you are working, or I will break your body, corrupt your soul, and banish you to an eternity of torment."

Every inch of my body broke out into a terrified cold sweat as I frantically looked around the room, desperate for some way to escape, or something I could do to distract Ariton long enough to get away. But other than Jim and Ariton's minion, we were alone. There were no weapons, no handy Demon-Lord-Begone spray, not even the slightest hint of an idea of what I was going to do to get out of this.

"I really wish I could help you, but I just can't. I'm not working with anyone," I told Ariton, desperation swamping me.

Ask him about his soul. A voice spoke into my ear. My head snapped around to the left, but there was no one there. *Ask him to show it to you.*

It's a pretty good indicator of the state of my mind that I ignored the suspicion that arose as to the wisdom of following the disembodied advice from who-knew-what being. For the first time in my life, I was truly terrified, not for my body, which I was sure would survive just about anything, but for my soul. If that was destroyed, it would mean Drake's death, as well. The other demon lord I'd had a brief brush with had been frightening, but everything had happened so quickly, I hadn't really had time to be terror stricken.

This time it was different.

"About your soul," I started to say. Ariton closed his eyes, lifted both hands toward me, and began to chant. Each word he spoke struck my body like a barbed missile, pain sweeping through me. Frantic, I pulled on Drake's dragon fire to give me strength. "If you're going to destroy me, the least you can do is tell me why demon lords have souls if demons don't. You're bigger and badder and infinitely more nasty than any one demon, so why do you get to have a soul?"

A little flicker of relief rose in me when Ariton paused his cursing, or whatever he was doing to destroy me, in order to answer my questions. "You mock me with these foolish questions, pretending ignorance for some reason I cannot fathom. You know of the Fallen. You know of the six classes of demons."

I wrapped my arms around myself, trying to keep from screaming for mercy. Ariton was clearly not going to believe me if I tried to convince him of my innocence in the ways of demons and their lords. "Of course I know. But you were born human, not a demon."

"And as a weak mortal, I was burdened with that most heinous of gifts—a conscience. Once I rid myself of that, once I purified myself by bathing in the pool of the Dark Master, then I became what you see. You wish to see my soul, Guardian?"

Be ready, the voice to my left spoke into my head.

Ready for what? Every inch of my body sweated beads of sheer terror. What was I supposed to be ready for?

"Behold, the true being, the One Form!" Ariton threw open his arms, a brilliant black light bursting from his chest, creating a corona of pure power around him.

Banish it! Banish it now! the voice screamed in my head. *Send it to Akasha and you will be free of him forever!*

Banish? Like I did when I sent Jim to the Akashic plain? I didn't stop to think, didn't reason out whether or not trying to banish a being so well versed in dark power was a smart move. I didn't pause for even a second to consider what such an act might do to me. I had no choice—either I saved myself or Ariton would destroy me, and by association, Drake and Jim as well.

The mental door in my mind was flung wide open as I welcomed the roar of Drake's fire. "Ariton, known as

Egyn, seventh prince of Abaddon, leader of the twenty-two legions, by this light, by my virtue, by my being, I do banish thee!"

Ariton clearly wasn't expecting that from me, because he stared at me in surprise for the count of three before releasing a roar of such hideousness, the walls around us cracked. "You dare?"

Power, black and evil, washed over me as he recommenced his chanting. I struggled to breathe, my body beginning to fail under the influence of his will.

Do it again! Banish him now! It is your only chance.

Through a miasma of pain and sorrow and abject terror, I saw Jim's face for a second. It was twisted with sadness, pain and regret so deep in its eyes, it made me weep.

It also brought me renewed strength of mind. I was a professional, dammit! I was not going to go down without a fight! I pulled hard on Drake's fire, flames erupting around me until I stood in a veritable inferno, one hand reaching for Jim. The demon didn't have any power as such, but it made me feel better to have my hand on it as I made a final, last-ditch attempt to save us. "Ariton, known as Egyn!" I bellowed, channeling the dragon fire straight at the demon lord. It met his dark power, colliding into a fireball. The resulting flash of light blinded me, but I didn't pause to wait for it to dissipate. "Seventh prince of Abaddon, leader of the twenty-two legions!"

"You will bother me no longer, Guardian! Begone!"

Little bits of me started to tear off. Not my body—bits of my soul, ripped from me and destroyed with the chant Ariton took up again.

Do it now! the voice shrieked in my ear. *Use the power! Banish him!*

I lowered my head, pulling on Drake's fire for all I was worth, but it wasn't enough. I could feel the chant working on me, pulling me apart, destroying not just my mind, but my very being, the essence that made up the core of my soul.

"No! I will not allow this!" My words ripped from my throat in a voice I did not recognize. The door in my head, open wide to allow me access to all the possibilities, suddenly was flooded with a hot, sticky warmth. Black and thick, it filled me with wrath, fired my rage to unimaginable heights, burning deep and dark alongside Drake's fire. "By this light, I banish thee!"

I lifted my head to look at Ariton, filled with so much power, it glowed around me in a strange, coppery aura. Jim said something, but I paid the demon no attention. That was solely focused on channeling this newfound power into the will to destroy the demon lord.

Ariton screamed back at me, words that cut into my flesh like honed blades, but I laughed at the pain. It didn't matter; none of it mattered—my whole being, my whole purpose was to destroy the being in front of me. And destroy him I would!

"By my virtue, I banish thee!"

A noise like a tornado ripping apart a house crashed over me. Ariton was screaming in horror now, his body twisting and whipping around itself as the power flowed from me, wrapping around his form in tendrils of destruction. "No! This cannot be! This . . . cannot . . ."

"By my being, I do banish thee!" My voice rose high

and piercing over Ariton's screams, painful even for me to hear. With the final words, I gathered up everything I had, every ounce of rage, every morsel of terror, every atom of spirit that dwelt within me, and blasted Ariton with it. He exploded in a nova of blackness that slammed Jim and me against the wall.

As I slid to the floor, my body rigid with agony, a voice spoke with quiet contentment.

Well done, Aisling Grey, prince of Abaddon.

20

"No," I told the voice, pulling myself to my knees. "Tell me you didn't say what I think you just said."

"I said you're crying blood. Your eyes are different, too. You . . . er . . . you didn't happen to channel any dark power, did you?" It was Jim's voice that answered me, not the voice that had spoken so urgently into my head.

"What? Dark power?" Oh, god! That was the warm, dark, thick feeling that had filled me a few seconds ago. Loathing rose within me to swamp all the other emotions twisting around my gut. I had used dark power! The most dangerous, most forbidden of all powers! The meat and manna to dark beings. I would be damned forever now! "No! I didn't mean to! I don't know—"

I looked around the room as if someone had written out the answers in big, easily read letters, but there was nothing. The room looked a bit worse for wear after the struggle between Ariton and myself, and there was a nasty black stain with rays that spread out across the floor where he had been standing, but nothing more.

And there should have been something. Someone whom I had last seen next to the door.

"Obedama?"

"No, although I used its form for a bit," the demon answered, but it wasn't in Obedama's voice. It was another voice, a familiar voice, once that made my stomach clench tight with dread. From the black shadows Ariton's passing had left on the floor, a figure gathered in the air and formed into that of a man.

I was still shaken by the events with Ariton—not to mention sick with the thought of having tainted my powers—but I was not a coward. "Peter Burke. I should have known you'd be bound up in this somehow. Who exactly are you? And why were you pretending to be Obedama? Why did you have me kill your master?"

Peter laughed. He looked perfectly normal, dressed in a conservative polo shirt and pants, but his face and eyes were as expressionless as ever. The feeling of power that rolled off him was bad. Very bad.

"Ariton was not my master. He was not, in fact, an overly bright being. I used Obedama's form to keep tabs on him for years, and he never noticed the difference. In truth, you did us all a favor by banishing him. I have every confidence that you will rule much wiser in his stead."

"No, no, no," I said, groaning as I got to my feet. I was more than a little bit surprised to discover that my towel was still covering me, smudged and dirty from the demon smoke and chalky with debris from the plaster walls, but still present. I tucked an end of it a little tighter, automatically brushing it off as if it was a dress. "I don't know why you've been trying to manipulate me to be the Venediger, but you're absolutely insane if you think I'm going to be a full-fledged demon lord. I'm grateful you showed me the way to destroy Ariton, but I am not now, nor will I ever be, a prince of Abaddon."

Peter's face was completely impassive. "I know it should be princess, but we've never had a reigning female demon lord. We tend to be very set in our traditions here."

"*We?* You mean you're not just a demon?"

"Do you really believe me to be so insignificant?" He laughed his peculiar humorless laugh.

"OK, let's back up a couple of steps." My head felt like it was going to explode. Maybe if I went through everything one point at a time, I could keep from actually going insane. "First of all, I'm not reigning anything— either the Otherworld, or a demon lord's position in Abaddon. I have one little demon, and it's not a particularly bad specimen. In addition, I have no intention of taking part in any of the politics you guys are so wrapped up in. And finally"—I took a deep breath, my faint control snapping—"*what the hell did you do to me to make me use dark power?*"

Peter just looked at me with cold, blank eyes. Jim's cold nose touched my hand in warning. I looked down at my demon, puzzled why it didn't speak. That's when the penny dropped. "You're a demon lord."

He bowed. It lacked all the panache of the dragon's courtly moves. "I have that honor, yes. I'm surprised you did not recognize me, since you've summoned me in the past."

"I have?" I racked my brain to think of the time I'd

summoned a demon lord. Yet another penny dropped. "You're Bael, also known as Beelzebub."

"I wondered if you would recognize me. I took great pains to disguise myself to you."

"But . . . I should have known who you were. I'm a Guardian. I should have felt something different about you . . ."

"There are some benefits to being the premier prince of Abaddon," he said with a faint scowl. The deathless look in his eyes made shivers go up my back, into my hair. "The ability to create glamours that can fool even other princes of Abaddon is one of them."

"Why are you doing this to me?" I asked, my question coming out a near wail. "Why would you try to get me to be Venediger if all you wanted was for me to banish Ariton?"

"My plans are many, and you have a significant role to play in them," Peter answered. (I couldn't stand to think of him as Bael, the head demon lord of Abaddon, the one who was going to be thrown down from power in a few days.)

I brushed away a few tears of horror. "This is about power, isn't it? You're due to be booted from the big kid's chair, and you don't want to go."

"Would you?"

I shook my head. "This isn't about me and what I want. You want power here"—my skin crawled at the re-alization of what was behind his manipulations to put me into the position of Venediger—"and in the Otherworld. You plan on using me to rule both worlds, don't you?"

Peter strolled past me and examined a bookshelf

behind Ariton's desk. "And there are some who say you are not particularly bright."

"Was it you who tried to kill me?"

"My dear, if I wanted you dead, you would have been so before the thought left my mind. That shot was just to bring you to Ariton's house in case he bungled his plan to use you."

"It doesn't matter." I shook my head. "I won't do it. I won't help you here, and I won't help you in the Otherworld. I am one of the good guys. I refuse to be a part of this."

"Do you really think you have that choice?" Peter snarled at me, slamming down a book on the desk. "Despite what you believe, you *are* now a prince of Hell. You have toppled Ariton from power. That automatically gives you his place on the council. Far from one demon, you now lead twenty-two legions of demons and demon-kind."

I stared at the demon lord before me, my mind crawling around, unable to shake off the horrible, paralyzing sense of shame, fear, and loathing that consumed me. "You tricked me into banishing Ariton."

"Tricked? Perhaps. I prefer to think of it as enlightenment. I showed you a possibility. You acted upon it." Bael made a dismissive movement with his hands that brought fresh tears to my eyes.

"How could I have done it? I'm just a Guardian. I have one demon. I don't have the sort of power needed to banish a demon lord!"

"Not on your own, no." Peter walked around the desk and shuffled through some of Ariton's papers. "But quite cleverly, you used Ariton's power against him."

"I didn't know . . ." I clutched the nearest chair, sinking into it as my legs went boneless. I wanted to weep until my tears washed away everything in my existence. "Channeling a demon lord's power is not anything I've done before. I didn't know that was what I was doing. I was just trying to save my life."

"And you succeeded extremely well. You show great potential, Aisling Grey. I will be happy to have you at my side as my lieutenant."

"I will not be *anyone's* lieutenant." Bile rose in my throat. I swallowed hard to shove it down. "I don't want to be a demon lord. I don't want legions. I don't want to be a prince of Abaddon. I hereby officially abdicate the position."

Hatred pure and deep flared to life in his dark eyes, causing me to recoil against the back of the chair. The hairs on the backs of my arms stood on end. Jim pressed tight against me, clearly trying to lend support.

It did little good.

"There is no abdication. You are, or you are not." He seemed to grow until he filled my vision, my body trembling in response to the threat he presented. It swamped me, drenched me in the absolute conviction that he could, and would, destroy my body and leave my soul in perpetual torment. "There is no gray area where Abaddon is concerned. Do not believe that you can put me off the way you did Ariton. You will either agree to support me as I continue to rule Abaddon, or I will destroy you. Right here. Right now. *Decide!*"

I believed him. This was my existence on the line. I looked at Jim. "What are my chances?"

"Truthfully?" Jim shook its head. "Nada."

My heart fell. I was trapped, bound, wrapped in the chains of my own ignorance, with no possible way out. I curled up into a little ball on the chair, my soul sick with the knowledge of what I'd become. It came down to a matter of survival, pure and simple. Either I agreed to do what he wanted, or he'd kill me. Period. Shame filled me at the knowledge that I was too weak to die with honor.

"I agree."

His body shrunk back to its normal size, the overpowering sense of threat lightening somewhat. "Excellent. Ah, it would seem Ariton has some outstanding debts. I'm sure you'll want to take care of those quickly. It seems he's borrowed money from the Furies, and we all know how unpleasant they can be when crossed." Peter dropped the stack of papers he was going through. "Such a long face. I think you'll find Ariton's position won't be too demanding upon you. He was the seventh prince, you know, not one of the Four. He held no important positions. To be honest, he was more concerned these last few hundred years with materialistic concerns than ones in Abaddon."

"If he was so minor and unimportant, why did you use me to get rid of him?" I asked, lifting my head from where it had been resting on my knees.

Peter smiled again. "You're much quicker than he was. This will work out very well, I think. It is true that Ariton held no special threat to me, but he was annoying in his persistent belief that he could hold the throne of Abaddon. I felt the time was ripe for him to be destroyed and another put in his place before I made it clear to the other demon lords that I would not be stepping down as they expected."

I sighed, sick, filled with anguish and pain, and with no idea what I was going to do to get out of the situation. "Can I leave now?"

"There is no need to ask my permission. You are my lieutenant, not a servant. Ah. This, I think, will summon it."

Peter pressed a bell set into the desk. In the distance of the house, a buzzing noise echoed dimly, almost immediately followed by the shuffling sound of feet approaching.

"You called for me, mas . . . eh . . . my lord Bael?"

The demon who opened the door appeared as a small and slight man, balding, with silver-rimmed lenses perched on a beaky nose. In its hands it held a PDA.

"Traci, isn't it?" Bael asked the demon.

"Yes." Traci looked from Peter to me, then to the spot on the floor. Its lips pursed in irritation. "I see. If I might be so bold to speak without permission, which of you has banished my lord . . . my former lord Ariton?"

"Aisling Grey is now your master," Peter said with a wave in my direction. "Serve her well."

He disappeared even before the last word was out of his mouth, leaving the demon named Traci alone with Jim and me. "You defeated Ariton."

I stood up, adjusting my towel. I had brought this on myself, but by god, I was not helpless. "Yes, I did. Who are you?"

"I am Traci, lord." The demon bowed. "I am . . . I was Ariton's steward."

"And what does a demonic steward do, exactly?"

Traci seemed to have a perpetually annoyed look on its face, but I could see it was struggling to keep its face as bland as possible. "I tended his lordship's business affairs, ran the house, and oversaw the work of the legions."

"Right. As of this moment, I am putting Effrijim in charge of everything. You can continue to run the business stuff and house. But everything else has to go through Jim or me."

Traci blinked through its glasses at Jim for a moment before turning its gaze back to me. "But . . . but that is a class-six demon."

"And?"

"A class-six demon cannot be in charge of the legions."

I my hands on my hips. If I was going to be a friggin' prince of Hell, I was going to be the worst prince of Hell there had ever been. "Who says so?"

Traci's mouth opened and closed a couple of times before it finally managed to say, "It has always been that way!"

"Well, things are going to change. I want you to spread the word to the rest of Ariton's minions that as of this moment, all demonic work is going to cease. There will be no damning anyone, no curses, no tormenting or torturing or rending the souls from innocent people."

I have to give the demon credit. It just stood there for a moment, its mouth slack, then shook itself. "What about the next release?"

"The what?"

"My lord Ariton . . . my former lord Ariton, I should say, had his legions at work in the software company. We haven't tormented or cursed or damned anyone for the last eleven years, ever since Ariton realized there was much more profit to be had from computer operating systems."

"He wasn't going by the name of Bill, was he?" I asked, suddenly suspicious.

Traci shook its head. "No, although I can see why you might think that. Ariton Enterprises produces operating software for corporate systems."

"Oh." I chewed on my lip for a minute. "Is there anything evil in the system?"

"Many things," Traci said bluntly. "There is a built-in system whereby the software is obsolete almost immediately, thus forcing the client to update twice a year. Also, specific bugs were planted in it, which will cause minor problems with the system. The patches to fix the bugs have been a particularly lucrative source of income the last few years."

I waved that away. "Is there anything dangerous to people? Anything really evil?"

Traci blinked a couple more times. "Ariton didn't see a profit in that, so we discontinued the damnation module."

"OK. Then you can keep everyone working on that. Just remember—no one is to do anything evil without permission from Jim or myself."

"As you desire," the demon said, making a note on its PDA.

"Great. Oh, crap, look at the time! I've got to get to the

fencing club." I eyed Traci for a moment. "I don't suppose you have any women's clothing here, do you?"

I could swear it looked startled. "No, I do not."

"Damn. Um . . . how about conjuring up something for me? Parading around in this towel is getting a bit old."

It frowned at me. "I am not a magician, lord. I cannot conjure anything."

"Well, that's just great. What am I going to use for clothes, then?"

"I would assume that's your responsibility," Traci said with an irritated sniff.

"Yeah? Assume again. Demon Traci, I order thee to get me something to wear!"

Five minutes later I narrowed a look at Jim that would have gutted a lesser demon. "One word, one single word, about Scarlett O'Hara, and it's off to the neuterer for you."

Jim walked around me, eyeing the togalike covering that Traci had fashioned for me out of the heavy, wine-colored velvet drapes. "I'm not saying a word."

"Good." I took a deep breath and tied tighter the gold braid that served as a belt. It wasn't haute couture—hell it wasn't even a real dress—but it was better than a dirty towel.

"Did you ever see that Carol Burnett show where she did her parody of *Gone with the Wind*? Your outfit is a hundred times funnier than hers."

"Shup," I told Jim, turning back to Traci, who was looking rather proud of itself as it tweaked a fold in my toga. I slapped its hand. "Is there any special power demon lords have about getting through rush-hour traffic really quickly?"

"No," it answered shaking its head. "You can alter time and space, though. Would that help?"

I looked at Jim. "Is that evil?"

"Naw. Kind of cool, really, although it hurts like a son of a bitch if you do it wrong."

"Right." I brushed out my toga and faced Traci. "Show me how to do that, please."

A few seconds later, I screamed my way into being, falling through the shredded fabric of space onto the sidewalk below, cracking both my elbow and my poor, abused head. "Son of a—"

"Told you," Jim said, grunting as it landed next to me. "Man, you have got to take portaling lessons. I just lost another toe!"

I pushed myself to my feet, glancing at the back foot it shoved toward me. Around us, the busy evening traffic of London pulsed past, a few people stopping to stare. I lifted my chin, brushed off my curtain, and turned toward the marble-pillared doorway of the London Fencing Association. The doorman eyed me warily.

"I believe I'm expected," I told him.

"Indeed, you are. I'm glad to see you have not suffered any harm," a voice said behind my shoulder.

I didn't need to turn around to guess who was behind me. Cool fingers took my arm in a grip that was borderline painful. "This is just not my day."

"Really?" Fiat looked me over. "Something is different about you. Did you have your hair done?"

"Oh, for god's sake!"

"This garment is fetching, but I preferred the other."

Fiat considered me for another few seconds, then shrugged. "I do not understand why you have done what you have so obviously done, but it is of no matter to me. If you do not do exactly as I say, you will not live to see another day."

21

I am, in general, an easygoing person. I try to take a reed-bending-with-the-wind attitude toward life, rather than fight everything. But these constant "out of the frying pan, into the fire, into a worse fire, into a worse fire than the worse fire before it" situations that had been riddling my life of late were beginning to wear me down.

"Just once, I'd like something to go right for me!" I snapped as Fiat and his men surrounded me. I looked around for any green dragon help, but the lobby of the fencing club was empty.

"If you do as I tell you, all will be right," Fiat said softly in my ear.

"Famous last words. You want to offer me a guarantee on my satisfaction?"

Fiat laughed as he steered me up a staircase, Jim following. I was just formulating a plan whereby Jim attacked two of Fiat's bodyguards while I went after him and the third one, but that idea died quickly.

"It would not work, *cara*. You are physically tired, and

Renaldo and I would easily overpower you, even assuming your demon could disable Pietro and his cousin Berto."

"No trespassing!" I growled, reinforcing the mental barriers to keep Fiat out of my mind. The fact that he'd slipped through them shook me more than I wanted to admit. Fiat on his own was dangerous enough—Fiat in possession of my thoughts just about made my blood run cold.

"You make it so easy . . . ah. Here we are." Fiat indicated a door. It looked like it led to a central court in the club. I waited until it was a few inches open, then screamed for all I was worth, the noise echoing off the high walls of the corridor into which we'd just stepped. Fiat caught the bulk of my scream in his right ear, but I didn't feel any pity for him. He yelled as Renaldo jumped me, slamming a hand over my mouth, but it did little good.

"Too late," I mumbled beneath the hand over my mouth, recognizing the distant voice that bellowed my name. "Now you guys are really in trouble."

Fiat snapped out some orders. The men quickly surrounded me, Fiat pulling out of his jacket a small black case, the kind diabetics carry around. By the time Drake appeared in the far end of the corridor, shoeless, wearing pants and the green silk tunic he wore at official dragon functions, and holding a wicked-looking saber, Fiat had a good grip on my arm, his men hemming me in on all sides.

Drake skidded to a stop at the end of the hallway, his eyes narrow as he looked over our little group. Behind him, Pál appeared, followed by a couple of dragons I didn't recognize.

"Aisling." Drake lowered his sword and walked slowly toward us, a frown darkening his eyes. "Where have you been? And what are you wearing?"

I pinched the back of Renaldo's hand until he released his hold on my face. "To hell and back, but that's a really long story, and not one I want to go into here. This is a curtain. I'd really rather not talk about it right now, either."

"Very well. We will leave the discussion of why you are clad in drapery for another time. The challenge has started." He stopped ten feet away, still scowling at me. My lips twitched. Drake was deliberately ignoring Fiat, something I knew would irritate someone of his pride. "What is wrong with your eyes?"

I touched the corner of my eye. "I don't know. Is something wrong with them? I imagine they're bloodshot as hell."

"They're washed out, almost white." Drake's frown deepened. "You will tell me later what happened to your eyes, too. But now you will explain why, when you were expected to be present for the start of the challenge, you were not. Where is István?"

"I have no idea. You'd have to ask my kidnapper that. Fiat?"

Drake finally looked away from me to Fiat, his gaze steady, his face mirroring nothing more than mild annoyance. "I hadn't expected to see you here, Fiat."

"I'm sure you didn't, but as you see"—Fiat waved the small black case at our group—"here we are. I ran into

Aisling earlier, and since I knew she would want to be here, I offered to provide her with safe transport."

"Oh, that's a good one. Safe transport." Jim snorted.

"What did you do with István?" I asked Fiat.

He waved a hand. "Your bodyguard took exception to us escorting Aisling here. Naturally, my men defended themselves against his attack."

My stomach, already twisted around on itself to a point where I doubted if it would ever again be normal, gave a lurch, my palms going slick with sweat. "What about Nora and Rene? What did you do to them?"

"We had no issue with anyone else in the house," he answered, relieving my mind on at least that point.

Regardless, I was still worried sick about István. "Fiat, so help me god, if you've hurt István, I will see that you suffer as no dragon has ever suffered before."

"You need not worry," Fiat said with a smile that made my bile rise. "He is no longer feeling any pain."

He patted the side of my face. I jerked my head away, rage filling me. With the rage came a familiar thick, black power. I pushed it back, pulling on Drake's fire instead.

Fiat burst into flames.

"I expected better from you," he said, shaking his head.

I snarled something that wasn't very anatomically possible and lunged toward him, Jim's harsh bark echoing as the demon leaped forward. Fiat's men grabbed me by the arms, holding me back.

"What is going on here? Drake, I assume you are defaulting on the challenge since you do not have the stomach to fight me further." Dmitri pushed his way forward through the people behind Drake, who continued to stand in a relaxed pose, leaning against the balustrade that ran around the upper hall.

Drake looked from Fiat to Dmitri, then to me. "What do you want with my mate?" he asked, looking downright bored.

I couldn't keep from smiling. Damn, I loved that man. I loved the way he bluffed; I loved the way he assumed the world revolved around him; I even loved the natural arrogance that was part and parcel of his makeup. Any other man would be demanding that I be handed over, but not my Drake. He had to first establish that Fiat was nothing more than a minor irritation; then he'd get down to business.

"It is as I have said—I have brought her to watch your challenge."

"Indeed. And what is your interest in a purely domestic matter?"

Fiat laughed. "Purely domestic? If Dmitri wins his challenge, then the green dragons will have a new wyvern. That will affect all of the weyr. Naturally, we have an interest in what happens. All wyverns do."

"Odd that the other two wyverns don't seem to share your level of interest," Drake said, waving his sword toward the people behind us.

"Do they not?" Fiat turned and looked behind him. "Perhaps you should inform our esteemed colleague."

"I'm sure Drake will understand just how important it is that a balance be maintained," a man's voice answered from behind Fiat's men.

Gabriel gave me a little smile as he joined us in the

hall, the smile fading as he took in the expression on my face.

Drake's eyes showed surprise for a fraction of a second, gone so quickly that I wondered whether I really saw it. Certainly his face gave no indication that he was taken aback by the recreant nature of his supposed friend.

I, however, had no such reservations in making my feelings known. "What on earth are you doing with this snake in the grass?" I asked Gabriel, nodding toward Fiat.

Jim snickered. Fiat's eyes narrowed.

"Something significant must have happened to you to change your eyes in that way," Gabriel mused. He shook his head and answered my question. "I know it must look bad, but I assure you that I am not here to betray either you or Drake. Fiat asked me to be here to mediate only. Since I know there is increasing hostility between the blue and green septs, I felt it was appropriate that I be here. We do not need another sept at war."

That sounded far too pat for my liking, but there wasn't much I could do until I saw exactly what Fiat wanted with me.

"I am in the middle of a challenge," Drake said, indicating Dmitri. "I cannot just set that aside to conduct negotiations with you that could well wait until morning."

Fiat made one of those elegant dragon bows. He didn't do it as well as Drake, but then, no one did. "I did not intend to disrupt the challenge."

"Shyeah. And monkeys might fly out of my butt, but I'm not ordering up any monkey chow," Jim said.

Fiat spun around to glare at Jim, his hand upraised as if he was going to strike it.

"Temper, Fiat. You wouldn't beat up an innocent demon in front of so many witnesses, would you?" Somehow, I knew that it would matter to Fiat what people thought of him.

He ground his teeth for a moment, then turned back to Drake. "We would be delighted to watch the challenge, if you do not object."

Drake was silent for a moment, his eyes flickering to me once before settling back onto Fiat. He waved toward the door he'd used to enter the hall. "Not at all. It is a straightforward-enough challenge, and not one that should take much longer. The points thus far have been to my advantage."

"Things change," Dmitri said suddenly, a smile on his face that I wanted to wipe clean.

"Come, mate." Drake held out his hand for me. "Your place is with the sept."

"I think not," Fiat said quickly, his hand hard on my arm as I took a step forward.

Drake's eyes narrowed. "You hold my mate hostage?"

"*Hostage* is such a harsh word. Let us say instead that I am looking out for Aisling's best interests. We will keep her safe while you determine the outcome to this challenge. After all, were you to lose, she would no longer be your mate, and who knows what evils your successor might inflict upon her."

I was speechless for a moment in the face of such absolute bull, but before I could rally my wits into responding to such an absurd statement, the third and final penny dropped.

"You're planning on using me to force Drake to lose,

aren't you?" I asked Fiat. "You want him to lose so a new wyvern will take his place, someone who has less honor and knowledge, and who could well turn out to be nothing more than your little puppet, right?"

Dmitri, who had started back toward the practice room, spun around and spat out an unflattering word.

Drake's sword tip moved so fast, it was nothing but a silver blur. The point of it pressed against Dmitri's pulse point on his neck. A thin line of blood appeared beneath it. "What did you say?"

Anger, hatred, and impotent fury all took turns on Dmitri's face. He swore, shoving the green dragon bystanders out of the way as he stormed back to the room.

"Someone badly needs to spend some time in his happy place." Jim's voice broke the tension.

I laughed at Fiat's carefully masked expression. "Oh, come on, Fiat—don't tell me you didn't think this idiotic plan through. You've known Drake for what—a few hundred years? Do you seriously think he's going to do something so asinine as to hand over his sept to someone else just for me?"

Fiat just smiled. Drake said nothing, but I could see the tension in his hands. "That's just about the most ridiculous thing I've heard today, and let me tell you, I've heard some pretty ridiculous things. The sept always has and always will come first to Drake. I know that. I accept that. You're deluding yourself if you think it's not true."

"I believe that the situation has changed now that you are breeding."

There were a number of surprised noises from the dragons behind Drake. I glared at Fiat. "I am not pregnant! And even if I were—and for the hundredth time this week, I'm not!—it still wouldn't make a difference. Drake is wyvern of the green dragons. He will be wyvern until the day he decides he wants to pass the job on to someone else. Isn't that right, Drake?"

Drake looked at Fiat, not me. "The sept and Aisling are both mine. I will not give up either of them."

"We shall see," was all Fiat said.

Gabriel stepped forward, putting his arm around my shoulder. "I think it would ease everyone's minds if I escorted Aisling to the challenge."

"Oh, don't for one minute think I don't have a thing or two to say to you," I told him as he gently pushed me down the hallway. Drake stood to one side, waiting until we had passed before following. "Mediating is one thing, Gabriel. But this is not mediation. This is siding with Fiat for some bizarre reason. Do you really want to see Dmitri in Drake's place?"

"Of course not. If I thought that would happen, I would have done everything in my power to stop Fiat. But you have not considered all the possibilities as a good Guardian should."

"All the possibilities? What other possibilities are there?"

He smiled, his dimples flaring. "Has it not occurred to you that a show of force by Drake will do much to weaken Fiat's determination to war with him?"

"Hmm." I thought about that for a couple of seconds. He had a point. Perhaps Gabriel wasn't the villain I'd begun to paint him.

"I see you appreciate the fact that while Dmitri may

have the letter of the green dragon law to back his claim to the position of wyvern, it has always been might that has held septs. Drake has shown time and time again that he has the might to keep the sept. He simply needs to remind Fiat of that. And this is a perfect opportunity for him to do so with little threat to himself or you."

It made sense, but it still left an unpleasant taste in my mouth. "You could have told us ahead of time what you were going to do."

"What makes you think I didn't?" His dimples deepened. I recalled the night when Gabriel had healed my wound. Obviously, one of the things he'd spoken to Drake about after I left the room was this situation. No wonder Drake didn't seem particularly disturbed about me being in Fiat's power.

But what about poor István? Was he in on it, too, or was he really dead? I had to know. If he was OK, then I could relax and just go along with things.

"Jim?" I gestured for the demon walking slightly behind me. "Heel!"

"For crap's sake, it's all I can do to walk missing three—that's *three*—toes now!" Jim grumbled, but obeyed and scooted over next to me.

"Would you like to go for four?"

"Bah!"

Gabriel laughed.

"Sorry, demon and demon lord talk," I told him, not wanting him to overhear what I was going to ask. "Would you think me horribly rude if I had a few minutes with Jim?"

"Not at all." He walked a few steps ahead of me,

giving us a bit of privacy. Behind us, Drake, Fiat, and the rest of the dragons marched along in silence.

"That time-and-space-ripping thing," I asked Jim in a quiet voice. "Can I do that for you, too?"

Jim shrugged. "You're the boss. Pretty much whatever you want to do, you can do."

"Great. I want you to go to Drake's house and look for István."

"Ew. What if his body is all bloody and stuff?"

"There may not be a body. That's what I want you to see—if he's there, fine, or hiding or something."

"All right, but if anything exciting happens here and I miss it, I'm going to hold that against you for the rest of your existence."

I stopped in front of the door I'd spotted and smiled a toothy smile at all of the people behind me. "Bio break! Be right back."

Drake frowned as I grabbed Jim's collar and dragged the demon into the ladies' room with me. "What do you need— No. I don't want to know."

"Smart man," I said, blowing him a kiss as the door closed. I turned the lock and faced Jim. "Right, let's do this."

I took a couple of deep breaths to clear my mind, focused on the thought of Drake's house, and reaching out, selected the possibility that I wanted to use.

Nothing happened.

"Hmm. I don't seem to be able to do it." I tried again, with the same result.

"That's because you're using dragon fire. This is a

demon lord skill, Ash. You gotta use demon lord power to do it."

"No." I shook my head. "I'm not using that dark power again. That stuff is bad, and if by some miracle my soul isn't already damned for having inadvertently used it to banish Ariton, I'm not going to risk using it again. It's evil."

"Power is power," Jim said, putting its paws on the counter so it could check its teeth in the mirror. "It's neither good nor bad. The person using it determines what it'll be."

"Oh." I thought about that for a few seconds. I wasn't quite buying what Jim said—I'd felt that power, and there was evil in it—but perhaps I had the ability to neutralize the bad. I weighed the revulsion I felt at using dark power with the worry that István could be lying injured or dead somewhere, and decided I'd have to risk using it once more.

"OK, once more. But just once more, and that's it. I don't want to take any chances." I cleared my mind again, focused, and allowed myself to be filled with the thick, warm power that seemed to ooze up out of the floor to wash over me. A horrible ripping noise filled the small bathroom, echoing off the tile walls and floor as I rended time from space, tearing a hole big enough for Jim to pass through. Overhead, two of the lights went out. The rip was right next to a sink, causing it to fall to the floor in an explosion of porcelain on tile. Two pictures fell off the wall, as well as a chunk of ceiling tile.

Water jetted out of wrenched pipe, arcing at an angle

that allowed it to hit the wall behind me, splashing everything—Jim and me included—within a ten-foot radius.

"Fires of Abaddon!" Jim exclaimed, looking with big
eyes at the damage.

"Later. Just go do what I asked." I put both hands on
Jim's furry derriere and shoved it through the opening.
The rip made an obscene sucking noise, closing up as the
last of Jim disappeared into its maw.

"Aisling?" The doorknob rattled. "Is everything all
right?"

I made an abortive attempt to shove some wadded-up
paper towels in the pipe, but it was hopeless. I'd simply
have to make restitution with the fencing people for the
damage my rip in space had caused. "Yeah, fine. I'm
coming."

The front of my curtain toga was soaked with water,
but I figured that was the least of my worries. I unlocked
and hurriedly slipped out the door, quickly closing it behind me.

Drake, Fiat, and Gabriel all looked at my sodden front.

"I had . . . er . . . a little accident washing up."

"If you are through with these games," Fiat said, his
eyes as chilly as his flesh. He waved toward a double
door at the end of the hall. "We can proceed."

"Right. Sorry."

I started after Gabriel but paused when Drake asked,
"Where is Jim?"

"It's . . . uh . . . cleaning up the water I spilled. It'll be
back as soon as possible." Or as soon as I had another
moment of privacy to yank it back through time and

space. I hurried after Gabriel, praying he was telling me the truth about everything.

It didn't explain why he didn't try to rescue me in Paris, but at least I'd feel a whole lot better about Fiat if I knew that Gabriel wasn't secretly siding with him.

22

"By rights, I could call the challenge as a default." Dmitri's voice rang out strong with self-confidence as we took our seats in the raised dais of what Gabriel told me was a training room.

That gave me a moment of thought. Why wasn't Dmitri a bit more concerned about battling Drake? Was he really so good at swords that he thought he didn't have anything to worry about? Or was something else going on?

Something nudged at the edge of my awareness, but I ignored it to focus my attention on Drake as he picked up his sword, testing its blade before walking to the far end of the room. "That would be foolish. You know the rules governing a challenge as well as I do. The challenge resumes once an interruption has been dealt with."

"You assume running off to see your woman is a valid interruption. I feel differently, but do not fear!" Dmitri held up his hand, an unpleasant smile on his lips. "I don't want to give you any grounds for crying foul. I am satisfied to have the challenge continue."

Drake nodded and stood waiting, his stance relaxed, but his eyes were at their most dragonish. I knew that every muscle in his body was poised to attack.

"Sit here, *cara*." Fiat's voice made the back of my neck twitch with irritation. He pressed me into one of the few chairs on the dais. "You will be able to see well from this spot."

The *something* nudged at my consciousness again. I frowned at Fiat, distracted enough by it to keep silent.

"En garde!" Dmitri lunged forward, his blade slashing through the air at Drake. My breath caught in my throat for a moment as Drake stood still, not moving to counter the attack, but when the blade was a hairsbreadth away, he swung around to the side, parrying the attack, sending Dmitri forward onto his knees.

"This challenge is to be fought, not to the death, but until the vanquished agrees to yield," Drake said, addressing me as Dmitri snarled an oath, leaping to his feet. "Normally a challenge is to the death unless it is agreed otherwise."

"I will kill you regardless," Dmitri spat, doing a couple of those big leaping fencing moves forward, his blade dancing through the air.

Drake seemed to have no problem parrying him, however. His sword, identical to Dmitri's, flashed silver in the blue-white lights. "My sept has lost too many members to the sword, however, and I am loath to lose another, even one who seeks to destroy me."

"Bah. You are weak, Drake. I would never tolerate a challenger to live after he had tried to take over as wyvern." Fiat's cool finger trailed down my bare arm. I snatched it away, giving him a glare. "Then again, you have much to fight for."

"I believe Drake's thinking to be magnanimous and humane," Gabriel said, secret laughter lurking in his silver eyes. "Only a man secure in his power would allow dissenters to remain within his protection."

Oooh. Touché. Fiat's face darkened, but he restrained himself from saying anything. He turned to watch the two men doing the peculiar fencing dance of back and forth, but I wasn't fooled. He had to make an effort to sit back in the chair and appear only marginally interested.

I turned back to watch Drake, admiring both the power and the grace of his movements, his attacks controlled, his defenses swift and sure. I had a feeling that he was playing with Dmitri, who had started to sweat. Drake's moves were still easy and clean, but Dmitri was starting to labor. His breathing was heavier, his movements slower, and twice more Drake knocked him to his knees.

"Do you yield?" Drake asked a few minutes later, after Dmitri had thrown himself forward into a particularly uncoordinated attack.

"Never," was the snarled reply.

Back and forth they went again, moving up and down the floor, Drake continuing to be sure-footed and fast in his strikes, Dmitri starting to make mistakes. Twin streaks of blood snaked down his left arm, his right shoulder stained red from another cut.

It was clear that Drake was drawing blood deliberately—not enough to endanger Dmitri, but enough to disorient and distract him.

"Enough," Fiat shouted, getting to his feet after a

particularly clumsy block by Dmitri that ended with the younger dragon bleeding from the chest. "I grow weary of this. End it now, Dmitri."

A roar of frustration filled the room as Dmitri, sweating, bleeding, and clearly at the end of his strength, made a last-ditch run toward Drake. Drake did no more than parry the awkward attack, but it was enough to send Dmitri slipping on the floor, sliding a few feet on his back. Drake held the sword tip to his throat again.

"Do you yield?"

Before I had time to even think, Fiat hauled me to my feet, a sharp pain accompanying the prick of something sharp against my neck.

"I believe that question is to be asked of you, Drake."

I rolled my eyes over to look at Fiat, careful not to turn my head.

"Fiat, do not be ridiculous." Gabriel's voice floated over my head. I couldn't see him, but I could hear the dismay in his voice. "Release Aisling. We will talk this over."

"The time for talk is long past," Fiat said loudly.

Drake still held a sword to Dmitri's neck as he looked across at Fiat. His eyes were dark green, almost glowing with an inner light. "What the hell do you think you are doing?"

"I am ensuring the future of the weyr." Fiat's voice was silky, rife with satisfaction. "I am doing something that should have been done long ago—eliminating the obstacle to peace, true peace, as enforced by one who holds the power to keep the septs in line, not that mindless democratic drivel you've been feeding us for the last century."

"Fiat"—Gabriel took a step in his direction—"please, do not do this. We will discuss your concerns for the future of the weyr—"

"Stay back! That's all you and Drake know how to do—talk. Now is the time for action, not endless discussions about how we should live in peace. You're both nothing more than politicians, your blood so diluted that you're more human than dragon. Well, I do not suffer from such weakness! In this syringe I have fugu venom, the most poisonous of venoms in the world, drawn from the ovaries of the fugu puffer fish. One step in Aisling's direction, and I will inject it directly into her bloodstream."

"What the heck is fugu venom?" I couldn't help but ask.

"A venom so toxic, there is no antidote to it. It causes paralysis which is lethal one hundred percent of the time when injected into the blood. Shall I describe to you the effects? The paralysis begins as a tingling of the skin, moving quickly to vomiting, dizziness, and weakness. The muscles in your lungs are locked rigid, making it impossible for you to breathe. Humans die of asphyxiation anywhere from five to twenty minutes later."

"I'm not human anymore," I pointed out, wishing like hell Jim was here to help me. I expected it to arrive with help at any moment. Surely Jim would have told Nora what was going on. She would probably call Rene, and the three of them would come bursting in at the exact moment I needed them.

Or so the scene went in my mind. Reality, unfortunately, had different ideas.

"No, you are not human. But what do you think will happen to your brain without oxygen?" Fiat leaned close, his breath brushing my face. "The fugu poisoning will strip your body of the ability to provide you with oxygen, leaving you in a coma after ten minutes without air. I believe an hour is all it will take to ensure that you spend the rest of eternity brain-dead, your being trapped in a living tomb from which there is no escape, unable to move, speak, even think."

A chill gripped me, horror crawling up my arms. I was banking on my immortality to keep me from being seriously damaged, but I'd never considered being trapped in my own body.

"You are so incredibly insane—" The needle burned as it slid a little deeper into my neck. I shut up.

"Fiat, this is folly."

"Stay back," Fiat snapped at Gabriel.

"I merely want some answers, nothing more. What do you mean you do not suffer from the weakness of diluted blood? Your mother was human just as ours were." Gabriel's voice was soothing, his body language deliberately relaxed to present no threat. He took a step toward Fiat.

"Why do you assume so? Because there is an archaic and asinine rule stating that no wyvern can be born of two dragons?" Fiat laughed, the movement jostling the needle so it slipped in a little more. I held my breath, my attention on Drake.

His face was a mask of indifference, but his eyes, oh, his eyes said everything his expression didn't. They burned with fury and deadly intention. Within him, dragon fire raged so greatly I could feel it across the room. His control of it was nothing short of miraculous.

Fiat laughed a cold, calculating laugh that made my stomach turn over. "Do not be so foolish, Gabriel. I am proof that the rule is just as outdated as your ideas of democratic peace. My uncle was born to be wyvern of the blue dragons, but he was too weak to stand up to me. I took his name, his fortune, his position within the sept, and when the time was right, I took the sept itself. And now I'm on the verge of ensuring that I will rule the weyr as was preordained. Dmitri, fulfill your destiny!"

Fiat really was insane. I knew that now, but being on the wrong end of a poisonous syringe meant I kept that thought to myself. As I watched, mute with horror and impotence, Dmitri shoved aside Drake's sword, getting to his feet.

"Do you yield?" he asked Drake.

Drake was silent, his eyes burning on Fiat.

"You must choose," Fiat told him, smiling. "Which do you value more? Your mate or your sept?"

"This is ridiculous," I said, very careful not to move. "Even if you do turn me into a zombie, I won't be dead, not technically. You won't have destroyed Drake."

"You think not?" Fiat looked back at Drake. "We will allow him to make the choice nonetheless. Do you yield the sept to Dmitri? Or will you sacrifice your mate?"

Dark power nudged at me, inviting me to use it again. I closed my eyes against the siren lure of it. There was something wrong with it, something that I instinctively knew was bad, something that would ultimately end in my destruction.

You are a prince of Abaddon now, the dark power sang to me. *You do not have to suffer fools such as Fiat. Use the power you have gained to protect yourself. Use the power to right the wrongs. How can something be evil that is used for good?*

I turned away from it, trying to pull Drake's fire to give me strength. I was a professional, dammit! I was a Guardian, not a prince, no matter what fate insisted. I was inherently a good person, and I would not walk the path of evil!

"I've told you before, Fiat," Drake said slowly, his voice deep and rough with emotion. "Both Aisling and the sept are mine. I do not give up what I hold."

"No? Perhaps this will help change your mind."

Before I could blink, before I could draw in a breath, Fiat shoved the needle into me. Burning warmth filled my neck as he pushed down the plunger, injecting the fugu poison into my blood.

"No!" Drake roared, a horrible noise that broke two of the nearest windows. He leaped forward, but Dmitri was evidently expecting Fiat's attack on me, for he threw himself at Drake, knocking both of them down at my feet. The green dragons swarmed forward but stopped when Fiat's men hauled Drake to his feet, their guns pointing directly at his heart.

Fiat released me. I staggered a step, then collapsed, my mind numb with terror.

Use me, the dark power suggested.

I was tempted. Oh, so tempted. I didn't want to be a vegetable. I didn't want to lose Drake and Jim and Nora and everything life had to offer me. But before I could make a decision that would damn my soul for eternity, Fiat jerked me upward again. Drake snarled and lunged forward, hauling Fiat's three men and Dmitri with him.

"Stop! Gabriel can draw out the poison!" Fiat yelled above Drake's continued roars of fury. "But he will not do so unless you yield."

I turned slowly to look at Gabriel. He stood a few feet away, his arms crossed, his face guarded.

"So much for being a mediator, eh, Gabriel?" I asked him.

His gaze held mine for a moment, then dropped. "There are things you do not understand, Aisling. If it helps, I genuinely regret you are caught up in this."

"How easily the lies slip off your tongue." I turned away from him, my stomach roiling at the thought that I had ever considered him a friend. No doubt it was Gabriel who had tried to kill me in Paris. Or perhaps it was a plan worked up between him and Fiat.

My breath caught short in my chest as I realized the sickness I felt was more than just Gabriel's betrayal. I was physically sick as well. . . . The poison was beginning to work.

"There is still time," Fiat said calmly, glancing at his watch.

He held me back with one hand, while it took three of Fiat's men and Dmitri to keep Drake subdued. I glanced beyond them to where the green dragons had stopped. They were huddled together, clearly unwilling to risk their wyvern's life. Tears pricked in my eyes at the thought that I wouldn't get to know them.

"Gabriel can save her. All you need do is yield."

Nausea hit me in the gut with the subtleness of a mule

kick. I fell to my knees, dry heaving as my body racked with the need to purge itself.

"See how she suffers. The paralysis will begin to take effect on her lungs soon. She will struggle to breathe, but it will be no use. Her muscles will not allow her to draw in the so desperately needed oxygen. You have"—Fiat looked at his watch again—"approximately fifteen seconds before even Gabriel's skills as a healer will be useless."

Another wave of nausea hit me. My stomach cramped so bad, I thought I would pass out from the pain. I wiped my mouth and looked up to where Drake was held, tears blurring my eyes. I was having difficulty breathing, my lungs not seeming to hold any oxygen. I panted, trying desperately to get some air.

Drake's green-eyed gaze held mine for a second.

"I love you," I told him, jerking with the attempt to bring air into my lungs. "I always will. Dead or alive or in a coma, I will continue to love you."

Drake's hands fisted, his jaw tight. Fire burst up in a ring around him, but it didn't faze any of the dragons present. I willed Drake to say the words I needed to hear, begged him with my eyes to acknowledge what was between us. He stared back at me, mute, and a little piece of my heart shattered.

I doubled over again, caught in an agony of vomiting, gasping painfully for air in between retches. This was it. My brain would die, but my body would go on, which meant Drake would continue to live.

Without me, my heart cried.

It doesn't have to be that way, the dark power answered, and to my horror, I started to pull on it for strength.

"I yield." Drake's voice was hard and filled with agony of his own. "Gabriel, help her!"

Thick, fetid power flowed up from the ground, wrapping itself around my tortured form.

"Get her on her side. I will draw the poison before it disperses any further." I was aware of Gabriel's voice, of hands helping me, of the sharp sting on my neck and subsequent hot flow of blood, but it was the dark power that caught my attention and held it. I pulled harder on it, focusing it to push the poison back, keeping it from spreading. I knew there would be a price to pay for using it, but at that moment, closer to death than I ever had been, I was willing to take that chance.

My soul wept.

23

"She will survive. The poison hadn't dissipated too much," Gabriel's voice said above my head.

I heard it but didn't pay much attention to his words. I was too busy being stunned. There was no other word to describe my emotions but *stunned*, although *stupefied*, *disbelieving*, and *flabbergasted* weren't far behind. As I lay on the ground, supported by Drake, my body gasping in great lungfuls of air, my brain stopped battling for a moment with the realization that I'd used dark power to save myself and pointed out the momentous event that had just happened.

Drake had given up his sept for me.

"Why?" The word croaked from my throat as I twisted my head to look up at him.

His eyes glittered hotly at me. "Why do you think?"

"Is this some sort of weird political move?" I couldn't think of any other reason for Drake to willingly give up the sept. I knew he was attracted to me, I knew he would honor me as his mate for the rest of our lives together, and while I suspected his feelings for me were deeper than he was comfortable with, I was under no delusions as far as love went. I wasn't absolutely certain Drake *could* love— as committed to the sept as he was, it was quite possible that it just wasn't in his chemical makeup to be able to love both it and me.

"You are crying," he said, touching my face. His fingertip was smeared red.

"Answer my question, Drake. Is this all a plan of yours?"

An odd, irritated look flashed across his face. "You know me better than that. I do not give up that which I possess."

"Then why did you do just that?" I tried to prop myself up but was still too shaky to do it on my own. Drake helped me into the nearest chair, giving me a glass of water to rinse out my mouth. Gabriel had Fiat cornered, arguing about something. I didn't care what their problem was. The two of them could go to hell for all I cared.

That can be arranged, the dark power whispered to me.

I shuddered and pushed it away, still sick at heart at what I'd done.

"You didn't have to do that. I wasn't going to die, so you were perfectly safe."

Drake sighed, capturing my attention again. "I do not like this rule of discussing my feelings that you have bound upon me, but I like less the assumption you have made. I yielded because it was the only thing I could do to save you. I was not in a position of power, nor could I count on Gabriel for assistance. I did what was necessary."

No. It couldn't be. I shook my head, still disbelieving. Maybe the poison had warped my brain and I was delusional after all. I pulled myself to my feet, swaying against Drake, allowing his warm, hard body to prop me up.

"You know what that means."

"I do." His jaw tightened, his eyes flashing with intermingled anger and passion.

My heart, leaden and sick, suddenly was enveloped in a gentle warmth that did much to dispel the ills that had possessed it. "Are you sure? Really sure? It's not something else? Maybe you're sick."

His face grew harder. "Do you think I'm a fool that I could mistake it?"

"No, but you don't look very happy about it."

"I'm not," he snapped, irritation rampant on his handsome features.

A smile curved my lips as I kissed the corners of his mouth, ignoring the presence of those around us. "Are you going to say it?"

"No."

"Come on. I want to hear it."

"No!"

I allowed all the love I had for him to show in my eyes as I rubbed my nose on his. "Please?"

His face took on the most martyred expression I'd ever seen. "If I say it once, do I have to say it again?"

"Yes. With increasing frequency. It gets easier with time, honest."

He sighed again. "I knew this would not come to a good end. Very well, I'll say it. But I reserve the right to refer you to this conversation on occasions when you wish me to say it again. Aisling, I love you."

I fought hard to keep the smile off my face. Drake's declaration of love was delivered in such a brusque tone, I knew it had to be costing him a lot to admit the truth. "I love you, too," I answered, and welcomed his mouth when it came to claim mine, my heart singing a joyous song of happiness and fulfillment. His mouth was a hot brand, burning mine, searing my lips and tongue with an intensity that was almost painful. I waited for the rush of dragon fire that would follow his touch, wanting it to fill me with his passion and love.

It didn't come.

"Release my mate," a cool voice spoke behind us.

I pulled away from Drake, frowning up at him for a second before turning to level the glare of a lifetime at Dmitri. "You annoying little crapbean!"

The room echoed with the sound of the slap I delivered to Dmitri's face. He looked surprised for a moment, then furious.

"Do you seriously think I would consent to being your mate after you sided with this worm to steal the sept from Drake?"

Fiat said nothing as I gestured toward him, but his hands tightened. I didn't care how much I insulted him—sept politics be damned.

"You have no choice," Dmitri answered, giving me an offensively possessive look. My hand itched to slap him again. "You are a wyvern's mate. I am the wyvern of the green dragons. By the rules that govern the weyr, you are now mine."

"Just two days ago you refused to acknowledge me as Drake's mate. You can't have it both ways!"

"I am the wyvern of the green dragons," he responded, giving me a slow smile. "I can have anything I want, including you."

"Like hell! If you think I'm going to stand around and allow a smart-ass upstart to ruin Drake's life, not to mention mine, you can just think again. I'm not a friggin' demon lord for nothing!" I snapped, spinning around to find Jim, remembering in time that I'd sent him home to check on István. I opened wide the door in my head and pulled on Drake's fire. "Effrijim, I summon thee!"

Nothing happened. No fire filled me with power, no demon popped into view. My being was empty of Drake's fire, completely empty. There wasn't even a smidgen left of the slow-burning banked fire that had been present ever since I'd accepted him.

"Goddamn it, you stole my fire," I snarled, wanting to lunge at Dmitri. I ran to Drake instead. Pál had been released by Fiat's men and stood next to Drake as well, his face hard and blank. I put my hand on Drake's chest. I could feel the fire in him, its warmth reassuring and comforting. "What happened? Why don't I have your fire anymore? Is it because you yielded? I know there's a stupid rule saying I'm not your mate anymore if you're not wyvern, but that's just a rule, right? It doesn't really apply to us."

His eyes were filled with pain. The sight of it sent my spirits plunging again. "No, *kincsem*. You are my mate.

You will always be my mate. Nothing and no one can change that. The law may say you are mate to Dmitri, but you are mine, and I will not let you go."

I leaned against him for a minute, drinking in his heat. "Then why can't I share your fire anymore?" I asked in a whisper. "Is it because of Dmitri?"

His fingers swept over my face, wiping away more hot tears. "I do not think so. I think . . ." He paused for a moment, his eyes so dark they looked black. "I think you have been proscribed."

"Proscribed?" I searched my mental dictionary for a meaning and shuddered at the answer. "You mean I'm condemned? I'm damned?"

"Not damned," he said quickly, raising his gaze to look at Pál. The two of them exchanged a look that left me shivering with cold. I rubbed my arms, aware, now that I'd lost it, just how much warmth and power Drake's fire had given me.

There is an alternative. You do not have to be helpless, the dark power said.

"What exactly is proscribed, then?" I asked.

Drake's hands were warm on me. "It is a form of condemnation. It is seldom seen now, but I recall my uncle telling me of a dragon who had been such. It is not . . . a desired state. But we will find a way to cleanse you, *kincsem*."

Perhaps not desired, but is it any worse than being helpless?

The voice of the dark power was growing stronger. Part of me wanted to push it back, ignore it, banish it from my being. But another part shrugged and asked what could be worse than what I'd already done? I accepted Drake's power before I knew what it was or whether I wanted to spend my life with him. What was different in this situation?

Nothing is different. Power is power. It is the person wielding it who determines whether it is good or evil.

"Aisling's well-being is no longer any concern of yours," Dmitri said in an odiously bossy voice. He snapped his fingers, adding, "Come here, mate."

Mate. Fury filled me at that word on his lips. I looked up at Drake and knew I had to do something. I was not a woman who sat around waiting for others to rescue me. Drake himself had told me I didn't need rescuing—he had confidence in my power and abilities.

You are a professional, the voice said silkily. *You have power at your disposal, great power unlike anything you have known. Do you wish for him to see that, without it, you are weak and helpless?*

"Aisling, do not do anything foolish," Drake warned as I turned around to face Dmitri. "He is not worth the price you will pay. We will work this out together."

And how many dragons will die in the inter-sept war that will follow? the dark power asked. *How many innocent dragons will die because you did not take a stand when you could have? Do you wish their deaths to be on your soul? Or do you wish to fulfill your role as wyvern's mate, and protect your sept?*

I walked to the center of the room and held out my hands, blinded for a moment as I accepted the power that flowed up from the floor. The sins staining my soul were my own concern, but I would *not* sacrifice others. "Effrijim, I summon thee!"

Jim's shape formed at my feet. It looked up at me, pursing its lips. "Man. I never would have thought that of you, Ash."

"Demon, see thee that dragon there?" I pointed to Dmitri, power rolling through me, filling me with its insidious warmth. I knew what I had to do, and although it was morally wrong, I had no choice. It was the only way I could change things back to the way they were.

Dmitri's smile dropped, a look of concern replacing it. He glanced nervously at Fiat, who leaned against the wall, a parody of Drake's bored look on his face. "Aren't you going to do something?" Dmitri asked him.

"I suppose," Fiat answered, strolling toward him.

It was my turn to smile. "You're next on my payback list, Fiat."

He bowed. "I look forward to it."

"Um. Aisling? I really don't think you want to go there," Jim cautioned, leaning against my leg to get my attention. "It's not a good idea, no matter what anyone is telling you."

You have the power. Use it for good.

"Mate, do not do this." Drake's voice was warm and calm despite the situation. "Come with me. We will work this out together."

I pulled the power hard, forming it, focusing it to do what I wanted, its slow heat burning hot in my veins as I narrowed my gaze on Dmitri.

"Fiat?" he asked in a high-pitched squawk, taking a

couple of steps to the side. His gaze skittered between me and the blue dragon.

Destroying him will be a pleasure, the voice said. *A pleasure and a duty. You must do it to save the others.*

I spread my hands, holding the power between them, ready to blast it into Dmitri.

"Do something!" Dmitri screamed, looking frantically at Fiat.

"Aisling! Do not do this," Drake commanded, starting toward me. "To do so will put you beyond redemption!"

Deal with that later. Right now you have a job to do.

"As you will," Fiat said as I hesitated, torn between Drake's warning and my own instincts.

"Ash, this is bad. Really bad. Don't do it," Jim said in a low voice, its eyes worried.

The power was warm between my hands. I held it focused, ready to be used, but was confused about what I should do. Use it to save Drake and the dragons and damn myself even further?

You've already used the power. How can using a little more hurt? Do not be weak, Aisling. Be instead an instrument of vengeance. Right the wrongs.

"By the laws governing the weyr, I challenge you by lusus naturae for your mate, Aisling Grey."

I turned to look at the man speaking the challenge. What was Fiat up to now? Why on earth would he want to challenge the man he'd just put into power?

"You . . . you what?" Dmitri asked, clearly as taken aback as me. "What do you mean? You can't do this!"

"No? Accept the challenge, and we shall see."

*More deaths. If Fiat wins, that's what will be the re-
sult. Do you want that?*

No! my mind screamed, sick of it all. I just wanted to
live happily with Drake, being a Guardian, working for
the good guys. I didn't want to be the instrument of
vengeance!

"I accept your challenge," Dmitri said, his voice loud
but a bit unsure. "Name the form."

"Aisling." Drake's hands were warm on mine. He
gently took them in his, pulling me toward him. "You
must listen to me. You said you trusted me."

I dragged my eyes from Fiat and Dmitri to the man I
loved with every atom of my being. "I do trust you."

The love was there in his eyes, filling me with more
happiness than I thought possible. "Then you must listen
to me now. To do what you plan is wrong. I know that you
desire it for the right reasons, but you must not give in to
this new challenge that faces you."

"You know," I whispered, mindless of everything but
him. "You know I used dark power."

"Weapons are so vulgar." Fiat gave a delicate shrug.
"Why do we not settle this in the mortal fashion? By fists.
That should provide a true test of strength."

"Very well." Dmitri adopted a boxing stance, his hands
up. "I am ready."

Drake's fingertips swept a strand of hair off my face,
the touch so gentle it made my knees go weak. "It is evident what you have done, yes."

"I'm damned forever." I wanted to cry at the look of
regret in his eyes. "I didn't mean to use it, I really didn't."

"I know, *kincsem*. Your heart is pure. But you cannot

risk tainting it, and that is what will happen if you continue down this dark path."

Beyond us, the two men fought, Dmitri grunting a little as Fiat danced around him.

"I only want to fix things," I told Drake.

"You wish to destroy Dmitri." Drake shook his head. "You have not used the dark power for anything harmful, but this is different. It is dangerous. I cannot allow you to do that. You must trust that in this, I am right."

I almost smiled. There was my bossy dragon, telling me what I could and could not do.

He is wrong. How can using power for good be dangerous?

I pulled my hands from Drake's, releasing the power, letting it wash from me. I felt weak but righteous, understanding at last what Drake was saying. He was right. I couldn't use power to destroy someone. Banishing a demon lord couldn't in any conceivable light be considered bad, but destroying someone for my own gain was entirely different.

"All right, I'll trust you. But it'll be a cold day in Abaddon before I'm his mate," I said loudly, nodding toward where Dmitri was trying to block a punch from Fiat.

The latter stopped. "I'm in complete agreement."

Before our stunned eyes, Fiat pulled out from his pocket a small gun and shot Dmitri in the face.

24

"Funky eyes and tears of blood aside, you're looking a bit odd," Jim said.

I dragged my gaze from the form of Dmitri spread out on the floor, a pool of blood beneath his head, to my demon. I was literally struck speechless.

Not so Jim. "Stuff always happens around you. Never a dull moment and all that. It's better than TV."

I shook my head, trying to clear my befuddled mind. There was just too much to take in.

"Gabriel?" Drake asked, nodding toward Dmitri's body.

"If his brain is destroyed, we won't be able to bring him back to consciousness," Gabriel answered, taking a step toward Dmitri.

"No," Fiat answered, holding up a hand that stopped Gabriel in his tracks.

The latter didn't like that. "Fiat, stand down."

"I think not. You made an excellent point. Dmitri could well recover from a single bullet to the head." Fiat glanced down at the man at his feet for a few moments, then cold-bloodedly shot him a couple more times.

I screamed and lunged forward to stop him, but Drake's hand shot out and caught my arm, reeling me back in until I was flush with his body.

"That, I believe, will dispense with any question as to whether or not Dmitri is still wyvern." Fiat bowed to Drake, who stood stiffly beside me. "You have your sept back. I hope you do not abuse it again."

"You shot Dmitri!" I all but yelled, unable to believe my eyes.

Fiat's attention turned to me. His face wore its usual pleasant, unperturbed expression, as if nothing at all untoward had happened. "I believe the evidence would be impossible to deny, *cara*."

"You just up and shot him!"

Gabriel directed a narrow gaze at Fiat, walking around him to kneel next to Dmitri. I turned my head away, sick both physically and at heart over what had happened, feeling as if for some reason, the fault for Fiat's actions lay directly on my shoulders.

"Yes, I did. You may thank me for saving Drake's sept for him."

"Thank you!" I exclaimed, outraged.

"Yes, thank me for returning to Drake that which he would not have regained without a battle," Fiat snapped, his blue eyes icy with disdain.

"You forced him to sacrifice the sept in the first place!" I shouted.

"There are powers at work here that are beyond your comprehension," he answered. "Do not make judgments.

In the end, Drake has back what he lost. Well . . . almost all. I assume now that Dmitri is incapable of serving as wyvern you will claim the post again?"

"Yes," Drake answered, his voice steady. I could feel the tension in him, however.

Fiat inclined his head. "I trust your people will have no problems in accepting you in the role again."

"Drake will always be our wyvern," Pál said, his voice filled with pride. "The sept loves him."

"Indeed. Lucky sept, then, to avoid the power struggle that would have ensued had Dmitri retained his position."

"No," I said, shaking my head. "That doesn't make sense. Why did you go to all the trouble of kidnapping me, poisoning me, almost making me a vegetable, to put Dmitri in power, only to effectively kill him a few minutes later? Why, Fiat, why?"

"Lusus naturae," Drake said slowly, his eyes on Gabriel as the healer bent over Dmitri's unresponsive body.

Gabriel looked up, his normally light eyes shaded and disturbed.

"Odd," Drake said in a distracted tone, almost as if he was talking to himself. "I always assumed it would be you who challenged for my mate, not Fiat."

"I intended to," Gabriel said, avoiding my eyes. I stiffened, my hands fisted. How dare he? "But after last night, when you told me Aisling would be having a child, I changed my mind."

"Is there anything you can do for Dmitri?" I asked him, deciding I couldn't deal at that moment with the implications of his statement.

"No, I'm sorry. There is too much damage to the brain.

He will live, but he will not be"—Gabriel gently touched the side of Dmitri's face—"cognizant."

Retribution can be yours, the voice said.

I ground my teeth, holding back both hot-tempered words and the bile that was raised by the violence of the day.

Revenge these sins.

I leaned into Drake to absorb some of his heat, turning away from the persuasive voice within me.

Right the wrongs.

"I will not do it!" I shouted out loud, startled by the sound.

Everyone in the room looked at me.

"Whoa, meltdown warning," Jim said, its voice flip, but concern visible in its eyes. "Everyone may want to stand clear."

I ignored Jim to glare at Fiat. There had to be a way to do this without using the dark powers.

"I spoke with a demon lord today. Two, as a matter of fact. I thought they were the coldest, most evil sentient beings I'd ever met, but I was wrong. You are, Fiat. And if there is any way I can bring you to justice for the crimes you have committed today, I will do so."

Fiat brushed off my statement as if it were a piece of lint. "Are you aware of how much your desires play a role in my plans for the future?"

"No." I frowned, confused even more. "How much?"

He didn't bother to look at me when he answered. "None whatsoever. Renaldo, Pietro, we depart. A pleasant evening to you all."

Fiat gestured toward the door. His bodyguards fell into place behind him as he started for it.

"Do something!" I demanded of Drake.

He raised both eyebrows. "What would you have me do? I am in control of the sept again. Dmitri will be taken care of the rest of his life, but he poses no more of a threat to us."

Jim shook its head. "Missing the obvious, man."

And how. I frowned up at Drake. "Yes, you're the wyvern again, but perhaps it's escaped your attention that Fiat challenged Dmitri for me, which, unless I'm confused about all those bizarre and outdated dragon laws, means I'm now a blue dragon."

"You are mine," Drake said, his eyes blazing. "You will always be mine. You belong to the green dragons. Nothing Fiat can do changes that. This is merely a political move on his part to gain leverage over me, nothing more. He does not expect you to fulfill any duties as the mate to the blue wyvern."

Fiat, for a change, said nothing. But he smiled.

It made my skin crawl.

"Don't think I'm going to let this situation pass without correcting it," I called after Fiat as he opened the door to the hall. He paused and glanced back over his shoulder at me.

I smiled a grim little smile of my own. Drake's arm tightened around my waist, giving me strength. "You may think I'm a pawn in this horrible game you're playing, but you're wrong. I have a whole lot more going for me than you can possibly imagine."

The condescending look on his face made my hand itch. "You have power, *cara* . . . but you are too pure of heart to use it."

The pressure of Drake's hand on my side kept me from making wild threats. Evidently I was back in the business of being politically correct.

"That does not mean you never will, though," Fiat added, his mind brushing against mine. *I have high hopes for your future.*

"Oh, thank goodness you're here," Nora said what seemed like an eternity later, as she opened the door to Drake, Pál, me, and two of the green dragons who insisted on escorting us home. "Someone attacked István, but he's going to be all right. Rene is with him now. Jim was here briefly, but it disappeared before I could ask what was going on. I was just leaving you a note and was about to find you . . ."

"Drake!" Catalina stood at the top of the stairs and glared down at us as we trooped in the doorway. "Where have you been? This woman here, this Guardian I do not know, has been giving me orders. Me! Make her leave."

I wrapped my arms around Drake and buried my face in his neck, allowing him to just hold me. The events of the day had taken away most of my strength, leaving me weak and boneless.

"She would not help with István," Nora said in an apologetic tone. "I was a bit sharp with her, I'm afraid. I apologized, but it didn't seem to do much good."

"Make her go away! She is rude to me. I don't like her."

"Mother, cease." Drake's voice rumbled in his chest. I melted against him, breathing in his delicious scent, filled with so much love it almost drove out the horrors of the day.

Almost.

"I will not be spoken to this way in my own home," Catalina huffed, twitching herself by Nora as she approached us.

"This is my home—mine and Aisling's. You will not insult our guests."

"She has bewitched you," she said, frowning at Drake. "She has cast a glamour on you to make you believe she is right for you, but we all know that is not so."

I sighed into Drake's neck and lifted my head to look at my future mother-in-law. "Boo!"

She gasped, a hand at her throat as she took a couple of steps backwards. Quickly she crossed herself. "*Madre de dios!* You are marked by the evil one!"

Nora's startled intake of breath quickly followed, her eyes huge with horror behind her glasses. "Aisling! Dear god. What have you done?"

"You know that bad-ass demon lord who was after her blood?" Jim asked.

Nora didn't back up the way Drake's mother did, but she did wrap her arms around herself, as if in protection. She nodded.

"Well, guess whose ass is the baddest now?"

The color drained out of her face as she reached blindly for a chair next to the window. "You didn't . . . you didn't . . . you're not . . ."

"She has sold herself to the devil," Catalina announced to everyone, her hands waving dramatically. "I hope you are happy now, son of my loins. You are bound to the devil! Pah! I wash my hands of you both. I am returning to Rio. If you come to your senses and rid yourself of the she-devil, you may call me."

I sank wearily onto the bench that sat between the arms of the stairs as Catalina made a grand exit, muttering under her breath about exorcisms and the possibility of demonic grandchildren. It was all so horrible, I just wanted to laugh, but I was afraid once I got started I wouldn't be able to stop.

"Aisling?"

"Yes, it's true," I answered Nora's unasked question. "I did. I am. You're looking at the newest prince of Hell."

She took a couple of steps toward me. Beyond her, Drake stood silent, his arms over his chest as he watched me. I gave him a minuscule little smile to let him know I appreciated his letting me deal with the situation. I knew from our discussion in the car on the way home that he would be much happier taking charge of my life for me.

"I'm sorry," Nora said, stopping several feet away.

"I know you are. It was an accident. Another demon lord tricked me into banishing Ariton."

She shook her head, interrupting me. "No, I mean I'm sorry that I won't be able to continue to mentor you."

"What? You said earlier that we'd just go on like before, even though the committee had stripped you of the official title."

"It's not that—" She looked from Drake to Pál, then back to me. "You are a demon lord, Aisling. I cannot harbor a demon lord. I cannot mentor one. To be near you is dangerous to me. The power you wield now . . . I am a mortal. It would be too much temptation for me. It grieves me greatly to say this, but I cannot remain in the same house as you."

"Why?" I wailed, hot tears forming in my eyes. My life was falling apart bit by bit, and I felt completely out of control, unable to fix the problems that tormented me. "I've been a demon lord since the day you met me."

"Yes, but that was with Jim," she answered waving a hand toward it. "Jim is a sixth-class demon."

"What on earth does that mean? Everyone keeps saying it, but I have no idea what a sixth-class demon is."

Nora straightened up, giving me a chastising look. "You have not been reading the texts I gave you."

"I'm sorry, I've been a bit busy, what with the imps after me, and the red dragons skewering me, and being kidnapped and poisoned and all."

"A sixth-class demon is the lesser of all demonkin," she said in a lecturing tone of voice. "They are Fallen."

I rallied my tired brain to focus on what she was saying. "Fallen as in . . . angels?"

"Not exactly, but it will do as a generalization."

I looked at Jim. "You're a fallen angel?"

To my surprise, it looked chagrined. "I was never an angel. Just a minor sprite, servant to a muse. A really cranky muse with absolutely no sense of humor who got me damned and sent to Abaddon. You think organized crime is tough—it's nothing compared to muses."

"You're a fallen sprite?" I asked, my mind muzzy and slow.

"Yeah, but don't let that give you any ideas. I was a bad-boy sprite, feared by all."

"OK." I turned back to Nora. "So Jim is a fallen semiangellike thing. I can accept that, because I've never felt anything truly evil in it. But, Nora, you know me—I'm not bad, either!"

"You are proscribed," she said simply, her eyes on mine. "You used the dark power."

I pushed myself off the bench, taking a step toward her. She braced herself as if expecting a blow. "Barely! And the first time without knowing what it was. I swear to you now, swear before everyone here, that I will never use it again."

"I'm sorry, Aisling." She glanced at Drake and Pál for a moment. "I'm really very sorry, but there is nothing I can do."

I begged, pleaded, and tried reasoning with her for two hours, but with no success. I even followed her into her room as she packed up her few belongings.

"Aisling, please—you are distressing yourself for no good purpose. I cannot change my feelings on this."

"But if I promise—oh, what is it, Pál?"

Pál held out a phone to me. "Call from Paris."

"It must be Amelie. I'm not through making a case yet," I told Nora as I left her room.

"It will do you no good," was all she said in response.

"Amelie? Hi. What's up?"

"Aisling, I wanted to be the one to tell you . . . today is the day the L'au-delà votes on Venediger, since no suitable candidates have come forward. I am afraid that you will be elected, my friend."

I sighed and slumped wearily against the wall. "I'd refuse, except it turns out that Peter Burke is worse than we thought."

"He is a demon, then?" Amelie asked.

"No. He's Bael."

Amelie swore. "*Mon dieu*, how could that be? Why did no one recognize him for what he was?"

"Evidently one of the perks of being the premiere prince of Abaddon is that you can work up a detection-proof disguise. What am I going to do, Amelie? I can't be Venediger. Things . . . well, things have happened that I can't go into now."

"I wish I had an answer; I truly do. But the L'au-delà is in uproar now, and someone must step forward before another such as Bael takes control. We are all extremely vulnerable until someone does."

The air before me shimmered a moment, then Traci the demon stepped out.

"I apologize for interrupting, but there are some pressing things for you to sign dealing with the patch out in two days," it murmured obsequiously, handing me a clipboard and pen.

I stared at in it bewilderment for a moment, quickly scanning the papers. They were all straightforward business-type things, dealing with the release of a new (bug-riddled) patch to the latest version of operating software.

"Aisling? Are you there?"

"Yeah. Hang on a sec." A thought appeared to me, a thought so bizarre, I almost discounted it. But deranged as it was . . .

"Can I nominate someone to take charge as Venediger in my stead?" I asked Amelie. "Kind of as a deputy? Someone who would be responsible to me, but do the job on his own until a real Venediger candidate comes forward?"

She was silent a moment. "Yes, so long as you are ultimately responsible."

Traci gave me a pointed look. "There are only four forms. You could sign them in just a few seconds, my lord."

"Then you can tell everyone there that I will offer someone to act in my name, someone who is bound to me. His name is Traci."

"Traci? This is a man?"

I smiled at the look of surprise on the demon's face. "No, this is a demon. My steward, as a matter of fact. It's too long of a story to go into right now, but you can tell everyone that my deputy for the position of Venediger is Traci."

"But . . . but . . ." Amelie sputtered a few phrases in French. "Aisling, you cannot place a *demon* in position as Venediger!"

"Yeah, it's an abomination, right?"

"*Oui!* Of the most major sort!"

"Excellent." I signed the forms and covered the mouthpiece to tell Traci, "I'll want to talk to you tomorrow about a little project I have for you in Paris."

"I shall wait in anticipation," it answered, looking appalled as its form disappeared into nothing.

"Excellent? You would put a monster of the dark powers in charge of the L'au-delà, and you say this is *excellent*?" Amelie all but shrieked at me.

I couldn't help a little chuckle. "Yeah. It's so bad,

everyone there will be scrambling to get a new, proper Venediger, won't they?"

"Oooh." She thought about that for a minute. "Yes, but I do not like it."

"Well, neither do I, but it's the only solution I have. Hopefully this will get everyone off their collective duffs and working on getting a real Venediger in place. I've got to go—there's a bit of trouble here and I need to talk to Nora. Love to you and Cecile."

"And to you."

I sighed as I hung up the phone, wondering whether I'd done the right thing. Black and white no longer seemed to be so absolute anymore. It was getting harder and harder to distinguish which was which.

Nora left an hour later, Rene's borrowed cab right behind the one Catalina had called to take her to the airport. I stood at the window in Drake's bedroom and watched as Rene helped put Nora's meager belongings into the back of the taxi.

"My life sucks," I said, leaning my forehead against the window. The door behind me closed. I didn't have to turn to know it was Drake. I felt his presence as a warm, tingling energy.

"You are having a bad period, I agree. But it will smooth out."

"Nora has left me," I pointed out, leaning back into him as he wrapped his arms around me, his hands on my belly.

"But she may return. You do not know what the future may hold."

"That's what Rene said. He also said István is OK."

Drake's warm breath touched my ear, making me shiver. His lips following shortly behind made me melt against him. "I know. I just spoke with him. He is getting proper care. It is you I am concerned about. Are you all right?"

"No. Everything is ruined."

"Everything is not ruined."

"Yes, it is. István is hurt."

His lips moved to my neck, hitting the one spot that drove me crazy. "You just said he is mending."

"I'm a prince of Hell."

He bit my earlobe. "That does not mean you have to remain so."

"Jim is calling up everyone it knows and is telling them it's second in command, and if they want any favors, to get the appropriate bribes in order now." I turned in his arms and buried my hands in his hair.

"You should never have given it a cell phone. I will cancel the service."

His eyes were so beautiful, so bright with emotion, it hurt to look at them. I dropped my gaze, but Drake wouldn't allow me to try to hide my shame. He lifted my chin and kissed each eyelid as hot tears squeezed out of them.

"I'm damned," I said, the words as hard and abrupt as the pain inside me.

"You are proscribed. There is a difference. *Kincsem*, do not hide yourself from me." His thumb swept gently along my cheekbone, brushing away the tears of blood.

"This, too, we will overcome. Do not give up hope, for I have not."

I shook my head, fatalism filling me. "I have no hope. I'm doomed."

"Is that what Rene said?"

I glanced up at him, a little confused. "No, as a matter of fact he didn't. He said something about one path ending and another beginning. Why?"

Drake was silent for a moment. "You said you suspected that Rene was not who he seemed. Have you not yet figured out just who he is?"

"No, other than I know he's not mortal. The guy at the Guardian place said he was a"—I dug through my memory for the word—"daimon. That was it. Do you know what it means?"

"Yes. It is Latin."

"For?" I bit Drake's chin. "Come on, this has been driving me nuts. I need to know who Rene is."

"*Daimon* is a word meaning fate," he answered slowly, his eyes smoldering with familiar passion.

"Rene is . . . fate?" I asked, nibbling on his delicious lower lip, my hands sliding down to his back, and farther down to his oh-so-delectable butt.

"One of them, yes." Drake's hands did a little exploration of their own.

My heart dropped as I thought about what fate had in store for me. I pulled away from him and turned to look back out the window. "I could just punch Rene in the nose for what he's done to me."

"He has done nothing. Fates do not make your life,

kincsem. They simply assist you to follow the path you've chosen."

"Oh. Well, that would explain a lot. But it doesn't change things, Drake. Not even your mind-numbingly fabulous kisses change anything. I'm still damned. Everything has been stripped from me. Everything I wanted and worked for is gone or ruined, all because of my incompetence."

"You have me. And I love you."

I slumped against the window again for a moment before turning and flinging myself in his arms, kissing him with every morsel of love in my being. "Boy, you sure know how to squelch a pity party, don't you?"

"It was an excellent attempt, but such a maudlin attitude does not suit my mate."

"The red dragons are at war with us. And now Fiat—" I started to say.

He kissed the words right out of my mouth. "That, too, we will deal with. We have been at war with the red dragons before. Sooner or later Chuan Ren will realize that war is not the answer. Until that time, I will keep the sept safe."

"And Fiat? If I'm technically his mate now, what does that mean to us?"

"Nothing. I will determine what to do about Fiat as soon as I know what his intentions are."

I looked at the man I held in my arms, his eyes blazing his emotions, every angle of his face as well known to me as my own, his being so closely bound to mine that I knew no one would ever be able to separate us again. Somewhere along the line, I'd taken him into my heart, and he'd filled the empty spaces in me I'd not known existed. I nodded, my throat tight with unshed tears. "Your heart rate is up," I said, my lips on his pulse point.

"You have that effect on me," he answered, a smile in his voice.

"Well, you know what they say: When two hearts race, both win."

He lifted my chin to kiss me again. "Who said that?"

"I don't know. I saw it in on the inside of a Dove chocolate wrapper. But it fits, don't you think?"

"Yes, it fits." His hands slid around to my stomach again. "Does my child rest in there?"

Fear pricked at me for a moment, but as I stood there clasped tightly to Drake, I realized that there wasn't anything I had to bear alone. Fiat, the demon lords, Nora and the Guardians, even Rene the master of fate—all of them could be faced so long as we were together.

"I don't know," I whispered, peeking up through my eyelashes at him. "I really don't know."

He nuzzled me, the gesture so unlike the stern, arrogant, unbending Drake, I turned into a big puddle of goo.

"I look forward to seeing what you make of your life, Aisling Grey. I look forward to being a part of it forever."

I smiled into his kiss. I had Drake, I had Jim, and I'd find a way to get Nora back as my mentor. Everything else, from cleansing my soul to ending the dragon war, I'd work with Drake on fixing. I was a professional, dammit. Nothing was so wrong that I couldn't eventually right it.

So naive, the dark power whispered to me. *We, too, look forward to what your life will become.*

Read on for an excerpt from Katie's next
vampire paranormal

The Last of the Red-Hot Vampires

Coming in May 2007

"Na then, t'get ta the faery circle, gwain ye doon the road past Arvright's farm—ye know where that be, then?"

By focusing very, very hard, I managed to pick out words in the sentence that I understood. "Yes."

"Aye. Gwain ye doon the hill past Arvright's, then when ye see the sheep, ye turn north." The old man pointed to the south.

"Is that north?" Sarah asked in an undertone, looking doubtfully in the direction the man pointed.

"Shh. I'm having enough trouble trying to get through his West Country accent." I turned a cheerful smile on the man. "So I turn left at the sheep?"

"Aye, 'tis what I am sayin'. Na then, once ye've skurved past the sheep, ye'll come to a zat combe."

"Zat combe?" Sarah's face was fierce with concentration. "I'm not sure I . . . a *zat* combe?"

I wrote down the old man's directions, praying we wouldn't end up wandering into someone's yard.

"Aye, 'tis right, zat. Full o' varments."

Sarah looked at me. I shrugged and said to the man, "Lots of them, eh?"

Behind my back, Sarah pinched my arm.

"Chikky, too. They needs a good thraipin', but none here'll be doin' it."

"Thraipin'," Sarah said, nodding just as if she understood.

"Well, thraipin' chikky varments is an acquired skill, I've always found," I said, continuing to take notes that made no sense. "So we go through the zat combe with the varments? Then . . . ?"

"Ye be up nap o' thikky hill."

"Ah."

Sarah leaned close. "I recognized a word in that sentence. I think I'm getting the hang of this language. It's good to know that all those years of watching BBC America are paying off."

"And that's where the faery circle is?" I asked the man, trying not to giggle. "Up nap o' thikky hill?"

"Aye." The old man narrowed his eyes, and spat neatly to the side. Sarah looked appalled. "Dawn't ye go kickin' up t'pellum on thikky hill."

"We wouldn't dream of it," I promised solemnly.

"Ye maids be master Fanty Sheeny t'gwain ye ta the faery circle. 'Tis naught good ye find up nap o' thikky hill."

"Well, now, that's just lost me," Sarah said helplessly, turning to me for translation.

I winked at the old man. "Really? Bad, is it?"

"Aye. 'Tis evil." He winked back at me, and spat again.

"That's a common fallacy, you know," I said, tucking away the notebook. Beside me, Sarah groaned. "Although faery rings have been considered places of enchantment for many centuries, they aren't really made by faeries. They are the result of a fungal growth pattern. Mushrooms, you know?"

The man blinked at me. Sarah tugged on my shirt and tried to pull me to the car she'd rented for our trip.

"I know this area is rich in folklore, and faery rings certainly have their share of believers, but I'm afraid the truth is much more mundane. It turns out that there are three distinct types of rings, and the effects on the grass depend on the type of fungus growing there, although not all rings are visible. . . ."

"Ignore her, she's a heathen," Sarah said, yanking me toward the car. "Thank you for your help! Have a good day!"

The old man waved a gnarled hand, spat again, and hobbled past us toward the pub.

"You are so incorrigible! Honestly, spouting off all that stuff about fungus to that very colorful old man."

I got into the car, taking a moment to readjust myself to the English-style automobile. "Hey, you started this bet, not me. I'm just doing my part to win serious 'I told you so' rights. Ready?"

"Just a sec . . . Oh, whew. Thought I'd forgotten this." Sarah folded a wad of photocopied pages and stuck them in her coat pocket. "I can't wait to see what effect these spells have on the faery ring!"

"I am obliged by reason to point out that some weird quasi-Latin words found in a Victorian book on magic are not very likely to have any result other than making your friend and companion don a long-suffering look of martyrdom."

Sarah lifted her chin and looked placidly out the window as we crept through town. "You can scoff all you want—these spells were written by a very famous medieval mage and passed down through one family over the centuries. The book I found them in was very rare, only fifty copies printed, and most of them destroyed. And I have it on the best authority that the spells are authentic, so I have every confidence that you'll be eating that long-suffering martyred look before the sun sets."

"Uh-huh."

By dint of Sarah consulting the hiking map she'd picked up in London, we tooled past the lazy river that wound around the town, headed over the stone bridge, and turned the car in the direction of farmland and the famed Harpford woods.

"Left side," Sarah pointed out as I strayed to the right.

"Yup, yup, got it. Just a momentary aberration. Let's see . . . down past the big farm, then take the road south to a bunch of trees. Beware of the varments. What do you think a zat combe is?"

"I have no idea, but it sounds fabulously English. Here, do you think?"

We pulled off the road and got out of the car to eye the field stretched out before us. It was the perfect day for a walk in the country, what with pale blue sunny skies; the bright green of the newly dressed trees; hundreds of daisies scattered across the field, bobbing their heads in the breeze; birds chattering like crazy as they swooped and swirled around overhead, no doubt busily gathering nesting materials. Even the sheep that dotted the hillsides were picturesque and charming . . . at least when viewed from the distance.

We gave them a wide berth as we followed what the hiking map showed as a right-of-way through a huge open pasture, up a hill to where a sparse crowning of trees waved gently in the June breeze.

"This is so awesome. It's absolutely idyllic! And the emanations—my god, they're everywhere. We have to be close, Portia," Sarah said emphatically, looking around us with happiness. "I feel a very strong sense of place here."

"Yeah, me too," I answered, stopping by a fallen tree to scrape sheep poop off my shoe.

"I knew you'd feel it too. I can't wait to try the mage's spells—they simply can't fail. Interesting arrangement of the trees, don't you think? They appear to make a circle around something. Shall we investigate?"

"Lead on, Macduff." I followed obediently as Sarah, glowing with excitement, broached a sparse ring of trees. In the center, a space of about eighteen feet, covered in lush, emerald grass, was open to the sky.

"There it is!" Sarah grabbed my arm and pointed. Her voice dropped to an awe-filled whisper. "The famed West Country faery ring! It's perfect! Just what I imagined it would be! It's like a holy place, don't you think?"

I left her hugging herself with delight and marched over to squat next to the bare earth that marked the boundaries of the faery ring. The ring was about four feet wide, a perfect circle of bare earth surrounded by lush grass growing on the inside and outside of it. There was nothing to indicate the cause, no mushrooms visible, but I knew they weren't always seen. I touched the sun-warmed dirt and mused, "I wonder if there's a lab around here where I could send a soil sample so we can find out just which fungus caused this ring?"

"Infidel," she said without heat, slapping her coat pockets, pulling out the spell pages, and turning around in the way women who have forgotten their purses have. "Do you have the camera?"

I cocked an eyebrow at her. "You took it away from me at Denhelm, if you recall."

"Oh, that's right—you insisted on taking pictures of the farmer's son rather than the bog man mummy. I must have left the camera in my bag."

"You have to admit, the son was much better looking than that moth-eaten old bog man."

Sarah straightened up to her full five foot nothing. "That bog mummy is said to have been used in a druid sacrifice, and thus could well contain the spirit . . . Oh, never mind. I can see by the mulish expression on your face that you are closing yourself up to any and all things unexplainable. Let me have the car keys so I can run back to town and get the camera."

"I'll do it—"

A little sparkle lit her eyes. "No, you stay and meditate in the faery ring. Maybe if you open yourself up to the magic contained within, you'll see how blind you've been all these years. Here, you can read the spells over while I'm gone, but don't try them out until I get back. I want to see everything the ring has to offer!"

I took the pages she handed me and plopped down to

sit with crossed legs in the middle of the circle. "All right, if you're sure you're okay with driving on the wrong side of everything." I plucked a piece of grass and chewed the end of it as I shucked off my light jacket. "I'll soak up a bit of sun while you're gone."

"Portia!" Sarah's eyes grew huge. "You can't do that!"

"Do what, sunbathe? I'm not going to take off my clothes, just roll up my sleeves," I said, suiting action to word.

"You can't eat anything that grows in the faery ring. It's . . . it's sacrilegious! In fact, I don't think you should be in the ring at all. I'm sure that's going to anger the faeries."

I rolled my eyes, chewing on the blade of grass. "I'll take my chances against the fungus. Remember to stay on the left."

She hurried off after delivering a few more dire warnings as to my fate if I continued. I sat enjoying the sun for a few minutes, but that quickly lost its charms. I made a search of the area surrounding the ring, but there was nothing but trees, grass, daisies, buttercups, and the wind whispering through the leaves.

"Right. A little scientific investigation is in order," I said aloud to break the silence. I seated myself again in the faery ring, plucking another blade of grass to chew while I consulted the photocopies Sarah had thrust upon me. The text explaining the purpose of the spells was couched in dramatically obscure language, no doubt fooling the more gullible reader into believing its authenticity. "It's going to take a lot more than some lame attempts at mysticism to fool me," I muttered as I ran my finger down the spells. "*Magicus circulus contra malus, evoco aureolus pulvis, commutatus idem dominatio aqua* . . . Oh, for heaven's sake, how hokey can you get? I bet this isn't even real Latin—"

A glimmer of something caught the corner of my eye. I turned my head to look at it, assuming someone had dropped a penny or bit of glass on the ground that had caught the sunlight, but there was nothing.

The hairs on the back of my neck stood on end, as if something that posed a threat was approaching.

"Honestly, Portia, how pathetic is it that you're letting Sarah's chat about magic get to you?" I rubbed my arms against a sudden prickling of goose bumps and gave myself a mental lecture about allowing someone's enthusiasm to sway my common sense.

A little flash of light in midair had me whipping around to look at it.

There was nothing.

"Oh, this is ridiculous. I'm spooking myself, and over what? Figments of an overactive imagination . . ."

Directly in front of me, something twinkled in the air again, just as if tiny motes of metal had reflected the sunlight.

To my astonishment, the twinkling continued, growing thicker until the air around me seemed to collect, flashing like a thousand tiny, nearly imperceptible lights.

"I'm hallucinating," I said, closing my eyes. "It's the sun. I'm sun blind, or having heatstroke, or the fungus in the faery ring is a hallucinogenic."

I opened my eyes, sure I would see only the top of a

sunny hill, but instead I gawked as the twinkling lights gathered themselves into an opaque form.

"It's got to be the fungus," I said quickly, getting to my feet and backing out of the ring. "It's from the peyote family or something—"

As I backed away, I stumbled over a lump in the grass, falling onto my butt. My mind came to an abrupt stop as the form turned into a person. I shook my head, blinking rapidly to clear my vision. "All right. Time to get some medical aid. This silliness has gone on long enough."

All your favorite romance writers are
coming together.

SIGNET ECLIPSE

Coming December 2006:
Philippa by Bertrice Small
Without a Sound by Carla Cassidy
If Only in My Dreams by Wendy Markham

Coming January 2007:
*The Rest Falls Away: The Gardella
Vampire Chronicles* by Colleen Gleason
Salvation, Texas by Anna Jeffrey
My Lady Knight by Jocelyn Kelley